ESMERALDA

THE ENCHANTED

by

ROCKY BARILLA

ROSQUETE PRESS

Cover design by Angie of pro_ebookcovers

Library of Congress Control Number: 2018900925

ISBN: 978-0-9904851-4-8

OTHER WORKS BY ROCKY BARILLA

A Taste of Honey

First Place Winner of the 2015
Latino Literary Now's Latino Books into Movies Awards for
Fantasy Fiction
Second Place Winner of the 2015
International Latino Book Awards for Fantasy Fiction

The Devil's Disciple

Award Winner of the 2018
Latino Literary Now's Latino Books into Movies Awards for
Suspense/Mystery
Second Place Winner of the 2016
International Latino Book Awards for Mystery

Ay to Zi

Award Winner of the 2018
Latino Literary Now's Latino Books into Movies Awards for
Romance
Second Place Winner of the 2017
International Latino Book Awards for Romance

Harmony of Colors

Second Place Winner of the 2018
International Latino Book Awards for Latino-Focused Fiction

All works are published by Rosquete Press and are available as Kindle or CreateSpace editions on Amazon.com

DEDICATION

This book is dedicated to my sister, Linda Yoshida, que descanse en paz, and to all those persons who have lost a loved one. Until we meet again.

.

"Some trails are happy ones,
Others are blue . . .

Happy trails to you,
Keep smiling until then . . .

Happy trails to you,
Until we meet again."

--- *Dale Evans and Roy Rogers*

TABLE OF CONTENTS

ACKNOWLEDGEMENTS

Another super-special thanks to my wonderful wife, partner, and editor-in-chief Dolores for her unending patience and fortitude in helping to create this manuscript. She is the godmother of all.

I am also grateful to the Monarch Joint Venture (MJV) Project that protects the beautiful Monarch butterflies. The Monarch Joint Venture is a partnership of federal and state agencies, non-governmental organizations, and academic programs that are working together to support and coordinate efforts to protect the Monarch migration that extends from Mexico, through the United States, and sometimes into Canada.

In Mexico, Monarch butterflies are an intricate part of the culture and symbolize the souls of the deceased. And in the Mexican culture, Death is seen as a continuum of Life, rather than as a finality.

What is called into question is "when does Life end?" What strata in the universe houses our departed souls? Do we really ever die? Life is good. But what about Death?

Until we meet again . . .

PART I

EL CAMINO

Chapter 1 - The Phone Call

Sunday, October 11, 1970

The sudden ring of the phone startled her. Her body lurched. The Sears clock radio sitting on Esmeralda's tiny wooden nightstand displayed 11:15. Pitter-patter. Pitter-patter. The rain was tapping on her attic bedroom window. Pitter-patter. Pitter-patter. This was the typical Eugene, Oregon weather with its four distinct seasons: Cool rain, cold rain, warm rain, and two weeks of sunshine. A second telephone ring.

Esmeralda's lithe body slowly slithered out from under her comfy-cozy down comforter. The smoky air from the downstairs wood stove reached her nostrils. They twitched. She was exhausted from her Sunday volunteer clean-up on the Willamette River trail. It had been foggy most of the day and the handful of her fellow wildlife club members had been less than enthusiastic. In fact, they were wimpy and whiney. Her group was good-naturedly called "The Tree Huggers." Although most Oregonians are genetically-coded not to litter, there are always the occasional Styrofoam food containers, plastic straws, empty Wild Turkey booze bottles, and orphan articles of clothing strewn haphazardly on the hiking paths. Es had graduated from the University of Oregon the previous June with a degree in Environmental Sciences and she was stone-cold serious about Nature. This was a trait that she had inherited from her Mexican father, Francisco Luna.

Another ring. She massaged her scalp. A few strands of green fell from her shoulder length hair.

The remainder of the almost-22-year-old Esmeralda's life was on hold. Although she had more or less enjoyed her four years of college, she didn't want to waste the effort of going to graduate school. In fact, she had been so involved with another "Save the Mother Earth program" that she was sort of a loner. She hadn't always been this way. When she was a young girl she attended the grammar school where her Aunt Chlora was teaching. Es was a cheerful and sociable child. Her best friends were Eileen, Sherril, and Lupe. The children played together and went to each other's birthday parties. After elementary school, Eileen moved to Portland, Oregon, and Sherril went to Santa Cruz. Fortunately, Lupe "Loops" did not move away also.

Then came junior high school where Es was labeled the "beaner" [a derogatory term to describe Mexicans] by some of her classmates. They would snicker if she brought a burrito to school for lunch. Sometimes she would be picked last in intramural sports. And they made fun of her clothing or her black hair color. Es couldn't understand why they characterized her as Mexican, even though she was half-Irish. During the summers, Es would join "Loops" and her family in picking strawberries to earn a few dollars. Es met other migrant farmworkers from Texas who were treated very shabbily by the growers and were often cheated by them. When she asked questions about the discrimination against Mexican-Americans, her mother, Kelly, said something about humanity and its interconnectivity with the universe. Es didn't understand what her mother was trying to say. But her father, on the other hand, was less circumspect and hinted at the pain he had suffered during his lifetime being a Mexican. The ugly and painful taunting, discrimination, and bullying had left terrible imprints on him. Her father, Francisco, then simply advised Es to treat everyone with respect; but that didn't mean she had to hang out with them.

By high school, Esmeralda had formed her own survivalist personality with a corresponding set of values. She stayed away from the hormonal boys and the bimbo girls. Her mother had passed away and her Papá had split, so part of her being a solitary person was ordained by fate. Thank goodness she had her Aunt Chlora and Tío Felipe as positive role models.

Later, in college, Es thought that most of her "green" friends were too liberal and self-absorbed. On the other hand, some of the other coeds made nasty innuendos about her dark skin and the last name of Luna. Being a half-breed put her in a different cultural comfort zone. She wanted her own space.

As to the rest of her personal life, she would tell people, when asked, that she was between relationships (this was a euphemism for not having much of a love life). For the last eleven plus years, since her mother passed away, she had lived with her Aunt Chlora and Tío Felipe who liked to be called Phil.

Es finally picked up the phone on the fourth ring. There was only one person who ever called her. It was still rather late for her father to be calling, but he was never predictable. Most of the time he called after 11 pm when the phone calls cost less.

She spoke into the white Princess console. "Hello," Es said groggily, her mouth opening wide.

"Is this Esmeralda?" replied an older woman. "Esmeralda Luna?"

Es was surprised by the strange voice, but she had been well-trained by her aunt and uncle not to give out personal information over the phone.

"Who is calling please?"

"This is Donna Rhodes . . . Mr. Luna's landlady."

Esmeralda's father, Francisco "Paco" Luna, had moved to Tubac, Arizona, after his wife Kelly's death. His brother-in-law Felipe was also his compadre. Felipe was a great spouse to his wheelchair-bound wife, Chlora. Chlora and Felipe had baptized

Esmeralda even though Paco and Kelly were not religious. Paco and Felipe became closer as Kelly's health started to fail. The compadres shared many experiences and secrets. Felipe was very surprised when one day Paco, within a year of Kelly's passing, asked him to take care of his daughter. Paco told him that he was leaving Eugene because he had things to do. Paco knew that Felipe and Chlora would act as great parents since they had no children of their own. Chlora, of course, was elated and alternated between smiles and tears at the idea. The following week the 11-year-old Esmeralda moved into to her godparents' home.

After settling Esmeralda in with Felipe and Chlora, Paco drifted from Eugene to Mesa Verde, Colorado, to Tucson, back to Mesa Verde, and finally to Tubac, Arizona. There he had started his own goldsmith business.

In the eleven years that had ensued, Paco and his daughter, Esmeralda, had drifted into what most people would call an estranged relationship with brief periods of reconciliation. But, unfortunately, in the last few years Paco had not been around much.

"This is Esmeralda," she responded timidly into the phone.

"Miss Esmeralda, do you know where your father is?"

"No, ma'am," Es found the inquiry very odd. She was hundreds of miles away from her father. *Geez! How would I know?* Esmeralda was starting to wake up. Her right hand stretched over her head. She stroked her right brow.

"Did he mention if he was going somewhere?"

"Not that I know of," Es' face was contorted. She was puzzled. "Why are you asking me these questions?"

"Well, nothing serious," the landlady sputtered. "It's just that we haven't seen anything going on at his place. We're a bit concerned . . . and his truck is gone."

"Maybe he went away for the weekend?" Esmeralda conjectured, rolling her eyes.

"I don't think so, dearie. He's been away for almost two weeks."

Esmeralda's head shook from side to side. *This doesn't sound too good.* She frowned, her nose making like a chipmunk. *Papá, what are you up to? Her father often did strange things, but always for a good reason, like the time he dyed his hair green. Was he in trouble? Why do people have to call me?*

"I can give you a call if I hear from him," Es was trying to be polite.

"Well, that's only part of the problem, dearie," Donna said, as she hacked into the phone. She sounded like a smoker, Es thought. "His rent is past due."

It was well past 1 a.m. when Esmeralda's eyes finally closed. *Whatever her father was up to, didn't concern her,* she thought as she tried to go back to sleep. *I'm not my father's keeper!* Still, she could not help feeling that something was wrong. Es had a strange but mystical connection with her father. She accepted the fact that he was prone to knock around from place to place on occasion. But tonight, she had a suspicion that something was not right.

In a moment of weakness, Esmeralda had told the landlady that she would drive down to Tubac and check out the situation. She would also bring the rent money, but it would take her a couple of days. After a few minutes of hemming and hawing, they sealed the deal. Esmeralda said that she had to make some arrangements and hoped to depart within the next few days. Donna the landlady was not happy, but she was in no position to quibble.

Chapter 2 – Family

Monday, October 12, 1970

Esmeralda tossed and turned in her bed during the early hours of the morning. Her mind kept churning a thousand questions about her father and his whereabouts. Maybe he had gone home to Mesa Verde, Colorado, to visit his mother? Maybe his mom (Es' grandmother) was sick or even dying. She started to panic in her semi-conscious state. Her skin was clammy.

Es' mind drifted back to the summers when she was a very small child. Her parents and she would spend a few weeks with her grandma Lulu Luna in the Mesa Verde, Colorado area. Her nana was a short, skinny Mexicana with black and grey braided hair and wrinkled, leathery skin who lived in a wooden hogan in the high desert. Her son, Paco, whose "Christian" name was Francisco, had a father who died at an early age of brown lung disease from working the mines. Grandma Lulu was now living alone.

Paco had inherited the maverick mindset and coexistence with nature from his father and the love of life and spirituality from his mother. Francisco was raised in an area that was a conglomeration of Native Americans, Mexicans, and whites. For better or worse, he was nicknamed "Paco the Taco" for being a Mexican. Growing up in the multiethnic, multilingual schools had opened Francisco's eyes. Sometimes the groups all got along; sometimes not. But unfortunately, the Natives always seemed to be shoved down to the bottom of the social and economic scales. It was the lack of jobs and the poor health services that drove Francisco to want to leave his birthplace. He had an itch to explore the world.

Paco's older sister, Teresa Redfox, lived in nearby Cortez, Colorado, in a Pueblo Indian enclave. Esmeralda always had a great time when Aunt Teresa, Uncle Jerónimo, and their two children came over to visit them at nana Lulu's.

Paco's carbon-eyed mother only spoke Spanish and always made Esmeralda giggle. During these visits, grandma Lulu would ask Esmeralda and her two age mate cousins, Linda and Olivia, what they wanted for breakfast. But no matter what the children requested, the grandmother made them fried eggs and bacon in a big iron skillet that she could barely handle. The exception was on Sundays, when she made tons of pancakes with fresh berry preserves and local honey.

Sometimes during these vacations, Teresa's husband Jerónimo, a Pueblo Native, would escort Esmeralda, her parents, and the nana to Native American powwows and other rituals that intrigued Es. As a result of these experiences, Esmeralda would ask her nana a million questions. Grandma Lulu would give her granddaughter answers that drew from spirituality, nature, and ancient legends.

At other times, her parents would take off for the day and leave Esmeralda and her nana to take little walks along a historic trail that snaked through the neighboring hills. They would sit and rest, drink water, and converse in the tall grassy fields. Nana Lu would speak in Spanish and Esmeralda would nod her head;

and likewise, Es would say something in English, and the grandma would smile.

"¿Cuál es tu color favorito, magita?" the grandmother looked into her nieta's eyes. [What is your favorite color, my little enchanted one?]

"Verde," [green] the girl would reply with a grin.

The pair would then continue on navigating the gravelly paths through groves of madrona trees. They gingerly stepped over the pieces of the fallen reddish bark.

In the milkweed patches they would find butterfly pupae and swarming Monarch butterflies. The flying creatures would land on Esmeralda and she would laugh as they tickled her arms and neck. Nana would give a big smile and remark, "Eres la niña encantada de la madre tierra." [you are the enchanted daughter of mother earth.]

After the long, hot day they would wind their way back home. When Paco and Kelly returned, they would find the adventurous pair eating cookies and drinking their Navajo tea.

Sniff! Sniff! Es finally awoke that morning when she smelled the aroma of freshly-brewed Mo's #36 herbal tea that permeated the house. She put on her plush Tigger slippers and went into the nippy bathroom.

Ugh! I hate this friggin' hair! Es gritted her teeth as she looked into the mirror. She brushed it and tied it back with a clip. Finally, she trudged downstairs, still in her animal-patterned flannel night gown.

"Buenos días, mijita," her uncle Phil aka Tío Felipe shouted out. The wood burning stove in the living room was being tended by him. The warmth was welcomed by all. The temperature outside was in the low forties. The rain had stopped.

"Morning," Es replied blearily. "Is auntie already at school?" Normally, Felipe would have gotten up really early, made his wife Chlora breakfast, and then driven her to the elementary school where she was the veteran third-grade teacher. But today, Chlora had taken the day off because of a cold that she had caught from her students. She did not want to infect all the children or her teaching colleagues.

"Nah, she catching cold," he plopped another oak branch into the wood stove, handling it with an oversized glove. "I made her some tea. You want some?" Uncle Phil's English diction still needed a little work since he was a non-native English speaker.

Esmeralda didn't say a word. She was in a foul mood. *Why did the landlady have to call me? I just want to be left alone!* She wandered over to the living room where an old brown shag carpet covered the wooden floor.

"What you want for breakfast?" asked Tío Felipe, who was the cook, bottle-washer, and self-appointed Suzy homemaker.

"Don't know," Es stated curtly as she plopped herself down onto the old cocoa-colored rumpled sofa. She was debating with herself about how to bring up the subject of her missing father. Paco was always a bit of a sore subject with her his aunt and uncle.

"I guess the usual," she retreated and grumbled sheepishly. Oatmeal with yogurt and blueberries dusted with cinnamon was her staple. Since her uncle ran the local health food shop and snack bar, she knew that everything would be super nutritious. She dragged herself over to the rectangular table that sat just off the kitchen. Her uncle had placed a big spoon and a small spoon on her tan cotton napkin, along with a big mug of herbal tea.

"Excuse me for a moment. I've got to make a phone call," Es suddenly got up from the table and went to the adjacent room. Her uncle's mouth twisted in surprise.

From the living room phone, Esmeralda called her aunt Teresa who was already up. Teresa had not seen her brother Paco for a few years. Es asked if her father could be at nana Lulu's. Her grandma did not have a telephone. Her aunt replied no; she had been with her mother the night before and nobody had heard from Paco in ages. Es chatted for a few more minutes and then hung up. *Rats!* She wandered back into the kitchen with her head down. She was not happy. And her oatmeal was now cold.

Suddenly, there was a clamor. "Good morning!" Chlora sniffled at the two as she rolled into the room. Chlora was Esmeralda's mother's older sister.

"Good morning, mi amor!" Felipe bent over and kissed his wife's forehead. "You ready for tea?"

He opened up a space at the kitchen table so that Chlora could maneuver her wheelchair up to it. Esmeralda looked at them. She was feeling guilty about the bomb that she was about to drop on them.

Chlora Valverde, née Glas, was born in Eugene, Oregon, in late 1922. Her Irish parents had emigrated from Cork County, Ireland, to look for the American Dream. Her father got work as a butcher in a small grocery store at Oak and 18th, in the southern part of Eugene. The family never wanted for meat, and often they ate it three times a day. Chlora's mother was a stay-at-home wife. They lived in a small two-story, two-bedroom house.

Twenty-two months after Chlora was born, a little sister arrived in the family. The two girls were always happy and smiling. Their mother thanked God every day for these precious gifts. The younger sister, Kelly, would follow Chlora around like a shadow. Their mother read stories to them every night and their father would always bring them a special treat on Saturdays.

When the two girls attended school, they gained the reputations for being well-behaved and smart. Kelly liked wearing her sister's hand-me-downs because it made her feel like a big girl.

Then it happened. It was Halloween night of 1931. The two girls were trick-or-treating in their neighborhood around Lincoln Elementary school. They were both wearing white sheets and carrying bulky pillow cases. It had poured cats and dogs earlier in the day and the night was terribly dark. Dozens of kids ran from house to house getting their shoes muddy trying to score popcorn, candies, and other diabolical treats.

Kelly was inattentively checking out her Halloween stash and lagging a bit behind her big sister as they crossed the middle of Monroe Street. The squealing of tires could be heard from down the street. A set of cross-beamed headlights came barreling down upon the two girls. Chlora ran forward impulsively to avoid the approaching car, but suddenly realized that Kelly was not with her. The engine of the car screamed louder and louder. Chlora's face contorted with horror as she saw her sister standing in the middle of the street, not moving, like the proverbial deer caught in the headlights. With a superhuman effort, Chlora twisted her body and sprinted back toward her sister. The noise of the car was deafening. This was followed by the loud sound of screeching brakes and smoking tires. Chlora dived and pushed her sister to safety. Unfortunately, the right front bumper of the car crashed into Chlora and she caromed off the car and landed thirty feet away. She was rendered unconscious. The car sped away. Kelly screamed. Porch lights went on and adults came running out. Other children started to cry. Some parents tried to comfort them; and others simply left the scene.

Several hours later, Chlora's parents were at the county hospital. Kelly had been left at a neighbor's house. Mr. and Mrs. Glas were unable to see their daughter because she was being operated on in the Intensive Care Unit (ICU). The mother chose to go to the hospital chapel to pray.

It was just past eight in the morning when one of the surgeons came to the waiting room down the corridor from the ICU. The place reeked of antiseptic.

"Mr. and Mrs. Glas," the doctor had his surgical mask dangling around his neck. "We have her stabilized. I won't lie to you. The injury was very serious."

"Can we see her, doctor?" asked Chlora's father with red bloodshot eyes and a tired looking brow.

"I'm sorry, Mr. Glas. Not at the moment," the doctor wanted to seem accommodating. "Chlora is under heavy medication. She is in great pain."

Chlora's mother broke down. Tears flowed down her cheeks.
"Is she going to be all right?" quivered the father.

"She has a complex fracture of the ilium and femur," the doctor went on to explain that there were dozens of small breaks in Chlora's hip and upper leg bone.

"Will she be able to walk?" Mr. Glas stared into the doctor's eyes.

"I'm afraid that it is worse than that, Mr. Glas," the doctor was measuring his words carefully. "There has been a lot of soft tissue and nerve damage. There has also been a significant amount of internal bleeding."

"Oh, my God!" screamed Mrs. Glas. "My poor baby!"

"We have called in a pediatric orthopedic surgeon from Portland. He's a specialist. He will look at the x-rays and make his diagnosis."

"Doctor, what are her chances of recovery?" Mr. Glas wanted to know now. He and his wife could not live with uncertainty.

The doctor hesitated in responding. "The best scenario is that all the bone fragments can be wired together and that with a rigid physical therapy program, Chlora can lead a near normal life."

"And the worst?" Mrs. Glas sobbed.

"We might have to amputate the leg," the doctor said matter-of-factly. "There is a high risk of infection and gangrene. Necrosis could be fatal for her."

The parents broke down into hysterics as the surgeon left. He advised them to go home and informed them that they would be notified when the specialist had rendered his conclusions.

"What are we going to do, papa?" the wife beseeched.

"I don't know. You keep on praying." He was concerned because they did not have any medical insurance. The hospital bills, the surgeons, and the specialist were all going to cost money. He was in no position to borrow any money from anyone.

The parents picked up Kelly on their way home. They had to make a few phone calls to arrange their affairs. Mr. Glas' boss was very understanding.

That afternoon two uniformed police officers came over to the Glas house to investigate the tragedy. Kelly was unable to supply any information because of her age and the fact that she had not been paying attention while crossing the street. The police had canvassed the neighborhood of the collision without much luck.

Two days later Chlora was reconstructed in a Raggedy Ann fashion. Wires ran through her lower skeletal structure. Bales of cotton bandages were wrapped around her body. A catheter and drip lines poked her.

By the following Friday, Chlora had started her physical therapy. She cringed in pain and tried to avoid taking the pain medication. At times she would stumble but the PT staff were always there to prevent her from injuring herself. By the end of the second week she could use the bathroom with minimal assistance. Chlora was overjoyed when she took her first shower and had her hair washed.

Within three weeks of the catastrophe, the medical bills started rolling in. A hundred dollars here. Twelve hundred dollars there. Ten dollars for five aspirin. The Glases were beside themselves. The workers at Mr. Glas' store generously chipped in forty-five dollars and change.

At the six-week mark, things went from bad to worse. Chlora had been making great progress in her physical therapy. She thought that she would be able to walk again, but the doctors decided that her bones were too fragile to bear all of her body weight. Besides, she was not finished growing and there was no guarantee that the bones would develop normally. The medical staff redirected her treatment to an iron horse wheel chair. The family was in despair, except for Chlora. She would just smile and sigh. Mrs. Glas continued to go to church every day to pray for her daughter's speedy recovery. On the weekends Kelly would accompany her.

The police finally caught a break when an angry young woman showed up at the central police station. "I know who hit that young girl."

The woman spilled her guts. She and a guy from Cottage Grove (about 25 minutes south of Eugene) had been drinking at a bar a few months before. He had given her a line about being in the insurance business. He came off as a big shot. They drank and drank. He wanted to go to a motel. She was agreeable. These little trysts became a weekly affair. However, one night at the No Tell Motel, she had found his wedding ring. He confessed and said that he was sorry, but that his wife did not understand him.

With the police department's assistance, the Glases retained legal counsel. The threat of criminal prosecution leveraged a big financial settlement. The perpetrator would pay all medical bills plus twenty-five thousand dollars. He would also pay a ten thousand dollar fine for the hit-and-run violation. The jilted girlfriend was set free with a stern lecture about the dangers of dating married men.

The Glases set up a trust account at the local bank for Chlora.

On Christmas Eve, the door to the Glas house opened and Chlora's father wheeled his daughter in to greet her tearful mother and sister.

"Auntie, I have something important to tell you two," Esmeralda held her spoon in a death grip as she tried to compose herself. Her eyebrows lifted. "I think my dad is missing."

Chlora and Felipe gave her puzzled looks. They knew that Es was not prone to exaggerate or fabricate stories.

"Es, what is going on?" questioned the concerned aunt with a worried look.

Esmeralda slowly recounted the phone call that she had received the night before and this morning's chat with her aunt Teresa. Uncle Felipe brought his chair closer to his wife. The two looked at each other quizzically.

"What are we going to do?" said Chlora as she went into her Type-A, take-charge mode. There were tensions between her and her brother-in-law. Francisco had dropped out of his daughter's life and only contacted Es sporadically.

"Well . . . I'm thinking of driving down to Arizona to look for him," she said without much conviction.

"But how can you find him?" the aunt pushed. "You don't even know where he is."

"But I gotta try."

"Why?" as soon as Chlora said this, she knew that she had crossed the line. While she, Felipe, and Paco had an informal arrangement for the care of Esmeralda, Chlora felt that the father was basically irresponsible. Sure, Paco took Es occasionally on two-week outdoor outings all over the western United States during the summers and on infrequent visits to see his family in Cortez and Mesa Verde, but there was no consistency. And there certainly was no money coming in from him.

Because of her accident, Chlora could not bear children. On her deathbed Kelly had asked Chlora to help raise her daughter after she passed. Taking care of Esmeralda after her mother's death was really a blessing for Chlora. Chlora and Felipe had the best of all worlds.

"He's my dad," Es defended herself. "He's still part of the family."

Her Uncle Felipe's face frowned with sadness. Granted he was only her uncle, but he loved her as if she were his own flesh and blood. He would do anything for her, but he understood that he was still number two behind Paco. That was probably the way it should be, he thought.

"Well, Es, you are almost twenty-two years old and certainly capable of making your own decisions," her aunt seemed to surrender, but her words were not heartfelt.

A half-hour later Esmeralda was upstairs in her small bedroom in the attic. The bed with the comforter was bordered by a small antique nightstand and lamp. The brown paneled closet was filled with her jeans, long-sleeved tops, and outdoor wear. The pressboard chest of drawers was stocked with at least fifty pairs of socks, in all sizes, thicknesses, and colors. The underwear drawer displayed more utilitarian than fashionable items. There was a dearth of bras.

Esmeralda pulled her hiking backpack from the back of the closet. Nobody in the household owned a suitcase because they never took touristy trips. They always roughed it, trying to save money. Es learned to prefer this more casual way of traveling.

Well, maybe she would find her father already back from a hunting trip with plenty of fresh meat. Then perhaps the both of them could spend a few days hiking in Arizona, she thought. Or perhaps back to the Grand Canyon? She started grabbing things and randomly plopping them on her bed. Her pack already contained some of her camping equipment essentials e.g., water bottle, all-purpose Swiss Army knife, flashlight with extra batteries.

She started to pack. First, came her clothes. She wasn't a fashionista, but she had a very methodical approach that her father had taught her. Work from the feet up. Shoes were the most important piece of clothing. "The battle was lost for a want of nail," he used to say (he had learned this in the Army). She took up the lightweight, tawny-colored hiking shoes from the closet. Next: *tennis shoes or flip flops? Hmm? Converse tennis shoes would be a little more versatile.*

Esmeralda then selected seven sets of socks (lightweight) and cotton pants from the little dresser. "Frig!" she smashed her finger closing a sticky drawer. She shook the index finger three times.

She resumed packing. *No bathing suit. Don't plan to swim.* Gradually, she had several piles of clothing and gear on her bed. Her father's second rule was to take half of what she had assembled. The extra sweater was discarded. Instead, she threw in a baseball cap because it was a necessity. Her ultimate goal was to have the backpack weigh no more than thirty pounds. Although she was 5'4" and 127 pounds and physically fit, she never wanted to test her limits.

Es thought that she could pile other provisions into her car, especially food. She should probably bring a few books. She had started "One Flew Over the Cuckoo's Nest" twice without going past the third chapter. *Okay, I'll bring that one since I'm going crazy anyway.*

The last rule, probably the most important instruction that her father had given her, was to be prepared for anything and everything. Research, research, research. *I don't know what the weather is going be like in Arizona. Don't have time to check. Assume it's going to be milder than here. Shouldn't be a problem.*

As Esmeralda, was adjusting and readjusting her belongings, there was a tapping on her bedroom door.

"Come in," Es yelled out.

It was her uncle. He was a slender, brown-skinned Mexican man. At home she called him Tío Felipe, but at his health food store where she worked part-time, she called him Uncle Phil, per his preference. Now he was standing in the doorway and looking at her with his sad brown eyes.

"Oye, mija, I guess you are going," he said. "Auntie is worried. Yo también."

"You don't have to be," she replied with bravado. "You both have taught me well. I can take care of myself."

"I know, mijita. I know. But sometimes things can happen."

She loved her Tío Felipe, just as much as her own father. Felipe was the pillar of the family.

Felipe Valverde was born in Guadalajara, Mexico, in 1923. In the early 1940's there was a shortage of agricultural laborers in the States due to the second World War. In 1941 Felipe and his older brother Telesforo emigrated to the Pacific Northwest of the U.S. looking for work. His first job was working at a fruit cannery outside of Salem, Oregon. There was a glut of fruit and vegetables that were growing all over the Willamette Valley. The pay was good, and the working conditions were decent, but he and the other Mexican workers were always being harassed by the sheriffs from Polk County. How many times had he heard the term "wetback"?

One day an Anglo foreman came up to him and told Felipe that he was leaving for a better job. He advised Felipe that he could stay at the cannery and hope to be a line supervisor one day or he could come with him to work at the new place. Felipe asked about the new job since he was doing okay and didn't want to lose his job by doing something rash. But finally, he agreed to depart also.

Fate was in his favor. There was a new grocery chain that was being established in Oregon. It had rough challenges fighting the giant food conglomerates that had sewn up big supply contracts with local growers. Felipe's store tried to brand itself as the independent and local grocer. Little by little, it increased its market share and became a player in the Oregon food industry.

Felipe started off as a warehouseman and then rose to be a shipping and receiving clerk. By that time, his English proficiency was improving. He also made special request deliveries to various account holders. One day he dropped off several crates of peaches, apples, and onions at the receiving dock of the Oregon College of Education (OCE) Student Union cafeteria in Monmouth. As he was driving back, it began to rain hard. As he peered out the wet windshield, he noticed a moving figure, clutching a satchel and struggling to move forward along the highway. The rain was blowing from left to right and this poor soul was getting soaked.

Felipe pulled over about fifty feet in front of what he finally recognized as a person in a wheelchair.

"Do you want a ride?" he offered as if he were Sir Walter Raleigh.

"No thank you," came the reply. "I can manage."

Felipe saw a sopping wet woman drowning in the rain.

"Come on . . . you're very crazy . . . going in this rain."

Eventually, Felipe convinced her to come with him. He helped her up into the front seat of his delivery van. He collapsed the wheelchair sideways and laid it in the back of the van.

As they drove off from the side of the road, the woman tried to dry herself off with very little success. The windows were now fogged up and Felipe had the defrosters going full blast.

"Thank you," she said shivering. "You are a knight to the rescue."

Felipe didn't quite understand what she had just said, but just smiled.

"My name is Chlora Glas," she offered her hand.

He drove her to her off-campus apartment. Chlora was in her fifth year of study at OCE. She was trying to earn her teaching credential. Her parents had wanted her to finish her education at the University of Oregon where she had earned a bachelor's degree in Comparative Literature, but Chlora wanted to be independent. Monmouth was about sixty miles north of Eugene. Good enough, she thought. Her parents were worried about her being wheelchair-bound, but she wasn't. Throughout her university tenure, Chlora had done just fine.

She and Kelly were fairly close during their high school years, but they became less connected when Chlora had enrolled in college.

Chlora invited Felipe to her dormitory's potluck luncheon the following Sunday. She did not expect him to come. Felipe arrived, bringing a big basket of freshly-picked fruit. He suddenly became the hit of the small gathering. Chlora and Felipe sat for hours talking about family. He never asked about her accident or the wheelchair. They continued to see each other for several months. Felipe liked Chlora's positive attitude on life and her determination to become a teacher. Chlora liked Felipe's big smile and his kindness. On Sundays, his day off, Felipe and Chlora would drive into the country and look out over the fields or hills or rivers while it rained. Sometimes Chlora prepared a little picnic lunch for them. One holiday weekend she brought him down to meet her parents in Eugene. Mister Glas was chagrined that Chlora had brought a Mexican to his house and moreover, that she was dating him. Chlora's mother, however, took her husband aside and pointed out that they should be grateful. Chlora was lucky to have a suitor at all. *Thanks be to God,* she said. She reminded Mr. Glas that as practicing Catholics, they had been violently persecuted by Oregon's powerful Ku Klux Klan factions in the 1920's. The lack of timber and farming jobs resulted in days of killings, beatings, and the destruction of property of innocent people. The image of the burning cross on Skinner's Butte in Eugene was still etched in their minds.

After a few more visits to the Glas household, Chlora's father relented and fell into line. Pure logic, self-interest, and crates of fresh fruit and vegetables seemed to have won Mr. Glas over. Felipe and Chlora would spend hours looking into each other's eyes and talking about how good life was and how grateful they both were. Chlora's younger sister, Kelly, was enchanted by the stories that Felipe shared with the two sisters about the ancient places in Mexico.

Unfortunately, both Chlora's parents died in 1946. By then, she and Felipe had become a serious item and they married at the end of the year. Felipe requested and was granted a transfer to his company's Eugene store. Immediately thereafter, the happy couple moved to Eugene. She began her third-grade teaching career. During this time, Kelly was a student at the University of Oregon and would sometimes visit them on the weekends and receive care packages of fresh produce from Felipe.

After a few years, Felipe became an expert in the organic food end of the grocery business. In 1952, Felipe and Chlora opened up their own health food store/snack bar near downtown Eugene. The adult customer traffic was insignificant, but the U of O students were always popping in for little purchases. Over the years, their small business grew, and local merchants and professionals would stop by for wheat germ, alfalfa sprouts, or some funky new product called tofu.

"Mija, your aunt and me talked mucho," Felipe said softly. "I drive you to Arizona tomorrow. Business not so good anyway."

Esmeralda knew that her uncle was fibbing to her, because she worked part-time in his health food store and knew that business was good. "Gracias, Tío, but no," Es sighed. "He is my responsibility and I have to deal with it."

"No problema, mija."

Esmeralda knew that this was really hard for her aunt and uncle. She couldn't have Felipe abandon Chlora on her account. *What if something happened to my aunt? It would be my fault. I probably need to grow up a little anyway.*

Chapter 3 – Hej

Tuesday, October 13, 1970

Aunt Chlora had a fitful night, sneezing and coughing. Her hacking echoed throughout the house. The wastebasket that sat next to her side of the bed was filled with mucous-drenched toilet tissue. She knew that she had kept poor Felipe up most of the night. Before retiring, Chlora had plied herself full of Echinacea and other homeopathic medicines. She just needed some rest.

The new situation with Esmeralda had stressed her out, even though Felipe had tried to comfort her. He walked in, carrying a mug of hot hibiscus tea with lemon and honey.

"How are you feeling, mi amor?" he tenderly asked her.

"Like an axe crashed through the middle of my head," she tried to smile.

Chlora had a stoic personality. Her outward façade appeared confident and controlled. But inside her soul, she was tired. *What can I do about Es' decision to look for her father? Why is he back in the picture?* She looked sadly at her husband. Felipe was a better father to Esmeralda than Francisco. Life could be so unfair.

After the accident on the Halloween of 1931, Chlora had never cried. She never complained. She did her physical therapy exercises religiously, trying to mobilize her leg. Her mother and little sister, Kelly, were at the hospital every day. Mrs. Glas was always in the corner chair quietly saying her rosary.

Kelly was at Chlora's bedside and accompanied her big sister whenever she had physical therapy. Kelly wanted to share her Patsy doll with Chlora, but the latter declined. During the lag times, their mom would read them stories. The sisters listened to "Tom Sawyer," "Anne of Green Gables," "Alice in Wonderland," and "The Wonderful Wizard of Oz." Fortunately, Chlora's mom managed to borrow all these books from the hospital library.

Mrs. Glas kept Kelly out of school during this challenging period, but Chlora's classroom teacher, Miss Walters, dropped by every week with classroom assignments. Chlora loved Mrs. Walters and always finished her homework early.

Finally, when on Christmas Eve, Chlora was allowed to come home, reality for the family set in. The prognosis was that Chlora would never be able to walk again. The specialists were afraid that some loose bone fragment near her spine might migrate and puncture an organ or sever a vein if she tried to walk.

The Glas family Christmas was happy, but also bleak. Everyone was thankful for Chlora's return, however, no one knew what the next steps would be.

Chlora's elementary school classes resumed in early January. Mr. Glas would drive the kids to school in his primer-colored jalopy. He would stow the wheelchair under a tied-down tarp. School was good for Chlora and she was an excellent student. Mrs. Glas continued to read to the girls every night. Chlora was still the model daughter who never complained.

Years later, when Chlora attended high school, she seemed to gain greater self-confidence and independence. She could choose some of her classes. Chlora developed a small core of friends that could be labeled brainiacs. But as a female, her future career choices seemed limited: teacher, secretary, nurse, or housewife. The latter three did not seem viable to her.

Life in the Glas household seemed routine and uneventful until Kelly enrolled in the same high school as Chlora in 1938. Kelly had an outgoing personality and quickly made friends at school. However, her crowd tended to be the non-academic, underachiever types. Likewise, Kelly was becoming more and more self-sufficient. She started to walk to and from school with some of her friends. Her father forbade her to ride in anyone's car.

Then there was the fall dance scheduled just after her 15th birthday. Kelly pleaded with her mother to let her go. A neighbor's daughter was attending, and her mother was going to be a chaperone. Kelly's parents relented and finally gave their permission. Mr. Glas was adamant about not wasting money on buying her a new dress. Kelly's mother through some magical maneuverings, made a beautiful dress using remnants from a fabric store.

Chlora had no opinion about whether or not Kelly should go to the dance. She never went to outside social functions because she did not want to be stared at or pitied. *I'd rather be reading a good book, than being a wall flower.*

There was no rain the night of the dance, but it was chilly. Kelly walked over to the neighbors' house around 7:30. Mrs. Glas had given her daughter a dozen admonishments about boys and alcohol. And definitely, no smoking!

Around eleven o'clock the front door of the Glas house crashed opened, and Kelly rushed past her parents who were staying up to make sure that she came home safely. Kelly ran straight into the bedroom where Chlora was sitting up in bed, reading a book.

"What is it?" Chlora said in a surprised tone as she turned and pulled off her thick black-rimmed glasses.

Tears were flowing down Kelly's cheeks.

"I'm sorry!" Kelly dived into Chlora's arms. "I'm so sorry!"

"For what, sis?" Chlora was dumbfounded.

"It was all my fault," the sobs were now uncontrollable from Kelly.

"What was?"

"The accident," Kelly said, knowing full well that it really hadn't been an accident.

Chlora stroked Kelly's hair. "You're not to blame," she tried to assure her younger sister.

"Yes, I am," pouted Kelly. "I wasn't paying attention."

"Hey, it wasn't your fault that that jerk was drunk and driving too fast."

"It should have been me, not you," Kelly had had an epiphany at the dance. While she was having a good time, her sister had to stay home. Kelly felt guilty. Chlora had suffered because she had saved Kelly's life.

"That's nonsense," Chlora's eyes started to moisten.

"Why you?" Kelly's voice quivered. "Why not me?"

"You're my sister. It was my duty," Chlora tried weakly to justify what had happened. "That's what family is for."

Kelly's dying wishes kept ringing in Chlora's ears as Esmeralda was preparing to leave. Chlora looked at Kelly's photo on her dresser. *Kelly, what do you want me to do? She wants to leave. I can't do anything to stop her.* She leaned forward and turned the photo closer to her. *Why are you letting him take her away from us?* She said bitterly to herself.

After breakfast Esmeralda said her painful goodbyes to her aunt and uncle. They had given her dozens of admonitions and do's and don'ts. *Don't pick up any hitchhikers! Call us each night (collect)! Take lots of breaks on the road.*

Tío Felipe helped load up Esmeralda's 1968 Anti-Establishment Mint green Ford Pinto. He stocked her with enough granola, trail mix, and stash tea to supply an army. He also slipped her an envelope that contained a $100 in small bills.

"Call us if there are any problems," they said as they waved goodbye. They were losing their baby. Chlora was sitting in the threshold of the front door way. The couple had forlorn expressions as they stared outward.

Before leaving town, Esmeralda went to her bank and withdrew $300 from her savings account. That left a balance of $24. *Oh, well, I already promised to pay for dad's back rent. Hope it's not too much.*

Her next stop was to fill up at the gas station. It was about fifty degrees outdoors with a little sprinkle dotting the environment. She made sure that her front windows were clean.

Es left Eugene just before eleven a.m. She tugged on the orange butterfly opal pendant that was hanging around her neck. *Oh, mother, help me! Help me find him!*

The highway was not too busy, but big logging trucks were constantly cutting her off. Esmeralda was not looking forward to the long drive. She had been on some arduous journeys, but never as a sole driver. *I'll pretend this is just a week-long camping trip.* A song titled "Easy Rider" played on her radio full blast. She was driving just over the speed limit. The weather had started to clear up, but it was still partially cloudy. She turned down the heat. She did not want to get too comfortable.

Esmeralda forced herself to pull over at a rest stop to use the bathroom. Her adrenaline was flowing. As she resumed her journey, she saw that a tall young man with long brownish-blonde hair and his slender female companion were hitchhiking at the on-ramp. They had a scribbled sign on cardboard saying "Ashland." Their backpacks were laying on the ground with little blue and yellow flag insignias sewn on them. Despite the cold weather, the pair were wearing shorts. Esmeralda felt sorry for them.

"Hey! Do you guys want a ride?" Es shouted as she stopped and rolled down the passenger window.

"Hej!" [Hello] replied the young man as he started to pick up his backpack.

"Hop on in," Esmeralda called out. For the next two hours she conversed with the youngsters who were traveling across the United States. She found out that Ann-Marie and Axel, were from Uppsala, Sweden, and taught English as a second language in Sverige. Axel spoke with an accent and seemed to gasp every time he would try to explain something. Ann-Marie was more relaxed and told Es about their three-month jaunt across the United States.

The Swedish couple talked about European politics, the beauty of the United States, and the very different foods they had encountered. Every once in a while, Axel and Ann-Marie would speak Swedish to each other in a sotto voce tone. "Ser du hennas hår?" [Check out her hair.] he said. Ann-Marie replied "Det är antagligen bara färgat." [It's probably just a dye job.]

The pair were eventually heading for San Francisco and then Disneyland down in Southern California. They were having such a good time that Es didn't even think about how quickly she had broken the "no hitchhikers" rule.

When there was a lull in the conversation, Esmeralda's thoughts drifted. She thought about her mother. Esmeralda didn't remember many details about her mother. She had passed away when Es was only eleven years old. But one of the things she recalled was that her mother was an independent soul, a perfect complement to her father. Kelly was a free spirit whose nature blew with the wind.

Kelly would listen to Es' father, Paco, trying to mentor their daughter and teach her the right way [i.e., his way] to do things. Paco and Esmeralda would sneak away on the weekends and after school while Kelly was working, would go hiking and commune with nature. Because of this, Esmeralda had all the trappings of a tomboy.

When Paco wasn't around, Kelly would tell Esmeralda, "The first rule to remember is 'Break all rules!'" The mother and daughter would then giggle conspiratorially.

Earlier that morning before her departure, Esmeralda's aunt had prepared four grilled cheese sandwiches for her. Esmeralda shared these with her new acquaintances. During this ride Es kept glancing at Ann-Marie who was seated in the front seat with the backpack on her lap. Ann-Marie's whitish legs had dark splotches. *Oh my God!* Es noticed. *She doesn't even shave her legs!*

The time flew by quickly, and eventually she dropped off the Swedish couple at a gas station right outside of Ashland. They could smell the pine in the air as they exchanged hugs and addresses. Esmeralda thought that she probably would never see them again. Es wondered if she would ever make it to Europe. She filled up her gas tank and bought a twelve-ounce cup of coffee. Or some kind of brown liquid, anyway.

As she pulled back onto the highway, she noticed that the afternoon was getting overcast and darker. The gas station attendant had told her that she wouldn't be needing chains going up the highway pass that abutted Mt. Ashland. But she didn't really know for sure as she drove at a normal speed. The radio reception was full of static. She stuck in a "Blood, Sweat, and Tears" tape into her eight-track player and hoped that it would work. It was so temperamental.

As she propelled on, flashing yellow signal lights suddenly appeared on both sides of the road. "Caution: Storm Warning. Chains May Be Required." *Rats! I didn't bring any dang chains!* Putting chains on the car was one of her least favorite things to do. She kept driving cautiously, trying to avoid the trucks that were going seven and a half miles per hour up the grade. There were a few cars pulled off the road. Finally, she came upon the highway patrol station. The uniformed officer with a full-length yellow coat waved her through. She breathed a sigh of relief and continued on her way.

For the next two hours she drove white-knuckled through the Cascade Mountains, crossing from Oregon into California. She put on her headlights as it was getting darker. Es kept vigilant of black ice and cars with their lights off or too dirty to be visible.

Blink! Blink! All of a sudden there were dozens of brake lights in front of her. Traffic had been brought to a standstill on both sides of the highway. Near Dunsmuir a big rig semi had jack-knifed in the middle of the road. Three black-and-white California Highway Patrol (CHP) cars straddled the south bound lanes with their lights flashing. The CHP officers could be seen directing operations with their powerful flashlights as a road crew cleaned up the debris.

Several drivers in front of her had turned off their engines. Esmeralda did likewise. She snacked on some of her stash. People were getting in and out of their cars to relieve themselves by the side of the road. No one seemed to care about modesty.

Esmeralda started to get cold as the temperature dipped into the thirties. She pulled her down feather sleeping bag from the back seat and wrapped it around her legs. She closed her eyes for a minute. One of her dad's rules was to rest when you could. She now had to use the bathroom, but she was afraid that if she left her vehicle, the traffic would start up again. It had been almost two hours since the mishap.

Finally, she saw one of the CHP cars take off. There were now a dozen flares on the right side of the road. An officer was now trying to direct traffic. It was difficult to ascertain whether there were two or three lanes merging. Some of the big rigs cut off the little guys because they could. Twenty minutes later Esmeralda was hightailing it down the highway.

Esmeralda couldn't hold it until the next exit, so she pulled over and did her business off the side of the road. Just like camping, she thought.

About forty-five minutes later she arrived in Redding, totally frazzled. She booked a room at the Motel 7, paying cash. She brought only her backpack into the lodging with her. Es hoped that no one would break into her car or even steal it.

Before taking a shower, she called her aunt and uncle.

"Es, we were so worried about you," gurgled her aunt who still sounded congested. "We hadn't heard from you."

"Just traffic," Es did not want to give them the gory details of her day. She didn't want to worry them.

They spoke for only a few minutes. Es didn't need to run up their long-distance telephone charges.

Ah! The hot water in the shower felt so good. *Hot! Hot! Hot!* She was able to thaw out. Now Es was ready to get something to eat. Since she never wore makeup, getting ready was easy. Es quickly towel-dried her hair. Thirty minutes later she left the motel to look for a local diner. She was hungry. Fortunately, she found the Mount Shasta Café just next door.

At home with her aunt and uncle, Esmeralda ate mostly vegetarian. When she was with her father, she was an omnivore. *I'm on my way to dad's. Might as well start on the red meat diet.* She ordered a cheeseburger and fries at the counter.

A young woman customer wearing a Shasta College sweatshirt remarked to Es as she walked by the counter, "Cool hair!" Esmeralda got those types of comments a lot, but over time had chosen to ignore them. *Whatever!*

She went back to her motel room, negotiating the slippery, slushy outdoor steps up to the second floor. She got ready for bed. Her tummy was full, and she was exhausted. However, she was still wound up from the stressful drive and couldn't go to sleep. She pulled out a copy of one of her mother's books that she had brought with her, "Green Mansions" by William Henry Hudson. It had one of her mother's "Famous Poems" bookmarks in it. Her mother was an aspiring poetess, who never shared her poems. Esmeralda unconsciously twisted her mother's orange fire opal pendant with the fingers of her right hand. It felt warm.

Chapter 4 – Bikersfield

Wednesday, October 14, 1970

The cracked and dirty motel clock radio that sat next to the nineteen-inch RCA brown plastic television blinked 4:04. Es got up and zigzagged to the bathroom in the dark, fumbling around to find the errant light switch. She crawled back into bed, but kept the covers off her. Esmeralda was still tired, but unable to go back to sleep because the room was overheated. She couldn't breathe with the overbearing warmth coming from the baseboard heaters.

Es laid in a semiconscious state thinking about her mother. *Mom, you asked me to take care of him. Why?* Es guessed that her father became a wandering soul when her mother had died. She knew that her father had loved her mother very much. What she couldn't figure out was why he had abandoned her, his only daughter! *To find himself? Gimme a friggin' break! I lost mom too!*

Esmeralda was born on Halloween night of 1948 in Eugene, Oregon.

As Kelly held her baby, she remembered a promised that she had made years earlier. *I will teach this child to revere nature and to care for the helpless creatures of this earth.*

When Paco came into the maternity ward, she changed her mood into a much light vein. "Well, I either got tricked or I got treated," Kelly said to her husband Paco as he held her hand.

"*Sugar and spice* and all things nice!" he smiled looking at Kelly and the baby. "Especially, Halloween candy!"

In the early years of their marriage, Kelly and Paco had developed a close relationship with Chlora's husband, Tío Felipe. Paco and Felipe always teased Kelly about how lucky she was to have two Mexicanos in their family. Especially, since they were so handsome. They would all laugh.

Kelly asked her sister Chlora and Felipe to be Esmeralda's godparents. At the baptism, baby Esmeralda kept moving her head to avoid getting wet. It even seemed like she gave the priest a dirty look.

Esmeralda grew up as a happy child, who was very liberated. She always wanted her own way. Paco and Kelly raised their daughter in an old rented house off East 19th Avenue and Alderwood in Eugene. Kelly had opened up a little bungalow ceramics shop in an art colony when Esmeralda was only three. Kelly originally had gone to the University of Oregon before she was married, but had eventually dropped out. She started to take pottery classes instead, at the Eugene Technical-Vocational School. Paco had gotten a job as an assistant naturalist with a long-term environmental project at the University of Oregon. His research professor from New Mexico Highlands University had helped him land the position. In the early years of their marriage, on the weekends, Paco split his time between doing metal work for Kelly and assisting a goldsmith who was suffering from senility issues. Sometimes he brought Es to the shop where she was entertained by her mother, fellow shopkeepers, and the customers.

Kelly had two kilns that Paco had set up. Paco made some metal stands for some of the flower pots or chicken legs for the ceramic birds. Kelly also did calligraphy posters, cards, and bookmarks utilizing some of her own poetry.

On occasion, Esmeralda might be left with Chlora and Felipe on a weekend. They loved taking care of her. Felipe would always converse with her in Spanish. She even had her own little room with books and toys at their house. They would take her with them to church on Sundays. Everybody always assumed that Es was their natural born child.

As time went on, Kelly, grew more and more anti-religious. She believed that Catholic priests were out of touch with women and birth control. She didn't believe in the notion of an eye for an eye in the Old Testament. She just believed in treating everyone else like she herself wanted to be treated, to be grateful for life, and to do good deeds. Paco wasn't so extreme, but he went along with the program.

Things changed a little when Esmeralda started school. Paco was the one who dropped her off and picked her up. After school Es and Paco would stop at the nearby park and play frontier adventures. He taught her how to knot ropes, to fish, and to hunt. Es became a star Girl Scout.

Having to assume the role of the bad guy, Kelly would have to gently remind Paco that their daughter also needed to do homework. On the weekends, Kelly recaptured her daughter. Es would hang out in her mother's studio, either playing by herself or making rudimentary ceramic animals. Customers would chat with the young girl about her artwork. Es did quite well. On those rare occasions when someone bought one her clay creatures, Es was allowed to keep the money.

Sometimes Paco would have to go into the forests for a couple of weeks at a time for the research project. Es would cry that her father was never coming back. That lasted a few hours. Kelly and she would sit in the stairwell of their little abode wrapped in each other's arms. The mother would tell her stories about magical butterflies, ill-tempered frogs, and a petulant

Chihuahua. Es would fall asleep and Kelly would have to gingerly carry her daughter to bed.

During these times Kelly would also allow Es to wear some of her beaded necklaces or bracelets. Es felt grown up.

When Francisco returned from his job wearing two weeks' worth of mottled black beard, Es hardly paid him any attention. So much for loyalty.

At other times, Kelly would participate in local arts and crafts exhibits throughout the State of Oregon and sometimes Seattle. Francisco would pack up their car, and if he could get a few days off work, would drive Kelly and her wares to the various markets. Es, meanwhile, would stay with her Aunt Chlora and Uncle Felipe, who took her out for pizza at a parlor owned and run by Guido and Lorenza. The place had delicious, thick crust pizza and was adorned with cheap prints of Da Vinci's "Mona Lisa", "The Last Supper", and many others. The restaurant was infused with garlic.

Esmeralda held her own in elementary school, although everyone called her a tomboy. A group of girls led by Laura Campbell tried to bully Es because of her Mexican ethnicity. Es never engaged and sometimes had to walk the long way home to avoid the nativists. Es kept this to herself and felt bad for the other Mexican students who were also being picked on. Es became more of a maverick and didn't have many close friends.

One day in 1958, her Uncle Felipe picked her up from school and took her to their house. Aunt Chlora seemed very pale and agitated. The ten-year old did not understand why she was spending a weekday night at her godparents.

The next day after school, instead of taking her home, Tío Felipe took her to the local hospital. After a little wait, Es was shown into a hospital room that had two beds. One was empty; and in the other, her mother was lying down with a tube coming out of her arm. Next to her, a monitor was showing fluorescent orange numbers and oscilloscope spikes. Paco was sitting beside Kelly. He had dark circles under his eyes.

Esmeralda started to cry. She didn't know why. She rushed to her mother's side. Her dad stroked her head.

"Guys, can I have some alone time with her, please?" said Kelly as she labored to speak.

The two compadres left with Felipe laying his hand on Paco's shoulder.

"Es, I have something important to tell you," Kelly held her daughter's smallish hand.

"Are you okay, mama?"

"Well, yes and no," Kelly didn't know how to respond and didn't want to lie to her daughter. "I have a disease. It's called cancer."

"Are you going to be all right?"

"Well, no," she took her daughter's hand and traced a pattern above her breast. "The bad germs have spread all over my body."

"Are you coming home?"

"I have to go away," Kelly said trying not to break down. "Remember how mommy has always taught you to try to live in the present? That means right now. And not to worry about things far into the future." Kelly was always telling people that she didn't know if she had 25 minutes or 25 years to live, but she wanted to live life to the fullest at each moment.

"Are you going to leave us?"

"Not really," Kelly sighed. "You just won't be able to see me like today."

"Are you going to die?"

"Yes and no. My body will turn into a bunch of old stinky bones," Kelly tried to make light of the subject. "But my spirit will always be watching over you."

Esmeralda's face contorted. She wasn't understanding all of this. And if she did, she didn't want to believe it.

Kelly reached over to the nightstand and brought out a small Mexican embossed leather purse. She unsnapped it and pulled out the orange fire opal necklace that she always wore. It was shaped like a butterfly.

"Here, mija, always wear this and I will always be close to you."

Kelly put it over Esmeralda's neck and retied the leather strap. Es knew that her father had one just like it. The necklace felt hot on Es' chest. She sniffled.

"One more thing, Es," she held her daughter's hand tightly. "You will have to take good care of your daddy after I am gone."

Her mother died a year later.

Es hadn't requested a wakeup call, but she finally decided to get up at six o'clock. She still had a long drive ahead and it would be good to get an early start. Her only concern was whether the roads were icy. She repacked her knapsack and headed over to the café next door. She wanted a hot breakfast to give her energy. This time she remembered to tuck her hair under her baseball cap.

She liked to eat healthily and was prepared to eat her routine hot oatmeal with fruit, but then the smell of bacon punched her in the nose. Thirty minutes later she was dipping her toast into the fried eggs and eating the greasy bacon. She felt like a truck driver.

Esmeralda gassed up the Pinto and did a visual check of the exterior of the car. She made sure that her windshield was clean after all the ice and grime that had accumulated on it the day before. She began the continuation of her journey south. There was a tall, bearded hitchhiker on the side of the road next to a black Schnauzer with a red bandanna tied around its neck. She thought for a second and then said to herself, "Naw! Not today, buddy."

A little drizzle began, and she turned on her windshield wipers as she sailed down the highway. There was still static on the radio, so Es put "The Abbey Road" into the eight-track player. She hummed along for a while, bobbing her head up and down. She made good time on the way to Red Bluff, zigging and zagging through the highway curves. The sky started to clear, and she could see snow-capped mountains to the east. The traffic was light, and the road straightened out, but the big rigs still splashed cars if they veered too close.

In Sacramento, Highway 99 detoured through city streets going past the state Capitol. Es missed a sign and went in the wrong direction for several blocks before she realized her error. Ten minutes later she was back on the highway going toward Fresno.

The road was now flat and straight again. The clouds in the skies were becoming greyer. Es passed a scraggly-bearded hitchhiker, but she didn't stop. Es thought about the Swedish kids that she had given a ride to. *I wonder how they are doing? It must be nice to be free spirits and travel around the world. That's what my mother always wanted to be . . . a wandering soul. And why my Mexican blood makes me be adventurous. Am I rebellious? Or just a combination of my parents?*

Esmeralda had always thought that her mother was cool. A precursor to the hippies, Kelly had been non-judgmental and tended to go with the flow in life. However, at times it seemed to Es that her mother lacked ambition or direction. Sure, Kelly ran a fairly successful ceramics business, but it seemed like more of a hobby than a real business venture.

Es, on the other hand, was self-directed and always worked hard. In high school and in college Es earned money working for her uncle part-time at his health food store. She stocked grains and nuts. She labeled packages. She made fruit smoothies for thirsty customers. It was work, but not really. Tío Felipe was overly generous in paying her. She felt bad that she had abandoned him this week to go find her father. In many ways her uncle had been more of a father to her than Paco. *I wouldn't give it a second thought to look for my uncle if he were missing. I'd look for him under every rock. Life isn't fair. Poor Tío Felipe!*

Es passed abandoned fruit stands, and big eucalyptus trees planted along the side of the road as windbreaks. The audio tape had finished playing and she fidgeted with the radio trying to get a good station. She wasn't a fan of country western or evangelical preaching. Es was surprised to find Spanish-speaking radio stations playing their norteño music. She had spoken Spanish with her dad, uncle, and her dad's family in Mesa Verde. She also had taken three years of Spanish in high school. She was proficient but still had a gringa accent. With little success of finding a decent station, she finally turned off the radio.

At Manteca she pulled over and drove into a gas station at the edge of town. The fuel prices seemed more expensive here. The restroom there was not wonderful, but Es made do. The gas station had a small food and beverage section. She looked for something to munch on, but all the snacks had tons of salt, sugar, and preservatives. Her Tío Felipe would have had a cow. She didn't want a soda pop, so she ended up filling up her water bottle back in the bathroom. Other travelers were coming in and going out. They had little kids who were bundled up or still wearing their pajamas. She noticed that most of the license plates were from out of state. Es wondered what they were doing in California at this time of year. Some of the patrons spoke Spanish. *This is a nice change,* she thought.

Es decided to take a break from driving and walked to the center of the little town. Her muscles were feeling cramped. There were no sidewalks and the path was muddy. Most of the foliage from the trees was gone, but the crows sat on the branches anyway, making their cawing sounds. The air was cold and smelled of truck fuel. Es picked up her pace.

There was a sign that hung over the entrance to the center of town: "Manteca – Gateway to Yosemite."

Esmeralda's eyebrows furrowed. She remembered that her father had cracked a joke when she was a youngster about why so-called smart people would name their town Lardsville.

Esmeralda was only about 4 or 5 years old when the family had driven to Yosemite National Park in an old 1950 Ford. She didn't remember the color of their car because it was so faded and primered. They liked to travel around the Southwest. Kelly always told her that travel was about searching for beautiful things. They approached Manteca.

"Yeah, mija, Manteca means lard," her father laughed. "These people are . . ."

Paco was interrupted by Kelly who gave him the "look" that meant he should not teach their daughter inappropriate terms. He nodded good-naturedly in agreement. The family had been delayed because Esmeralda had become motion sick with the twists and turns of the road. The poor girl had vomited several times, both inside and outside of the car. Kelly made her suck on a lemon. Kelly did her best to clean up the stinky mess while Paco gave her a piece of wild licorice from his leather medicine pouch.

Later that afternoon they checked into a campground in the middle of the Yosemite Valley. Since it was getting dark, Paco immediately started to set up their tent. Kelly went to the campground faucet to wet some towels to further clean Es up. Es was asleep in the back seat of the car. No one was taking the time to look at the beautiful scenery that surrounded them.

Paco built a little fire and started to roast hot dogs. He started singing songs. Esmeralda was awake and now feeling better. She joined her father and made sure that their combined vocals scared away any mountain lions for miles away.

After brushing their teeth in really cold water, they retired to their tent and snuggled into their sleeping bags.

"Don't let the bed bugs get you!" shouted out Paco as he tucked his daughter in.

"Ugh!" whimpered Es. "Not in my bed!"

"There's no bugs," Kelly rolled her eyes as she smiled. "Daddy is just teasing you."

The night was uneventful except for the perfunctory walk with a flashlight to the outhouse in middle of the night. There was also some intermittent clanging of trash cans. In the morning the mischief of errant bears was evident.

Esmeralda was not a happy camper as her mother bathed her in the shallow Merced River that ran through the Yosemite Valley.

"Mama, I'm freezing!"

"Look at those beautiful mountains," Kelly tried to distract her daughter. She pointed to Half Dome and the black-streaked granite monolith walls that ascended thousands of feet above the valley floor.

Esmeralda looked upwards and for the moment forgot her discomfort. Then all of a sudden, she heard splashing. She was getting wet as the Loch Ness monster approached. No, wait! It was her father diving into the ice-cold water.

"Grr!" Paco snorted as he tried to attack Esmeralda who was using her mother as a shield. "Brr!"

The horseplay lasted but a moment with everyone getting soaked and freezing to death. They jumped out of the river that was laden with small round stones. They quickly grabbed their towels.

"Papá, you're a monster," Es laughed.

"Okay, you two, get dried off. Breakfast in twenty minutes," ordered Paco.

A half hour later the family was sitting in clean clothes on cutup logs scarfing down pancakes.

Later in the morning, Es and Paco trekked up the river about eighty yards and found themselves a fishing hole that was a pool surrounded by moss-covered rocks. Paco baited the two small fishing poles with little bits of cheese. Kelly stayed back at the camp and worked on her poetry.

The sun beat down on the fishermen even though they had hats on.

"Papá, when are we going to catch some fish?"

"Soon, mija," Paco smiled as he lied. "See those dragonflies over the water. They are trying to tell the fish to come this way."

Suddenly, out of nowhere, a kaleidoscope of Monarch butterflies surrounded the pair and slowly landed, one by one, on both Paco and Esmeralda. This occurrence was truly amazing because butterflies usually shied away from humans. And as swiftly as the butterflies had appeared, upon some sort of indiscernible signal, they dispersed and disappeared!

Around noon, when Kelly came to bring them some cheese sandwiches and a water bottle, Es began jumping up and down. She shouted, "Mom! Mom! I saw the pretty things you said. The butterflies jumped on me and Papá. They told me that I was their friend."

Kelly looked askance at Paco, but then smiled. She looked at her daughter in a loving way and said, "I'm so glad that you are seeing the beauty of nature."

A noisy neighbor interrupted them from a nearby pine tree. A yellow bird with black wings sang a funny song.

"Mom, it's face is funny," Es said, pointing to another bird. It was the orangish-red head of the tanager.

Kelly left them and wandered back to camp. She would talk with Paco later to hear his side of the butterfly story.

Esmeralda eventually fell asleep on the shore. Paco gave up on fishing and carried her back to the camp.

"What kind of fish are we having for dinner?" shouted Kelly as the two approached,

"The kind that we are going to find at the lodge," Paco retorted.

The wildflower meadows trail was about .7 miles long. They walked among the green plants with the small yellow flowers as they smelled the evergreens.

A colony of ants cut them off at the pass.

"Papá, why are the ants so big?" Es asked.

"Because they eat little girls that ask a lot of questions."

For dinner the trio shared a roasted chicken at the restaurant. They walked back to camp singing under the moonlight.

That night after Esmeralda was fast asleep, Kelly and Paco talked about the butterfly sighting. Paco admitted that he was thoroughly surprised to see the large flotilla of butterflies that had swarmed them. Most of them had fluttered around Es and landed on her. Es had talked to them as though they were playmates. Paco didn't think anything of it. What surprised him most was that they were indeed Monarchs. As Paco was talking, Kelly had a preoccupied look on her face as she clutched her opal pendant.

The next day came early. Kelly had rinsed out their bathing suits and washed some of their clothes from the day before. She hung them out to dry on some small shrubs.

Suddenly, there was a scream by the water. Es had disappeared from the sight of her parents. They were in a panic. *Where was she? What happened?*

They saw movement at the edge of the water. Then there she was. She was crying.

"What's wrong, sweetheart?" her mother hugged her. "Are you all right?"

"The socks are going away," Es sputtered.

"What do you mean?"

Esmeralda pointed downstream. Paco could see one of his woolen socks floating down the river. He pointed his chin for Kelly to see. They both smiled and then laughed.

The day ended on an auspicious note with Esmeralda licking a vanilla ice cream cone. They never did eat trout.

In downtown Manteca, Esmeralda bought herself a vanilla ice cream at the drugstore on a whim. It was cold outside, but it still tasted good. The Pinto beckoned to her and she resumed her journey.

Es took her time traveling down the road and decided to stop early. She was exhausted from the constant defensive driving mode that she had had to assume. Pickup trucks flew by her at ninety miles per hour, four-cylinder Nash Ramblers hauled small Streamliner travel trailers at 35 miles per hour, and miasma spotted her windshield from running over road kill.

Going through Bakersfield, she found the Ming Lake Motel a few blocks from the main highway. Es checked in with the hayseed clerk with his slicked down hair who asked a grocery list of questions before taking her cash. She decided to call her

aunt and uncle early, before she took a shower or went hunting
for some dinner.

"Hello, mija!" belted out her uncle who sounded like he had
a big smile on his face at the other end of the telephone line. She
assured him that she was doing fine and that she missed them.

After talking her ear off for several minutes, Tío Felipe
finally handed the phone off to Aunt Chlora. She was feeling
much better and had gone to school. Teaching was a better
distraction than staying at home worrying about her niece.

"Do you need anything, Es?" her aunt asked. "Have you
been eating?"

"All's good, tía," Esmeralda wondered what her aunt could
possibly provide her, being so far away. After a few minutes of
small talk, Es said goodbye and hung up.

Esmeralda's clothes were getting a little ripe. She was
leaning toward hitting the shower. *Naw! I'll get some food first!
This way I can relax and sleep better.*

A block away from the Ming (aka the Merciless) Motel there
was a big parking lot that surrounded a twenty-four-hour diner
and bar. As she walked there, the full moon lit her path. *It kind
of reminds me of a pizza. Yeah, I could do pizza tonight.* As she
opened the worn door, the sound of loud laughter and Western
music hit her. She covered her nose to avoid the smell of
cigarettes. *Ick! Better eat and run.* The place was half empty and
there were a few cowboys standing at the bar, adjusting their hats
and stomping their boots every few minutes. Esmeralda didn't
want to take up a whole table by herself, so she sat at the counter.
Everybody in the place seemed at least ten years older than her,
except for the pony-tailed brunette who took her order at the bar.
Her name tag said Missy and she was skinny with a pimpled
face. She didn't look over sixteen.

Esmeralda ordered a tuna melt. Pizza was not going to work
in a place like this. She had asked for wheat bread, but the diner
only had white. Her meal came with French fries, a leaf of
iceberg lettuce, and a slice of tomato (that had no color red in its
DNA). Not bad, not good, it was food, thought Esmeralda.

Halfway through her meal, Es felt a cold draft of air gush in as the front door opened. There was a clomping of boots coming up behind her. A barrel-chested biker wearing a blue calico head scarf and sporting a frizzly brown beard plopped down on the stool next to her. He gave her the once over as he took off his "Sons of the Devil" leather motorcycle jacket.

Es was focused on her meal. *Hmm. These fries aren't too bad.* She hadn't really noticed the guy who sat next to her until he spoke to her.

"Hey, you wanna beer?" the redneck blurted out, staring at Es. Esmeralda began to feel a warmness from the orange opal pendant on her chest.

She nodded no, without speaking.

"Come on now," he continued. "You're old enough. I got no problems with Mescuns."

Es repeated her head shaking. The opal necklace started to get hot.

She and the biker sat in silence while the biker ordered and received his meal. The guy kept pouring more and more catsup onto his hash browns. She noticed the tattoo on his left knuckles that spelled out a four-letter bad word that started with the letter "f." Breakfast was served all day and he had ordered the three-egg special with all the sides. Some of the red condiment burrowed into his beard. The smell of this guy and the grease from his food was beginning to turn Esmeralda's stomach. *What a jerk!* Her normal response was just to ignore these types of people.

"Hey, you wanna ride on my Harley?" he smiled with his tar-stained teeth. "It's parked right outside. I told you I got a thing for Mescuns." He swung his left arm around and pointed to the door.

Es shook her head no a third time. The opal necklace started to vibrate on her chest.

"What the hell's the matter with you? You can't talk?" he was raising his voice in a huffy tone. "You think you're too good for me, you f__ing Mescun," He gave her a death ray stare.

Es remained silent and kept eating.

"Ronny, do you want a refill?" the waitress came over and asked him. He grunted yes.

Missy picked up his coffee cup and started to pour.

Es felt a jolt erupt from her chest. The guy's hands flew up in the air. "Aww! God darn it!" Missy had dropped his cup and the hot coffee had landed on the intruder's lap. "You . . ." He got up and tried to wipe the crotch of his pants using his paper napkin. That didn't seem to work. He left angrily, cussing all the way to the restroom.

Esmeralda got up and grabbed her jacket. She slipped a ten-dollar bill to Missy (over twice the amount of the bill) and silently mouthed the words "thank you" as she left the premises. The opal necklace was cool again.

Chapter 5 – Green Hair

Thursday, October 15, 1970

Sunrise found Esmeralda paying her motel bill as she checked out. She wasn't going to stay and have her breakfast around there. She would grab something to eat on the way. Her stomach would just have to wait. A handful of granola would hold her over.

As she handed over her room key, Es heard someone in the back office of the lodging rattling on, ". . . last night this biker's Harley had its tires slashed real bad."

"Probably a rival gang."

"Yeah."

Esmeralda hurriedly left the motel, jumped into her car, and headed out of town. Before Es hit the Grapevine climb, she gassed up her car at a local station. Although she had checked the directions for how to get to Arizona, she wasn't sure how to avoid going through Los Angeles proper, since she heard that the traffic down there was the pits. "What's the easiest way to catch the highway going east?" she asked the cashier. He pointed to a map on the nearest wall without uttering a word. She sauntered over to it. The current location was a ragged empty hole surrounded by black smudges. Esmeralda wasn't able to make heads or tails of the map.

"Excuse me, sir?" Es stopped an older man wearing a red and white McFarland Cougars cap, a blue work shirt, and jeans with frayed cuffs. "Do you know anything about how to get to Arizona?"

He stopped and looked kindly at her. After a moment's conversation she smiled and thanked him.

"Hear there's tule fog on the way," he yelled after her.

Es went outside and made a visible inspection of her car. The pungent stench of the roadkill was gone. The weather was cloudy and cold. All systems go.

The mist dotted her windshield as she chugged up the Grapevine slope. The Christian radio station was indiscernible, so Es traveled in silence. Patches of fog assaulted her as she continued toward the Tejon Pass at an altitude of four thousand plus feet. Her hands gripped the steering wheel tighter. Es turned on her headlights. She didn't remember where the switch for her fog lights was. She did not dare try to pass the big rigs that were barely going twenty miles per hour.

Finally, the road leveled off. Just before Esmeralda got to Gorman, the fog lifted and the traffic sped up. She noticed a tallish girl hitchhiking by the side of the road. Actually, it could have been a guy with long hair. She did not get a good look. *Can trust Oregonians. Not sure can trust Californians*, she thought. She didn't stop.

Thanks to the stranger at the gas station, she made all the correct turnoffs on the spider web of the Los Angeles freeway system.

The weather became clear and warmer. Es decided to take off her jacket for the first time in a few days. Now she was driving through towns of concrete. She sighed and decided to stop and gas up around Rosemead, just south of the San Gabriel Mission. She took a little walk after filling up. Es saw a place with white five-foot high letters over the front door advertising barbeque. She hadn't had any BBQ in a long time. She walked in and within minutes was eating the featured barbequed chicken. It costed her almost $3, but it was worth every finger-licking bite. She even had a couple of stains on her navy-blue top to prove it.

Once she hit Palm Springs, the hot winds hit her straight on. Now there was nothing but arid desert in front of her. She saw a light blue pickup truck with its hood up parked off the side of the highway. The average speed on the freeway seemed to be in excess of ninety miles per hour. Esmeralda was doing 70 when she saw a very young man in a white tee shirt and blue jeans carrying a gas can a quarter of a mile ahead of her. It took almost a minute for her to stop on the shoulder of the road. The guy ran up to her car huffing and puffing in his cowboy boots.

"Need a ride?" she yelled.

"Yeah," he gasped. "Ran out of gas. Thanks for stopping."

They took off.

She drove him to the next exit which fortunately had a gas station.

During the short ride, Esmeralda found out that Jim was a high school dropout who worked at a motor oil change place in Indio. He was late for work and hoped that he wouldn't get fired. He wasn't the brightest bulb in the box, but he was polite and thanked her for the rescue. She could relate to him. However, she did not offer to drive him back to his truck.

Es was feeling perky and wondered how far she could push it. She knew that her aunt and uncle didn't want her to set any speed records getting to Arizona. The radio had more Christian, cowboy, and Mexican music. Back to the eight-tracks she went, starting with the Kingston Trio. As she drove through more of the Californian version of the Sahara Desert, Es spotted another hopeful hitchhiker with a dog. Poor guy, she thought, and poor mutt. He reminded her of her dad, but at least this traveler had a companion.

Her head was getting hot under her hat. She dared to take off her cap, allowing her green locks to flow to her shoulders.

After her mother died in November of 1959, Paco tried to take care of Esmeralda, but his heart was not in it. He was devastated. A part of his soul had died with Kelly. Esmeralda was equally distraught, and she cried continuously. She wouldn't eat, she wouldn't smile, and her aunt and uncle were afraid for the child's health. The greatest shock was when Esmeralda's hair turned green overnight. Es went berserk and cried even more.

"I hate my hair!" she would scream. She wanted her head shaved, but Aunt Chlora drew the line. Es did not want to go to school. She acted out and went ballistic. Es and her aunt finally reached an accommodation: Es was allowed to wear a cap to cover up her hair.

Paco took her to a doctor who examined her, but he couldn't give a straight answer as to the cause of the girl's green hair.

"Trauma," surmised the medical person. "Brought on by her mother's death."

"How long will it last?" asked Paco.

"Can't tell," continued the doctor. "Too many factors to consider."

"What do you know for sure?" Paco was getting frustrated with the physician.

"Well, we could run some tests."

Aunt Chlora and Uncle Felipe took her to the priest for a spiritual consultation.

"Why did this happen, father?" Chlora asked the young priest.

He grasped her hands in his. "It is God's will," he propounded. "There are many things that are not known to man. But there is a reason for everything. This child may be spiritually blessed."

"Then she not possessed, padre?" blurted out Felipe.

The priest smiled and nodded no.

Chlora and Felipe took her home and tried to comfort her. The next day when Esmeralda came home from her aunt and uncle's, her eyes lit up. There, in front of her, was her father with his long ponytail, dyed a bright green. He had colored it with food coloring. Esmeralda smiled for the first time in several days.

The adults tried everything to try to get her natural hair color back, but without success. Even when they tried cutting it, the hair grew back green. Finally, things seemed to be settling down until two weeks later. Paco received a letter from the principal stating that Esmeralda was refusing to remove her cap during class time. Actually, Es was coping with the situation in her fifth-grade class until one day she accidentally forgot and subconsciously removed her hat. Most of her schoolmates thought her green hair was cool, especially the other girls. However, a few of the boys started taunting her. The fact that she bloodied Jeff Jones' nose after school did not engender sympathy for her at school.

The principal, Gary Doerfler, had stated that Esmeralda's green hair was a nuisance and was causing disruption in the classroom. He wanted Es to either shave her head or have it dyed a "normal" color!

Since Chlora was a teacher in the same school, the aunt went berserk. She got her brother-in-law Paco to write a letter to the school board requesting a hearing on the matter.

A week later on a Wednesday, Paco was able to plead his case to the school board. Principal Doerfler said that it was the responsibility of the school to maintain order. In rebuttal, Paco painfully explained the recent death of his wife and the strange physiological change in Esmeralda. The school board went into closed session and came out a half hour later. They then voted 3-2, that Esmeralda did not have to shave her head or dye it, but that she would have to wear some type of head covering at all times.

After the hearing, Paco drove Chlora back to her home. She was all right with the decision, and Paco was just glad that Es was okay. When they told Felipe, who had been watching over Es, the uncle became unglued.

"They no gonna to treat mija like a second-class citizen," Felipe ranted. "They always do this to me. No! Not to mija! ¡Pinche c*abrones!"

Felipe had a friend of a friend of a friend who knew an attorney. The friend twice-removed did not know what kind of lawyer Dana Minsky was, but he knew that she was good.

Chlora and Paco met with the attorney in her downtown office that was furnished with funky leather couches and ragtag Oriental carpets. Chlora explained the situation to the lawyer.

"I can't guarantee any results, but I will do my best," Ms. Minsky smiled. She was going to charge them a couple of hundred dollars, far below her normal rate.

Minsky sent a legal demand letter to the school board alleging that Esmeralda Luna's constitutional rights had been violated, and that she would hold each board member personally and severally liable.

The school board's attorney David Paulus called back and left a message with Dana's secretary/paralegal. The one-word response was "No!" The school district was infuriated with the legal challenge and took a strong opposition stance against the complaint.

Calmly, Dana sent another letter to the school requesting another school board hearing. This was to be an open and public hearing, and Minsky wanted the opportunity to question Principal Doerfler. The school board saw that the problem was creating bad publicity for the school and decided reluctantly to grant the request for the audience.

At the next regularly scheduled school board meeting, many parents and members of the community showed up for the spectacle. A reporter from the Eugene Register-Guard was also present.

Dana Minsky made an opening statement. The school's attorney, Paulus, followed and stated that hair color was not a protected class under any civil rights laws and that Esmeralda's appearance was offensive and disruptive to the classroom environment.

Then the gloves came off during rebuttal. "Would you kick a black child out of school because he or she was unacceptable to the majority?" Dana asked. The hearing room became silent. The board members squirmed in their seats.

"How about left-handers? Would you kick them out too?" Minsky walked in front of the school board members, each who looked uncomfortable.

"How about kids over six feet tall?"

A half hour later the school board members went into closed session. When they returned, they voted 4-1 to allow Esmeralda to have her hair any way she wanted. Dana shook Chlora's and Paco's hand. Paco gave Chlora a big hug with a big smile.

Afterwards, the cub news reporter asked questions of the school board chair. The newsperson later questioned the lone dissenting vote, Joyce Bowers, who stated for the record, "the youngster must have sinned and offended God in order to have her hair change colors."

For the next few weeks, Paco seemed to be upbeat. Then he went to pieces again. He became depressed all the time. Luckily, Tío Felipe took Esmeralda to and from school. Half the time she spent the night at her godparents' house because Paco would come home late. He didn't drink, but he seemed to be having trouble at work and often had to work late to finish his tasks.

Since Paco didn't know how to do ceramics, he couldn't make pottery. He tried to sell off Kelly's remaining inventory. Finally, he decided to close up Kelly's business because he couldn't afford the rent. He volunteered more and more for assignments at work that would take him out into the forests for weeks at a time.

Paco seemed to be drifting more and more apart from Esmeralda and the in-laws. Chlora and Felipe tried their best to counsel and encourage him. Chlora and Felipe were especially worried about Esmeralda and her tenuous state. Finally, it was agreed that Paco would move back to Mesa Verde and try to get his head straight. He bought the equipment of his goldsmith friend who was now in a rest home. Chlora and Felipe would now have full-time, physical custody of Esmeralda. They would take a wait-and-see approach on legal custody. They had Minsky draw up a power of attorney that allowed the godparents to take care of any emergency needs for Es.

When Paco explained to Esmeralda that he was leaving, she did not cry. "It is the first step," he told her. Es did not understand. She just grabbed at her opal pendant that was the twin to her father's. It started to get warm and vibrate.

Es stopped in Blythe near the California-Arizona border at an International House of Pancakes. It was late, and she was debating on whether to continue or to stop for the night. The blueberry pancakes were tasty, even though the syrup was overly-sweet. She had decided not to have the eggs and sausages because they looked too greasy. Afterwards, Es purchased gas and hot-dogged it all the way to Arizona. The night was pitch black and there were no highway lights. The sky was smitten with a million stars and the moon was bright. It seemed that most people drove lightning fast with their high beams on.

Esmeralda was feeling bad that it was so late and that she had not called her aunt and uncle. They would be worried. She passed a highway patrol car with its flashing lights. The AHP had pulled over what looked like a red Corvette. It was hard to tell in the dark. She decreased her speed a notch. *Wow! I was doing eighty!*

As Es approached the mountains, she was starting to get tired. *Come on! Just a few more miles!* Finally, around ten o'clock, the Pinto pulled into the O'odham Motor Lodge that had a lit "Vacancy" sign over its front porch. The room rate was rather cheap. Es decided that she didn't need anything else to eat that night.

"Es, where have you been?" her Aunt Chlora answered the phone.

Chapter 6 – Tubac

Friday, October 16, 1970

Es was drowsy the next morning from her long drive. Her back ached. Aunt Chlora had reprimanded her the night before for taking unnecessary chances. Es knew that her aunt was right and that she shouldn't worry her godparents. *Así es la vida,* as her uncle would say.

From the front desk clerk of the Tucson motel, Es received directions to Tubac. She had never been there even though her father had lived there for several years. The clerk also recommended Chero's, a Mexican restaurant just about a half mile down the road, for breakfast.

Moments later as she entered the hole-in-the-wall tan adobe building, she was reminded of her grandmother's house in Mesa Verde. The sweet smells of onions, bacon, and garlic drenched her senses.

"Buenos días, señorita," smiled a young dark-skinned girl. Her black hair was braided in coils with red, white, and green ribbons.

Esmeralda nodded and mumbled something unintelligible as she followed the young woman to an empty booth with brown-marbled vinyl upholstery. There were very few patrons in the place. Es was given a bilingual English-Spanish menu.

Oh, my God! I'm in hog heaven! She perused the menu, savoring every entry. Chilaquiles! Tamales! Huevos rancheros!

A young busboy came by and dropped off a basket of totopos [tortilla chips] and red chile salsa on her table. Es picked up a chip and dipped it. Then another, and another. Within a few minutes the locusts had devoured half the basket.

"¿Lista, señorita, para ordenar?" the girl had come back to take Esmeralda's order.

"Sí," Es was having a hard time deciding. "Huevos divorciados por favor." Es wanted the "divorced" eggs with two types of sauce.

"¿Tortillas de maíz o harina?" Es was given the choice of corn or flour tortillas.

"De maíz por favor." She chose the corn.

"¿Y para tomar?"

"Té de manzanilla," Es ordered chamomile tea to drink. "Con limón y miel, por favor." She took her tea with lemon and honey. Her Spanish was coming back to her. Her dad, her uncle, and nana would be proud of her. She pushed the basket of chip crumbs away.

Within ten minutes the young boy brought out a hot, midnight blue plate topped with a red sauce on one side and a green sauce on the other. A fried egg sat under each dollop of salsa. A demarcation line of jib sail chips over refried beans marked the middle of the "divorced" eggs.

Es broke up the egg yolk with a corn tortilla. She was in heaven. The red sauce made her mouth water. Then she tried the green sauce. It was tangy. She kept eating. Her stomach was full, but she wanted a piece of pan dulce, Mexican sweet bread. *Can't. Gotta stop eating.*

The meal was less than two dollars with the tip. *How can these poor people survive down here?*

Es was totally relaxed (and quite full). Her stomach ached. The sun smacked Esmeralda in the face as she exited the restaurant. She took her time driving down to Tubac, arriving around nine o'clock. Tubac looked like a small Wild West town with one-story adobe buildings and a sandy road. There were even a couple of horses being ridden on the side of the lane. She had her dad's address, but it still took her fifteen minutes of driving around to find his place. There were a set of sand-colored adobe bungalows down a double-tracked path off a main street. She parked in front of the biggest cottage and got out. She stretched her legs. Es was glad that she had finally made it.

She knocked on the worn, wooden door of the manager's office, using the rusted copper cattle head fixture. Nobody responded. She knocked a second time, only this time louder.

There was the sound of footsteps approaching. The door swung open slowly.

"Hi, can I help you?" greeted a greyish-blonde, fair-skinned woman garbed in a long Western skirt and blouse accessorized with a silver squash blossom necklace.

"Yes, I'm Esmeralda Luna," Es introduced herself. "I'm Francisco's daughter." When Es saw a blank look on the woman's face, she added, "Paco is my dad."

"Oh yeah, I still haven't heard from him," said the 5'6", 145-pound, gum-snapping landlady as she turned away. "Come on in . . . I'm Donna Rhodes . . . Did you drive all the way from Oregon [mispronouncing it Or-eh-gone]? Won't you have a seat, dearie?"

Esmeralda nodded her head as she sat down on a couch upholstered in a Native-American motif. The living room was filled with dozens of framed photos sitting on top of the mantle, tables, and every space available.

"See that handsome guy with the crewcut," the landlady pointed to an 'étagère' in the corner of the living room that housed dozens of curios and a few portrait style photos. "That's my ex-husband, Gordon." Donna was a talker and she knew that she had a captive audience that wasn't going anywhere. Within the first few minutes, Es found out Donna's whole life story.

Donna had grown up in Denver, Colorado, and went to the University of Colorado where she majored in "let's find a husband." She met Gordon Rhodes from Durango at a mixer at the Colorado School of Mines, where he was studying Earth Science engineering. They were married even before they finished school. After he graduated, they moved to northern New Mexico where Gordie worked for a turquoise excavating company. She became involved in the art and crafts movement in Santa Fe. She soon developed an ongoing affair with a local artist and she quickly filed for divorce. Gordie left the state to work in a gold mine back in Colorado.

The new lover was offered a position to work for R.C. Gorman in Tubac where the artist had a gallery. The two moved to Tubac ten years prior and Donna got a job with the Tubac Center for the Arts where she was still working. The lover boy split after a year, but Donna stayed. She was getting alimony from Gordon and investing the money in property, both residential and commercial.

"Where's my manners? You must be exhausted, you poor thing," Donna's eyebrows furled. "Can I get you a coke or something to drink, dearie? . . . Maybe a beer?"

Es nodded no.

To Esmeralda's chagrin, Donna started again to make small talk. Es was anxious to find out about her father.

"This town reminds me of 'Gunsmoke'," Es involuntarily remarked.

Donna's big pearlies broke through. She explained that Tubac had once been a Spanish colonial garrison and part of the Camino Real from Mexico to California. Es tried hard to remember her U.S. history, but drew a blank. In recent years the settlement had sprung up from mining, farming, and ranching. It was also an up-and-coming artists' colony mixed in with a bunch of cowboys.

"Before I forget, Mrs. Rhodes," Es decided that she had heard enough to last a lifetime, "I promised you that I would pay my dad's back rent."

"Oh, I almost forgot about that," Donna feigned almost convincingly, "and his studio rent too?"

What friggin' studio rent? Frowned Esmeralda. *Nobody had mentioned anything about that. But I guess, it must be true.*

"How much is it?" Es face showed dejection.

"Both come to $120," promptly responded the landlady. "Since you drove all the way down to pay me, I'll waive the late fees."

Esmeralda pulled out her leather lanyard wallet from underneath her navy-blue top. She counted out six twenty-dollar bills.

"Thank you, child," Donna showed her pearlies again. "I'll get you a receipt."

A minute later Es had a paid-in-full slip in her hand.

"Mrs. Rhodes, did you ever contact the police or the local hospital about my dad?"

"Nope. Hadn't even given it nary a thought," she said matter-of-factly. "All of his things are still in his room. I think Magdalena still has copies of his keys, if you want to go over there to check out his place. I know she's home because I saw her just before you knocked on the door." Donna's mouth made a little laugh as she added, "Nearest hospital is 'bout 25 miles away."

Esmeralda got up to leave and thanked Donna.

"Oh, dearie, do you want to pay next month's rent just in case?"

Es smiled politely and nodded no. She let herself out. *Así es la vida*, as her uncle would say.

Esmeralda wandered over to the tan adobe bungalows. A small dog was running in circles as it barked.

A tiny Native-American woman with liquid black eyes and wrinkled skin appeared out of nowhere. She had long black-braided hair with little yellow ribbons tied at the end. She was dressed in a flowery native design blouse and skirt. Her little Chihuahua ran toward Es and barked threateningly.

"Hello," the woman's weak voice called out.

"Hi, I'm looking for my father's place. Paco Luna," Es responded as she approached the Apache woman. "I'm his daughter Esmeralda."

The woman beckoned Es to follow her to the second bungalow on the right of the court. The dog kept himself between the old woman and Es. It finally stopped barking. The woman extended her small right hand and signaled Es to wait. Several minutes later the woman came out of the casita.

The lady pointed to herself and said, "Magdalena." The two women plus the dog walked back to the last bungalow. Magdalena gave Es a paper clip with two keys on it. She pointed to the house.

"One for house," she spoke in broken English and broken Spanish. "La otra para la tienda." The other key was for the shop.

"Magdalena, do you know where my father is?" Es tried to ask in English. "Or where he went?"

The older woman nodded "no" and started to walk away. The dog followed her. Magdalena shooed him away. She pointed to Esmeralda. Es was baffled by this gesture.

"Magdalena, isn't this your dog?"

"Su papá!" the older woman blurted, as she started to walk away. "Su perro." The dog was her father's.

"What's his name?" Es shouted after her, but the old lady did not turn around.

Oh, brother! What am I going to do with this creature? She bent over and snapped her fingers. The Chihuahua came over and licked her hand. *Oh, brother! You're my best friend now.* She noticed he had a flea collar and a little medal. She reached over and squinted to read the tag. The tag read, "My name is Xolo." Es read it and thought, *my dad must be nuts! Why did he have an oversized rat as a pet?* She thought.

ESMERALDA – THE ENCHANTED

"So, your name is Xolo!" *I think this is pronounced with a "ch" sound.* His little brown eyes gave her a warm and fuzzy look. *Papá, what have you done?*

Soon thereafter, Esmeralda used the bigger key to open the front door of the bungalow. The small living room looked intact, although the threadbare throw carpet looked like it was two hundred years old. There was dust and grit on everything. Es found the dog's plastic water bowl and poured in some fresh water. She also found some dry dog food in the pantry and filled Xolo's other bowl. *Geez! I guess he does live here.*

Es did a visual review of the house. The refrigerator, that had food in it that looked like it was left over from prehistoric times. She dumped this stuff into a trash bag in the kitchen, including the hundred-year-old eggs. She picked up another trash bag and started to discard things as she made her inspection.

The living room had no newspapers or magazines. There were a few dust-covered books on a brick and board bookcase. The writings included "The Teachings of Don Juan" by Carlos Castaneda, "I am Joaquin" by Corky Gonzalez, and "The Blessing Way" by Tony Hillerman. The unencumbered low-level coffee table had several water marks and was flanked by a flimsy sofa and two chartreuse bean bag chairs.

The bathroom was fairly clean for a guy, but the toilet needed work. Es emptied out the trash bin. *Gross!* She noticed that his tooth brush was gone. So was the tooth paste.

At first glance, the bedroom seemed innocuous. An Indian blanket hung in place of a curtain. A few posters were taped on the dingy off-white walls. Joan Baez. Judy Collins. Grateful Dead. Santana. There were a few poems written by her mother tacked to the wall. Es read them. They were good, but sad in a way. Es saw "The Giant Peach" poem in a frame in front of her.

> There was a peach,
> That I couldn't reach,
> Atop the tree,
> High o'er me . . .

Kelly used to read this rhyme to Es at bedtime every night. They both would giggle and then Esmeralda would fall asleep. The other poem "25/25" hadn't made much sense to Es as she was growing up. Her mother was always saying "twenty-five minutes or twenty-five years, we don't know how long we have to live. We have to experience life now. We can't wait until tomorrow." Later in her teens, she understood that her mother was a free spirit who lived for the present moment. Her mother had copied a saying that stood over their bed stand:

> Life is a gift,
> Today is the present,
> The present is today.

A wrinkled Mexican sarape had been thrown on top of the bed. The closet had a few empty spaces in it. Es noticed that her dad's big backpack seemed to be gone. It looked like her father had packed for a trip.

Es went to the pressed-board dresser. It was gritty with a sandy residue. *I guess dad doesn't have a housekeeper.* On top of the chest, in the middle, was a small Navajo storyteller doll. On one side of it were framed photos of Kelly and Esmeralda that now smiled back at her; on the other side was a blue calla lily ceramic dish (from Kelly's collection) with coins, a matchbook, and a dozen little things. She opened up the drawers. There was a lot of empty space in the underwear and sock drawers. The bottom drawer was a junk drawer. It contained an old fishing reel, a wire strung with over forty keys, and at least a hundred valueless collectibles.

Finally, she strayed over to a makeshift desk in the corner of the bedroom. It had a little lamp on top. The light did not work. There was a stack of invoices piled on the middle of the desk. Es picked them up and started to examine them. Some were for the house, like telephone and electricity. She guessed that they were past due, but she was in no position to worry about them. Her dad would have to deal with his creditors when he returned. There were also business-related invoices: bills for a caliper, a polishing buff, and a ten-power loupe. He owed a lot of money. There was also a carved "Mimbres" wooden business card holder complete with cards for the "Dancing Winds," her dad's goldsmith shop. It listed his business address, but Es had no idea where it was or how to get there.

Es noticed that there was no money of any kind around or anything of value. She couldn't even find his checkbook. Her dad did not own a television or a radio. *How did he live without music?* Her thoughts went back to her dad's business. *What happened to his inventory? It must be worth a lot. Mrs. Rhodes did not mention anything about it.*

There was barking by the front door. Xolo wanted out.

"Okay! Okay!" Esmeralda's neighbors back in Eugene had a German shepherd. She knew the routine. At least around here it didn't seem that one had to put a leash on the dog. She opened the door and the Chihuahua ran over to a saguaro cactus where he did his thing. A scrub jay flew away. Es followed Xolo. He left little tootsie rolls behind. Other dogs in the vicinity starting barking and howling. While Es was outside, she thought that she would go back to Mrs. Rhodes' place and ask a few more questions about her father's business.

However, as she passed Magdalena's unit, she decided to pay the native woman another visit. She knocked on the weathered door. A few moments later the Apache woman gave a half-smile showing that most of her teeth were missing. The dog barked at the older woman, but she commanded him to shush, and he obeyed.

Esmeralda asked her if she knew where her father's business was. The lady gave a circuitous explanation in broken English, but the good news was that it was only two blocks away. Esmeralda thanked her and started to walk away.

"Se fue a México," the older woman weakly yelled out after her. "¡Cuídate mucho, Ixzonxoxoctic!" She said that he left for Mexico and *"Be careful, girl with green hair!"*

Es had heard her, but she did not look back. *What all did she say? Why would her dad go to Mexico? Something doesn't sound right. This is crazy!*

Esmeralda decided to walk into the center of town to find her father's shop. Xolo was happy and jumping around. He seemed to know the way. As she approached the art colony units, the first business in front was a painting gallery. It had lots of Native American art that included works by Gorman and Peña.

Esmeralda walked into the art studio. After greeting the owner, she asked, "Have you seen my father, Paco Luna, lately?"

"Not for a couple of weeks," came the response from a dark-skinned young man with a braided ponytail who was sitting at a table, writing on three by five cards.

After leaving there, she went to the next shop, "Linda's Lovelies," that had loads of Navajo, Zuni, and Hopi ceramic works. Es grabbed at her mom's opal necklace pressing against her chest. It was warm. She sensed the nostalgia of Kelly's studio back in Eugene. In this shop she was surrounded by tribal masks, greeting cards, and beaded necklaces. She also spied a kiln in the back. Her face sagged with sadness. This shop's proprietress had not seen her father recently either.

Es continued to the last unit on the left side of the art colony. She met the "flower lady" with the big straw hat. Her shop was just across from the "Dancing Winds." The woman said that Paco had asked her to keep an eye on his place because he was going to be gone for a while. He was going on a trip. The lady had asked him where he was going, and he had replied "Mexico."

Uh-oh! Not liking what I'm hearing. Have to talk to auntie and uncle.

Before going to her dad's shop, she decided to hit the remaining two businesses in the complex: a wood carvings place and a sculpture garden. Nobody knew anything more at either place.

Finally, she walked back to her dad's shop that had a big picture window with its blinds drawn. There was no sign on the door stating that the owner would be gone for an extended period of time. After fumbling with the key for a minute, she unlocked the front door and opened it. Stale air hit her in the face. There was no jewelry in the display cases. The place looked abandoned. *Rats! Was his place robbed? I don't want to call the police.*

Es walked to the back of the shop and found a little office with a desk. The walls had business licenses and artsy posters. There was also a family photo of Esmeralda's parents on one wall. A grungy, empty coffee mug with a New Mexico logo was stuck to the top of the desk. And there were more invoices. Es found a closet and opened it. She found a bicolored wind breaker jacket hanging on a hook. On the floor was a fair-sized safe. Aha! This is where he must keep his jewelry. But Es was not confident. Xolo jumped in front of her and started to sniff the safe. *Oh, you're such a great help.*

Okay, safe, what is your combination? Her nimble fingers twirled 6-29-22. This was her father's birthday and she guessed that her father would want an easy number to remember. *Umm! No such luck! Well, he really loved my mother. Let me try her date of birth.* 9-16-24. *Curses! Foiled again!* Maybe the combination is hidden somewhere in or on the desk, she thought. She looked around but could not find any clues. Her tummy growled. She was starting to get hungry. She looked around the shop. The only food items around were ketchup and mustard packets, a jar of powdered decaffeinated coffee, and Navajo greenthread tea. Her stomach continued to grumble.

Es found a rolodex in one of the drawers. Maybe the combination was here. After ten minutes she was about to give up when she found her name and phone number on a card. *That's it*, she thought. *The combination is MY birthday!* She was excited. She spun the dial. 10-31-48. It didn't work. She tried again. *Rats! Double rats! Papá!* She continued to explore the shop while Xolo guarded the front door with his eyes closed.

Finally, Es gave up and left her dad's shop after she locked the door. She spied a fast food place across the street. She ordered a Navajo taco with black beans. It was so tasty and greasy. It wasn't on her diet, but she had to live for today, as her mother would tell her.

Ten minutes later, Es was back at "Dancing Winds," looking at the safe. Her right index finger and thumb turned the knob right to the number 25, and then reversed direction and stopped at the zero. She inhaled and concentrated as she went back to twenty. 25-0-25. The safe popped open like it was Christmas morning. Twenty-five minutes or twenty-five years!

Oh, my God! I have the Treasure of Sierra Madre. There were boxes and boxes of gold rings and necklaces. *Thank, God, her dad wasn't robbed.* She found several journals. One was for Paco's business. Another was a personal one. Es set that one aside to take away with her. There were a few books with her mother's handwritten poetry. Near the front was a stack of letters from Mexico, written in Spanish, held together by a tan rubber band. On top was a slightly worn folded-up map of Mexico. *I need to take this stuff with me and check it out.*

Es also found a small metal cashbox. It didn't have a key, and it opened up easily. There were three silver dollars and a standard letter sized envelope with a wad of cash. Es counted out $476. She wondered if she should take it all for safe keeping or just leave it. Well, she was really entitled to a $120 reimbursement for paying for her dad's rent on the house and on the business. After more deliberation, she decided to take $250, just over half. She had a feeling that she was going to need it.

When Es returned to her dad's bungalow she noticed something on the wooden porch. Actually, it was a canvas horse feeding pouch. *How strange?* Es picked it up and looked inside. There was a partial bag of dried dog food and a little brown sack with a tied bundle of sage in it. *Hmm! Something my dad would have in his medicine bag.* There was a bark next to her.

"Xolo," she gasped. "You hungry again?" She opened the front door and led him in. She found his food bowl and poured him some dried dog food. He barked and dug in.

Esmeralda knew that she had to call her aunt and uncle, which she did. She related the story of exploring her dad's little house and his shop. The pleasantries went on for a few minutes until her aunt asserted herself.

"Es, what are you going to do now?" Chlora was being aggressive. "There's nothing more to do there, sweetie."

"I don't know yet," Es said trying to collect her thoughts. Es then shared with her aunt and uncle about Mrs. Rhodes and Magdalena.

"Your tía is right," added Tío Felipe. "You come back home now. Your papa gone."

"But I'm still working on finding him, Tío," she didn't want to be pressured, even though she loved them and trusted them.

After she hung up the phone, she jumped in the shower. It was funky and a little moldy. The water started off a little muddy and cold. Luckily, she found an old, dirty bar of soap that had more cracks than the average dried prune. She shivered as she washed her hair and dried it. Es put on one of her father's tee shirts as nightwear. The temperature had dropped. She climbed into her dad's lumpy bed. It had his smell. She began to peruse the various journals and booklets that she had taken from her dad's shop. One was a ledger. The last entry was at the beginning of the month. The other one was cordovan leather-bound and seemed to be Paco's personal journal. *Maybe I shouldn't read this without his permission. But this, on the other hand, could give me a clue as to where he was going. Hold off,* said her good angel.

She also found a navy-blue spiral-bound notebook with numerical calculations scribbled in it. It didn't make any sense to her. In the middle of the notebook there were a few loose poems written in pencil. Es recognized her mother's handwriting. There was also a faded, folded photo of her parents at some sort of pyramid. They looked so young, she thought. On

the back of the picture was inscribed "25 minutes or 25 years."
She also found an article about a recently found Suzuki-Sato-
Seki comet tucked in the back cover. The author stated that this
heavenly body had been prophesied by the Aztecs and was
associated with their Day of the Dead celebration. Es was about
to close the notebook, when she noticed the date "October 31,
1970" in large letters circled in red on the back of it. *This is only
two weeks away!* She thought. Es was trying to determine if this
was an important clue, when Xolo jumped on top of the bed.
Xolo made himself comfortable at the end near her feet.

"Down," Es commanded.

"Arf."

"Down!"

"Arf!"

"Down, I said!"

"Arf! Arf!"

Rats! I lost that battle. What am I doing with this rodent?

She picked up a stack of letters tied up with a navy-blue
ribbon that she had recovered from her dad's dresser. Most had
Mexican postage stamps in the corner. There were also a few
travel brochures in Spanish with pictures of a snow-capped
mountain. Esmeralda started to read the letters. The
correspondence was sorted chronologically from newest to
oldest. She began at the back. Her Spanish was fairly good, and
she could decipher the letters easily. They all began with flowery
salutations and ended with best wishes for good health. What
she eventually gleaned from the six letters, was that her father
was trying to plan for a trip down to Pico de Orizaba, near
Mexico City. *Where in the heck was that? Why there? For what
purpose?* She couldn't ascertain. She jumped out of bed and
found a pad and a pencil in her father's desk. Brr! It was getting
cold.

Back under the sarape blanket, she began to take notes.
*Where is this place? When was he supposed to be going?
Why???*

She looked through the brochures that she had found with the journal. They were for lodging and mountain climbing excursions to Citlaltépetl. Citlaltépetl was the highest mountain in Mexico, located 120 miles east of Mexico City on the border of the Mexican states of Puebla and Vera Cruz. It was a dormant volcano that last erupted in the mid-16th century. Citlaltépetl came from the Náhuatl citlalli (star) and tepētl (mountain) and thus meant "Star Mountain." Its Spanish name was Pico de Orizaba. It peaked at an altitude of around 17 thousand feet and was branched with nine glaciers.

Curious, she then unfolded the map of Mexico. As she scanned it, her eyes got bigger. *My dad is not crazy enough to go down there, is he? He would have told me. Or would he? I hope he's not going nuts. Nobody around here seems to think so. No evidence here, but I don't know. Rats! It's the highest mountain in Mexico. He can't be going there.*

Esmeralda looked through the last two booklets, but they were business-related. She started putting everything back in the paper bag where they had been, but surprisingly discovered a smudged, folded-up piece of paper. It was a map drawn in blue ink. The word "Citlaltépetl" was accentuated with a thick black arrow. On the back side was written the date "El Día de Los Muertos, October 31 – November 2, 1970." *Holy crap!*

She found a telephone number for Posada Las Estrellas in Guadalupe Xochiloma in one of the brochures. The number had been circled. An October 7, 1970, date was scribbled in the margin. Esmeralda tried to call. There were lots of numbers. It had to be long distance. Really long distance. Mexico? The ring tone seemed labored. She hung up after a dozen rings. She looked again through the other brochures, but she didn't find any other names.

Esmeralda dialed again. After seven rings, an older woman answered, "Bueno! ¿Quíen habla?" *Hello, who is calling?*

In her best Spanish, Es asked for her father and gave his name. She was told to wait.

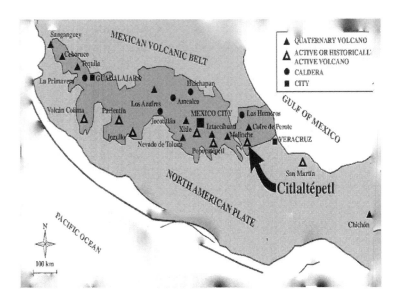

"Vete y trae a alguien!" she heard the older woman shout in a harsh tone for someone to go and get someone. Es surmised that this was a communal telephone. *Oh, my God! I hope this place is not at the end of the world!*

Five minutes later a young boy came on the line. This was going to be an expensive phone call, she thought. She made a mental note to pay off her dad's outstanding telephone bill in the morning. Probably would need the service just in case.

"Is this Posada Las Estrellas?" she inquired in Spanish.

"Sí," said the youthful voice of a pre-teen.

"Do you know if my father, Paco Luna, is staying there?" She continued.

"Sí."

"May I speak to him, please."

"Sí."

"This is his daughter, Esmeralda."

"Sí."

"I'll wait for him while you get him."

"Sí," he hung up the phone.

Es was surprised and angry. Upon reflection, she surmised that the kid did not speak Spanish.

It was past eleven p.m. when she called her aunt and uncle again. They were startled and thought something unfortunate had happened to their niece.

"You're coming back home, of course, aren't you?" Aunt Chlora half-asked, half-ordered.

"I don't know," Esmeralda replied.

"You don't know! I don't understand!" her aunt was angry. "What are you going to do?"

"I'm thinking about going down there to look for him."

"You're kidding!" Aunt Chlora exploded. "To Mexico by yourself?!"

"Mija, we don't think you should go," her uncle jumped in with a softer, sadder tone. "It's muy dangerous. You've never went there before. A lot of things could go wrong."

Like what? She asked. She was her own person now. This was her dad. Her mother would go. She had made a promise to her mother. *This is what family does. What can go wrong?*

Chapter 7 – La Frontera

Saturday, October 17, 1970

Esmeralda was startled by the barking in the middle of the night. She turned on the light. Her hand bounced around feeling for her trusty hunting knife. She finally found it and then started to look for Xolo. She walked barefoot into the living room. The floor was cold to her feet.

The Chihuahua was standing by the front door. He gave Es a friendly bark and wagged his tail.

"Rats!" Es pulled the sarape over her shoulders and opened the front door. Brr! It was in the 40's. The dog bolted out and waited for her. "Dog, you're crazy. I'm not going out there."

He ignored her and ran away to do his business.

Six hours later she awoke with the sarape over her face. Es got up and fed the dog. There was nothing in the house for her to eat and she did not want to raid her supplies. She had seen a Mexican restaurant down the street and would try it. But before she left, she found a quarter-inch thick Yellow Pages telephone directory in her dad's desk. She looked up "bus transportation – international." She perused the listings and picked one. Orion

Express. She called and asked if they went to Mexico. The answer was affirmative, but qualified. The passenger had to walk from the Orion's U.S. bus terminal in Nogales, Arizona, across the border to the Orion's counterpart terminal in Nogales, Mexico.

"Does the bus go to Citlaltépetl?" Es asked.

"I don't know where that is, ma'am," the young man addressed her politely.

She tried to describe where she thought it was and apologized for taking up a lot of his time.

"No problem. I got time. Just going to school part-time and need the money. Don't get that many calls," he replied.

"Where are you at right now?" Es was curious.

"Omaha, Nebraska."

"You're kidding," Es was incredulous.

"Nah, it's true," then he paused and came to life. "Hey, I think we can get ya down as far as Puebla. But you gotta change buses in Mexico City."

"How long is the trip?"

"It looks like about three days."

Esmeralda was beside herself. She knew that driving would take at least as long and that it was out of the question. She asked about how to buy tickets and other logistics.

"When is the next bus to Nogales?" she asked. *Am I crazy? Do I really want to go? What am I going to do with this pain in the ass dog!* Her mind told her to abort her trip and go back home to Eugene. Her heart was breaking. *What would my mother do?* said a voice inside of her. *I'm not my mother!* said another voice. She grabbed at her opal necklace and squeezed it. She started to feel its warmth. It reminded her that every once in a while, she would see a Monarch butterfly in her garden back in Eugene. She had thought it very odd that the Monarchs would travel that far north. She had asked her Tío Felipe who knew everything about bugs and flowers about it. He told her that he believed that the power of Nature is so strong that all things are possible. He hinted that maybe the butterfly was Es' mother's spirit coming to visit her. Es felt energy sizzle through her body. It was prompting her to go on.

For the next hour Esmeralda was swapping out her backpack. *I think that I am going to have to pack for cold weather and high attitudes.* She had hiked in the Colorado Rockies with her father, but this trip looked much more challenging.

The next bus to Nogales, Arizona, left at 1:15 pm that afternoon. She would need to hurry to make that one, but there was another at 4:30 pm. However, she really didn't want to get to the border at night. *Hurry! Hurry!* She told herself. *Rats! I should wash some clothes first!* She had noticed a little shack set off at the back of the bungalows' property. She ran outside to check it out. She was in luck; it had a washer and dryer. Es ran back into the house to look for laundry detergent. She found some under the kitchen sink. She grabbed her dirty clothes and some items from her father's light blue plastic laundry basket and went back out to the shed. Before she started loading the washer, she noticed that the machines required quarters. *Rats! I only have one! What's my Plan B?* Her father had taught her that when backpacking, as in life, one had to have a Plan B. A backup plan. One had to be flexible. Paco often paraphrased Robert Burns: "'The best laid plans of mice and men often go awry' within the first fifteen minutes."

Esmeralda was famished. She hadn't eaten breakfast yet. She looked for and found a tiny leash that she attached to Xolo who seemed happy that he was going out for a walk. In the next hour Es wolfed down a breakfast burrito at the Mexican taqueria down the street, procured five dollars' worth of quarters, and got directions to the nearest grocery store. She went back to her dad's place and started a load of clothes in the washer. She then jumped into her car and went to a small mom and pop grocery store. Xolo was not happy about being left back at the house. Es bought some cheese, a salami, a bag of nuts, granola, a jar of peanut butter, a packet of raisins, and a few other items that she would need for her backpacking trip. She passed the pet food section. *What am I going to do with my Papá's mutt? Nobody seems to want him. Crap! And besides, how am I going to feed this pest?* It startled her that these questions jumped into her mind. When did she decide to take Xolo with her in the first place? Was the little guy already working his way into her head (and heart)?

She was also concerned about the packing weight. For her body size, she didn't want to carry more than thirty pounds. Her father's rule of thumb for packing was less is better. One-third weight load for food; one-third for clothing; and one-third for gear. *Okay, I'll take a bag of dry dog food. What a pain! He may have to eat peanut butter. Grr!*

Es drove back at the house and put the groceries on the little kitchen table. She ran outside and put the wet clothes into the dryer. More quarters! Then she went back into the house to finish packing. She had emptied out her backpack and put most of the things that she was going to take on top of the bed. She started discarding items onto the chair by the desk. No flip flops, no shorts, no sleeveless tops, etc. Only one book.

What am I missing? What else do I absolutely need? She went through a mental checklist in her head. For her clothing, she visualized going from her feet to her head. *I probably need an extra pair of socks, and I have mom's old scarf.* She went over to her dad's chest of drawers and pulled out a much too large set of thermal underwear. They would have to do.

For equipment, it was clear that she wasn't going to lug a stove and a tent. She checked her flashlight and made sure that she had extra batteries. She went to her dad's bathroom and grabbed a roll of toilet paper. Her dad had some old camping gear in a closet in the back of the house. She grabbed an aluminum mug that had a lid, some nylon cord, a small roll of duct tape, and a canteen. Es went back outside and collected her clothes from the dryer and put them in the laundry basket. She grabbed what she needed and threw the rest onto the bed. She carefully folded her clothes so they took up as little space as possible.

Es started placing the food items into large garbage bags. Then she started loading the backpack. Whoops! She almost forgot the sleeping bag which she usually tied to the top. She would strap the canteen and hunting knife onto her belt. Es would hand carry (or shoulder carry) Xolo in his horse pouch part of the time. *Oh, brother! What a pain in the patoot!*

It was almost one o'clock. She wasn't going to make the 1:15 bus. She had the address of the bus stop. She grabbed the telephone directory again. It had a town map of Tubac and she found out that her destination was only three blocks away.

She called her aunt and uncle and told them that she was taking the bus down to Mexico to find her father. Es could sense that they were very apprehensive. *I have to do what I have to do. Even though he has screwed things up, I miss him. Mom would want me to.*

Es made a final inspection of the house. She wrote a note and put it on the kitchen table stating where she was going. She put her car keys on top. Es had a last-minute thought and went back into her dad's bedroom. She found an old black ski cap which she swapped out for her baseball cap. She put her hair up. This did the job of completely covering up her green hair that she really didn't want people to see.

She locked up the house and went over to Magdalena's and knocked on the door. Nobody answered. She fastened her dad's keys that were still on the paper clip and a small note with a rubber band over the door knob saying that she was going to Mexico to find her father. *Rats! I was hoping that she might take Xolo off my hands.*

Esmeralda made her way to the bus stop with Xolo by her side. The way was dusty, and the Chihuahua barked at everyone and everything. Es found an antique bench in front of the gas station and waited. She wasn't sure about the rules for carrying a dog on the bus. She would put him in the horse bag when the time came.

By 4:25 that afternoon Esmeralda was riding on the fairly comfortable Orion bus on her way to Nogales. She had sat across from a young Hispanic mother and her daughter, even though there were only a handful of passengers aboard. The driver wearing a black bow tie, was busy chewing his gum a mile a minute as he sped down the highway in the fast lane. Es felt drained but did not want to take a nap. Xolo was sound asleep in the horse pouch. Es reached up to the console overhead and turned up the air flow.

They were halfway to the border when Xolo woke up and yelped. The little girl across the way awakened and looked around. She finally spotted the dog and whispered something to her mother. The little girl reached out and pointed to the dog extending her right hand.

"My dog," she said.

Es drew her head back. What was the little girl saying?

"My dog," the young one repeated.

"Your dog?" replied Es.

The small one nodded. Her mother leaned over and said, "She means that she has a Chihuahua back home that looks just like him."

Es smiled, "what's your daughter's name?"

"Coralina."

"¿Cuántos años tienes, Coralina?" Es asked the child her age in Spanish.

"Five," Coralina held up her right hand to demonstrate how old she was.

"She's such a cutie pie," Es smiled.

"Yeah, we like her."

For the remainder of the trip to the border, Es had a pleasant conversation with Araceli Lopez, the mother, with an occasional question given to Coralina. Araceli had been born and raised in Phoenix, Arizona. Every summer her family would travel down to Guadalajara to visit relatives. Araceli was truly bilingual as was her daughter. After she graduated from high school, Araceli went down to Jalisco to stay with her cousins for a while. Six months later she was married to a local Tapatio [someone from

Guadalajara]; twelve months later Coralina was born. They now lived in Guadalajara.

Araceli's family wanted her to move back to Phoenix. They would find work for their new son-in-law. She declined. This past year, Araceli's mother was diagnosed with diabetes and was unable to travel. Araceli went up to spend a month with her mother, bringing along Coralina. The grandmother and granddaughter bonded and became inseparable. The grandmother started to take better care of herself.

"Mom, you have to eat better and exercise if you want to see Coralina grow up," Araceli would tell her.

"Sí, mijita," was the constant response.

Finally, Araceli decided that she had to go back to Mexico. She had spent the past two days shopping for her family and relatives who lived back in Guadalajara. There were a thousand requests, but Araceli only bought essential clothing items. Nobody needed expensive running shoes or designer blouses. *¡A la fregada! No friggin' way!*

Es pushed the horse pouch across the aisle. Coralina tried to pet Xolo on the head. Instead the dog licked the girl's hand. Coralina cringed and giggled.

It was getting dark when the bus pulled off the main highway and arrived at the Orion bus terminal in Nogales. The ride had gone by quickly, especially talking with Araceli and her daughter. Before the bus had even stopped, the remaining passengers were up and about, dragging their suitcases and packages from the overhead bins.

Xolo barked. Es and the mother and child were the last ones off the bus. Araceli was laden with more bags and bundles than a caravan camel. They said goodbye to Esmeralda. In the meantime, Es looked for a deserted place for Xolo to do his business. The poor thing had been cooped up in the pouch for almost two hours. Everyone else had departed and Es went back to the depot office to ask directions to the Orion bus depot on the Mexican side of the border. She was told that it was six blocks straight ahead. She could see bright lights in front of her.

Es started down the left side of the street. On the right, the Coyote Blues Cantina was playing loud music. Es wanted to avoid the rowdy bar. Across the street, straight in front of her was a brick wall under a street light. Figures were leaning against it.

"Hey, cutie, you need a place to stay?" called out a greasy-haired young guy wearing cowboy boots.

Es just ignored him and walked on by. Her right hand moved slowly down to the hilt of her knife that was on her belt. Xolo growled.

"Want some weed? I got some good shit," said another unsavory character as he started walking toward her. Es went off the curb onto the street, ready to run if need be. She could barely make out his face, but it looked like he had blood shot eyes that kept squinting. He seemed to be staggering. She thought that he was probably stoned.

Her opal butterfly necklace started to quiver and get warm. She didn't get another thirty feet before a slickly-dress guy wearing a Stetson cowboy hat blocked her way.

"Need a job?" he had a sly smile. "Easy money."

She gave him the dirtiest look that she could muster and walked around him without saying a word. Her dad had taught her never to show fear with animals or human beings. She would defend herself if she had to.

The sidewalk was dark now since there was not another street light for a couple more blocks and the moon was covered by clouds. She took Xolo out of the pouch and let him walk. He seemed to pee every ten steps. Es was paying attention to him when she thought she heard some noise in front of her.

Esmeralda saw the outlines of three figures in front of her. Then she heard a young child scream. The opal necklace was now growing hot against her chest.

Strange! Es thought. *That sounded like Coralina.* Xolo took off toward the trio. Es suddenly felt energized and hurried after him. As she got closer, Es saw Araceli struggling with a young man in a white tee shirt. Esmeralda's shoulder muscles became taut. She balled up her fists. Her neck strained.

"¡Déjanos solas, cabrón!" Es heard Araceli scream. *Leave us alone!*

One of Araceli's big brown paper sacks fell to the ground. The youngster scooped it up and started running in Esmeralda's direction. Xolo went right for him. The teenager tried to avoid the dog who chased him into the street. The culprit was about twenty feet in front of Es, when she jumped into the street also. He was huffing and puffing trying to make his getaway with the purloined package. He gave a quick look at Es. He never saw the lightning fast leg come out to trip him. He flew in the air, dropping the bag, and getting the wind knocked out of him. A few seconds later Xolo was nipping at the delinquent's right Achilles' heel. The youngster made a desperate attempt to get up, screaming sounds coming from him. He got up limping and skulked away.

Es picked up the brown paper bag that now had a torn handle. She walked toward Araceli who was now approaching her. Esmeralda's normal mental and physical states slowly started to return. Her pendant started to cool down.

"Thank you so much, Esmeralda," said Araceli in the most appreciative way, holding her crying and scared daughter. "That bastard tried to steal my family's clothes." She started a litany of expletives in Spanish.

They walked gently together toward the border with Esmeralda carrying the torn bag. "We probably should stick together," Es suggested. Araceli nodded in agreement. Coralina had stopped crying and walked close to her mother.

They found the border crossing just ahead of them. There was a convenience store that had a sign in the window that read "Last Chance." Araceli told Es that she had to go in and grab a few items before they crossed the border. Es used the pay phone outside the store to call her aunt and uncle one last time (collect).

"I'm at the border," she informed them. "Going into Mexico." Their reaction was what she expected: they were not happy. When she told them that she didn't know when she could call again, her Aunt Chlora broke into tears. After the phone conversation, Es felt guilty. She never wanted to hurt them. She loved them. But she had to find her dad. And she was grown up enough to do it alone.

Esmeralda met her traveling companions back in front of the store. Araceli handed Es something. It was a chocolate bar. "Gracias, Esmeralda." Es wanted to say that this was unnecessary, but she did not want to be ungracious or rude by not accepting the gift. And besides, it was chocolate.

The three walked to the United States side of the border crossing. There were dozens of people in the various lines crossing into Mexico. The U.S. border agents mechanically waved everyone through. There were large families with a million suitcases, young teenage girls, and short, dark-skinned guys who looked like they worked in construction, all looking tired and weary.

Then the trio approached the Mexican immigration officials. Esmeralda, who was carrying Xolo and the torn paper bag, walked closely to Araceli. The khaki uniformed Mexican official did not pay attention to them as they passed.

"Aquí estamos, mija," Araceli told her daughter when they were on the street. "The bus station is real close," she told Es.

They passed crowds of people on the street and arrived at the humongous Central de Autobuses. The smell of stale cigarettes permeated the large terminal. A hunchbacked old man in a tan worker uniform had the never-ending task of trying to sweep the innumerable butts into his dust bin.

"Follow me," Araceli directed. They found the ticket window for El Expreso de Orion [the Orion Express]. Araceli bought tickets for herself and her daughter to Guadalajara. The next bus left Nogales at midnight and arrived in Guadalajara at four o'clock the next afternoon.

Then it was Esmeralda's turn. She tried to get a ticket to Pico de Orizaba, but the young sales person didn't understand where that destination was. In the end Araceli intervened and found out that Orion did not go there. Es would have to Mexico City first and then buy another ticket from another bus company to her destination.

Es capitulated and attempted to buy the ticket to the capital of Mexico.

"Lo siento, señorita," apologized the clerk. "pero no se aceptan dólares." Esmeralda had another problem now, the ticket clerk could not accept U.S. dollars.

Rats! Araceli said that she didn't have enough Mexican pesos to lend her, but she pointed Es to a money exchange counter nearby.

"He charges a fee," Araceli advised Es. "But he is honest and gives a fair rate."

Esmeralda tried to do advanced calculus in her head. She was good at math, but not great. *I'll exchange a hundred. But the ticket is going to be expensive. Hundred fifty.* Her dad had taught her that one had to be prepared for the unexpected. *Rats! Two fifty. Maybe I can exchange it back if I have some left.* Her dad had also warned her that slippage was a way of life and the cost of traveling.

Es exchanged the money and had to stand in line again to buy her ticket to Mexico City via Guadalajara.

"First or second class?" the clerk asked in Spanish.

"Second!" Araceli interrupted. She whispered that nobody was going to be on the bus anyway and the price was half as much.

Both Araceli and Esmeralda were glad that they were traveling together on the same bus, at least as far as Guadalajara. Now they had time to kill. People were wandering all around them. They found an empty bench and camped out. Esmeralda asked Araceli to watch over her dog. Xolo sucked up to Coralina who petted him and talked to him. Es went to the bathroom that was relatively clean and used the facilities. She also brushed her teeth. Her mouth still had the taste of the chocolate. She wasn't planning to eat dinner that night. *Oh, I better make sure to feed Xolo before we leave. Hope I can sleep on the bus.*

As it grew later and later, the crowds of passengers and families dissipated. Coralina had her head on her mother's lap and was sleeping peacefully away. Finally, there was an announcement over the loud speaker (in Spanish) that the bus to Mexico City via Guadalajara was departing from Platform 3. Araceli picked up her daughter and Es helped her new traveling companion by carrying two of the brown bags. They waited in line for twenty-five minutes.

The bus driver finally opened the door of the Orion bus that was decorated with red, white, and green striping on its sides and a tall figure of the mythological warrior in a star constellation. The olive-skinned driver was short and had a round face and a pencil moustache. He wore a company uniform that bulged around his stomach area. He looked like he was in his early thirties.

The passengers started climbing aboard. A woman who was about 4'10" and weighed at least 140 pounds took up about 30 cubic feet of space with her packages. A couple of scruffy old men with yellow-stained teeth, straw sombreros, and leather huarache sandals came on board. They were smokers. Then came a family of six. And finally, three laughing teenage girls, rounded out the group of passengers.

Araceli helped Coralina, who was now awake, get aboard. Esmeralda followed. She was getting tired. They picked rows across from each other.

"Not too close to the toilets," Araceli whispered. "They stink."

Es nodded her head in acknowledgment.

"Back is too noisy and bouncy," Araceli added as she put some of her packages in the overhead bin area. She took out a small pink sweater to put on Coralina. The air conditioning was on.

Esmeralda gave a silent sigh of relief. She had made it this far. *Papá, I'm coming. Where are you?*

PART II

MEXICO LINDO

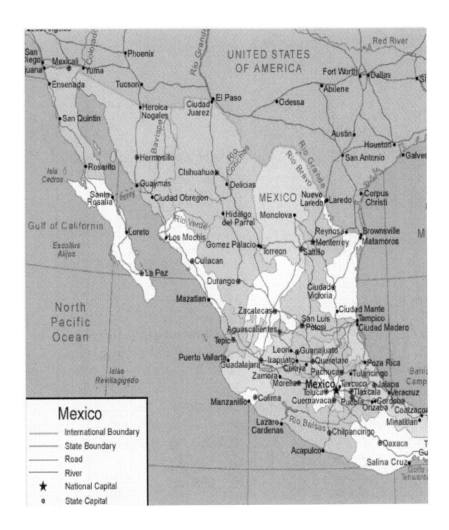

Chapter 8 – Stuff Happens

Sunday, October 18, 1970

The bus departed from Nogales, Mexico, a few minutes past midnight. The carbon black night sky was lit up by a million stars as the bus made its way southward. The planets and constellations were readily visible. Esmeralda could identify several of them. The weather was in the low seventies when they left the station. Esmeralda had her windbreaker on. Her scarf was in her jacket pocket.

The stocky driver dimmed the interior lighting of the bus. There were not many vehicles on either side of the highway. Neither were there traffic lights. The road was invisible, and cars flicked on their high beams randomly.

The ride was fairly smooth until they rambled through the town centers. The ubiquitous topes (speed bumps) tended to wake the passengers up from their deep sleeps and snoring. During the daytime, the passengers might be able to experience the 80-degree weather as they sped through the Sonoran Desert, but now, there was just cool air coming from the vents. The bus driver was playing norteño music at a low volume.

Es got up around three to use the toilet at the back of the bus. It was very challenging to walk down the aisle while the bus was zooming along. Her finger tips used the overhead bins as support. She had left Xolo alone. She wondered how long he could hold it. She didn't need him to have an accident. The toilet was clean but reeked of disinfectant.

Just after five a.m. they arrived at the Sonoran city of Hermosillo. The bus driver was going to take a one-hour break. They were instructed to be on the bus no later than six. Anyone not aboard would be left behind.

"I'm hungry, mamá," the little one said.

"Okay, mija, let's eat."

Es, of course, joined them. She didn't want to be separated from them. Besides, she could always eat. They found a little snack bar inside the bus terminal that was almost completely abandoned at this time of the morning. Es could already tell that the weather was getting warmer. She remembered that Sonora was mostly desert. *Geez! I don't think I brought any warm weather clothes.*

Getting off the bus, the first thing she did was to let Xolo go the bathroom outside the terminal. She quickly gave him some dried dog food and water.

A few minutes later Es joined the mother and child at the only little eatery that was open. Araceli ordered avena (oatmeal) and hot chocolate for the little girl. She also spread out a handful of Cheerios for the girl to pick at. The mother ordered huevos rancheros, beans, rice, and corn tortillas.

Es ordered a platter of fresh fruit (papaya, pineapple, and banana) and a soft-boiled egg. She also had white toast and tea. The food was tasty. The price was dirt cheap.

As the morning light rolled in, locals started wandering into the terminal, setting up little spots to sell corn, chicharrones, and tamales. Es found a little food stand and bought two bottles of water. She knew that water was important and that she had to keep Xolo hydrated. Before reboarding the bus, she bought a pork tamale and slowly removed the hoja wrapping. Xolo barked.

"No, you can't have any," Es knew that greasy food would not be good for him. She made a quick bathroom stop, leaving the dog with Araceli.

At five minutes to six, the trio was on the bus and resumed their original seats. A few new passengers had joined them. A young man with unkempt black hair stood at the doorway of the bus, offering peanuts in the shell and warm bottles of agua for sale. The hustling youth gave the driver a complimentary water before he escaped down the stairs.

The sun accompanied them down the highway. The sky was clearer, albeit a little hazy in the lower altitudes. The bus was making good time and the ride was smooth. If the passengers looked out of the windows they could see fruit stand vendors on the side of the road or boys riding bicycles with mounted crates carrying soft drinks. Two men in the back of the bus were smoking. The driver was playing his music a little louder now. "El Conjunto Bernal," mouthed Araceli silently across the aisle. *Okay. Who is that?* Es wondered. *I prefer Santana, thank you.* She put her head down on her backpack that occupied the window seat. Es eventually went to sleep. She had troubled dreams. She dreamt about the frustration and distress that she was giving her aunt and uncle by deciding to take this journey in spite of their advice. They were probably right. They loved her dearly and did not want anything to happen to her. *I'm an adult now. I can take care of myself. As long as I am careful, nothing will go wrong.* Subconsciously, she gently tugged on her fire opal pendant that used to be her mother's. She thought she could feel a little warmness from it.

It was about 8:20 that morning when the bus pulled into a Guaymas gas station that served as the de facto bus stop. People got off. Everybody went to use the bathroom. The women's restroom hadn't been cleaned in a while. The place reeked of diesel mixed with humid air.

While she was waiting for Araceli and Coralina to come out of the bathroom, Es looked around and saw the ocean from afar. Actually, it was the Sea of Cortez, but she didn't know this. A little breeze hit her face. She smiled. She put Xolo down to find the nearest bush. It was hot outside, so she made sure that she poured some fresh water out for him. He slurped it up in record time. Araceli bought Coralina a coconut paleta [popsicle]. A quarter of an hour later they all returned to the bus, waiting for the driver to open the door. The driver threw down his cigarette and stamped it out with his brown cowboy boot.

As Esmeralda climbed up into the bus, bullets of pain shot through her head. She hastened to find the way to her seat. Araceli and Coralina were happily yapping away across from her. Es closed her eyes. Her face started to feel flushed with heat. She looked up and tried to get more air from the AC vent. She dropped her eyelids again.

Ow! Es wanted to cry out. Something had stabbed her in the stomach. *Ow!* A sharp pain shot through her intestines. She writhed in pain. Araceli and her daughter were now asleep. The cigarette smoke drifting forward from the back of the bus made her feel nauseous. Sweat beaded up on Esmeralda's forehead. *Is this friggin' air conditioning working! Rats! It's so friggin' hot.* All of sudden she had an urgency from her digestive tract. She suddenly dropped Xolo onto her seat and ran to the back of the bus to use the lavatory. She didn't have time to put a paper liner around the toilet seat. She made a half squat. A hot, fetid liquid was expelled from her body. She waited a few minutes. Another rush came, albeit smaller. The odor was rancid, and she felt like she wanted to vomit. More time passed, and a third movement came. Finally, she cleaned herself and returned to her seat. She plopped herself down, nearly squishing Xolo and his horse pouch against the backpack. She took a deep breath.

"Esmeralda," Araceli leaned over her child. "Are you okay, mija?"

Es nodded and pointed to her stomach. Araceli nodded her head as if she understood what Es was going through. Es shut her eyes and tried to sleep. A half hour later there was another kick in the stomach. *Ow!* Back to the toilet she hurried with similar results. *I just want to die! Why did I disobey my aunt and uncle? I'm being punished!* She placed her hand over the fire opal pendant. It was hot, hot, hot! *Oh, mom!*

She tried to sleep for the next few hours. By now, all the passengers knew that Es had a grave problem. The miasma from the back of the bus was bad news.

Esmeralda could barely see the beautiful coastal sunset as they arrived at the bus terminal in Mazatlán. It was now six o'clock. The bus driver advised them that the layover was for one hour only. Es didn't want to get off the bus. Araceli persuaded the driver to let the young woman sleep on the bus. The driver didn't really care, so he nodded okay. The sweet Araceli also grabbed Xolo and took him with her. They had a Chihuahua back home and she knew how to take care of him.

"We'll be back, Esmeralda," Araceli showed her maternal side. "Do you want anything? Make sure you drink some water." Araceli gave the impression that she'd "been there, done that," having made several trips to and from Mexico and Arizona. It was no fun, especially if one had a child that caught *turista,* aka Moctezuma's Revenge.

As she slept, Esmeralda had more troubled dreams about her search for her father. In one dream, Xolo appeared and looked at her with deep, penetrating eyes that seemed to glow red. Everything was jumbled up. She could see her dad in the distance, but she could not catch up to him.

Just after seven that evening, the front door of the bus reopened. The old passengers returned still dressed in their sweaters. New passengers came in wearing beach garb.

Es was in a semi-fetal position. Araceli put her palm on Esmeralda's forehead and then felt her neck.

"I think you have a fever," said Araceli sympathetically. She took out a small towel and poured water on it.

"Mamá, what's wrong with her?" the little one said kindheartedly.

Araceli pulled the ski cap off of Es' head. Es did not resist. The mother's eyes widened in shock. She saw the green hair. Es was not moving a muscle.

"What's wrong, mamá?" the little girl repeated.

"Nothing, mija."

"Why is her hair green, mamá?"

"I don't know," Araceli whispered. "¿Está hechizada? She wondered if Es was bewitched. She didn't know what to think. In any event, Araceli kept wiping Esmeralda's forehead and neck with the damp cloth. Es' lips looked chapped.

The bus started up and within minutes was continuing its journey.

Es stirred and started to wake up.

Araceli handed her some pills. Three different sizes in three different colors.

"Here, take these," said Araceli offering her a bottle of water. "These will make you feel better."

Without questioning the good Samaritan, Es did as she was told.

For the next few hours, Es sat upright. Her stomach was gurgling. She felt hungry but was apprehensive about eating anything. She knew that Xolo needed some food. She reached into her over-the-shoulder bag, and after rummaging around for a minute, pulled out a small handful of dog food. The smell of it almost made her gag. Xolo barked and attacked the food. Es was lucky that she didn't lose a finger in the process.

Every once in a while, Es would feel a painful twinge in her bowels. She would rush to the bus toilet as fast as she could. They turned out to be false alarms.

Since she had slept most of the day, she was wide awake for the next leg of the trip.

Papá, why are you putting me through all of this crap!

Chapter 9 – Chilangaville

Monday, October 19, 1970

The luminescent hands on her watch shone 4:10 a.m. as the bus entered the Guadalajara terminal. The bus driver's weary eyes stared without expression. The passengers piled out carrying their luggage and possessions. Esmeralda, Araceli, and Coralina were the last to get off. They walked down the disembarkation area into the central terminal. Esmeralda would have to transfer to another bus for the continuation of her trip to Mexico City. Araceli helped her look for it. It was platform number 7 and the bus to Mexico City did not leave until 6 a.m.

"¡Mi vida!" someone yelled.

Araceli looked up and saw her husband running toward her. Es noticed that he was a papi chulo aka handsome stud. He was of medium height, had black hair and a slight build, and wore a skinny moustache. They embraced, flying at each other at a hundred miles an hour.

"¡Mi amor!" Araceli smothered her husband with kisses.

"¡Papi!" Coralina ran up to her dad and hugged his legs.

A few minutes and a few breaths later, Araceli introduced Esmeralda to her husband.

"Mucho gusto," he shook her hand. "Antonio. Para servirle." He told that it was a pleasure to meet her.

"El gusto es mío," her Spanish was starting to fall into place. Es was almost feeling human again.

Araceli then explained to Antonio that Esmeralda had rescued them from a dangerous robber, and that the pobrecita had gotten sick from something she ate. Es was anxious to break away and give Xolo an opportunity to relieve himself.

Antonio then insisted that Es come home with them until she was fully recovered. *Actually, it sounds like a good idea,* Esmeralda thought. *I could use a day or two of rest and recuperation. I don't want to go through another day like yesterday. Nasty!*

But Esmeralda graciously declined. She felt the obligation to find her father overwhelming.

"How about we take care of your dog?" Araceli suggested. "We have a Chihuahua también and there is no problem taking care of it. Coralina would love it."

Wow! That seemed very tempting. Xolo is going to hold me back. He is worse than traveling with a child . . . so needy! She thought it over for a few moments and then said "no." *I know that I'm going to regret this!*

"We understand," remarked Araceli compassionately. "We have a hard time leaving our dog behind too."

They spent the next five minutes hugging and saying goodbyes.

"You have to eat a little something," suggested Araceli in a maternal way. "Tortilla soup with lots of saltine crackers." The mother then had a litany of foods for Es to avoid: Fruit. Vegetables, Dairy products.

Rats! thought Es. *What can I eat?* But she wasn't hungry anyway. So, it didn't matter.

Araceli and Coralina finally gave Es some farewell abrazos as they separated.

"Don't forget the pills if you have any more problems," advised Araceli.

"Thank you for everything."

"By the way, don't be surprised if you are constipated for the next few days," Araceli shouted as they left.

Oh, great! Es exhaled slowly.

As they all parted and went their separate ways, Araceli began telling Antonio in hushed tones about Esmeralda's green hair. "I think it's real, mi amor. It looks real. But I didn't touch it. It doesn't look like pelo teñido. I don't think she dyes it. But, I don't know."

"Is she some type of bruja?" Antonio's eyes widened. Maybe Es was a witch.

Meanwhile, Es needed to tend to her own needs. Es looked around and finally found a little restaurant that was almost closing. She ordered tortilla soup in which she soaked five packets of saltine crackers. Afterwards, she took Xolo outside.

Back in the terminal, she didn't feel like brushing her teeth, but she did go to the bathroom and snagged some toilet paper, *por si acaso,* just in case. And then Es bought another bottle of water. She caught the next bus to Mexico City leaving from platform number seven. The driver was clean-cut, but his face had a thousand pock marks. The bus was almost half full as it left the station just past six that morning.

Fortunately, Es was now feeling better. She twisted her mother's fire opal pendant between her fingers. *Life is good! I can do this.*

As the dawn was breaking, Es looked out the window. The scenery was more and more open lowlands, occasional small towns, and tree groves. Every fifteen kilometers or so (the equivalent of ten miles) the bus would slow down. There was road construction going on. Dozens of dark-skinned workers with big sombreros and neckerchiefs over their mouths were bent over, doing manual labor. Only one lane of traffic was allowed to proceed at a time. This made for endless delays and unhappy truck drivers. At one such detour, an enterprising woman wearing a native huipil had a basket on her head and her two-year-old boy by her side. She was selling tamales. The bus driver opened the front door during the delay and several patrons bought some, including the driver. Es declined. She had learned her lesson well.

Two viejitas with prune-skinned faces were sitting in front of Es. They wore multicolored shawls over their heads. The heavy one, Julia, wore thick black glasses. They were both talking a mile a minute. And loud. Neither seemed to be listening to the other. Maybe they were hard of hearing, Es thought. She could understand every other word they were saying in Spanish.

"¿Oye, comadre, did I tell you what happened to Panchita's daughter?"

"¿How about that sinvergüenza Juan Francisco? His wife was barely in the ground. His bed never got cold. How shameless!"

"Y los precios de maíz suben . . ." María complained to Julia about the high prices of corn.

Es tried to endure the endless chatter until she finally fell asleep. The bus suddenly came to a grinding halt. Both sides of the highway were at a standstill. The passengers on the bus tried to rubber neck.

Finally, one of the viejitas told the other, "The driver says that a motorcycle crashed at the end of the pavement. The pobrecito couldn't stop in time. ¡Ay Dios mío!"

"Anyone hurt, comadre?" asked Julía, la gordita.

"They say a girl. She was a passenger on the back of the moto," replied the other.

"¡Qué lastima, María!" remarked Julia.

"These kids today have no respect for anything," continued María. "Except, of course, Carmen." Carmen was María's goddaughter and Julia's daughter. The two ladies lived in the village of Culiacán and were traveling to D.F. (El Districto Federal aka Mexico City) to visit Carmen's sick brother. The brother worked at a Chilango (slang for something or someone pertaining to Mexico City) meat packing plant. He had slipped on a wet factory floor and had injured his back.

Since traffic wasn't moving, Es decided to pull her book out of her backpack. Oh! It was her dad's journal that she had found in his office safe. Back in Tubac, she had swapped it out for the Ken Kesey book she had been reading. At her dad's place, it had been a weight issue and the journal weighed less than the book she had brought from Eugene. Sorry, Kesey. *Another time, another trip*, she thought. *Just call me crazy.*

Normally, Es didn't read while she was riding in a car. She got motion sick, especially if she sat in the back seat. She hadn't brought any anti-motion sickness medication. She sipped a drink of water and filled her hand with some more. Xolo lapped it up. *Should I feed him? He won't say no.*

A white police car passed the bus on the shoulder. It had on its yellow and red lights. The two ladies in front had stopped talking. Julia looked like she was falling asleep. She started to snore.

Es casually opened to the first page of the journal. She flipped through a few pages. It almost looked like a diary. The title said, "The Effects of Pesticides on Mexican Monarch Butterflies."

Esmeralda knew that her father had gone to New Mexico Highlands University in 1944 after his service in the military, but she didn't know the details. Her father seldom talked about the war or his youth, but she thought he had been stationed in the Aleutians, wherever that was.

Paco's family was not happy that he wasn't going to stay in Mesa Verde after leaving the Army in 1944. They thought that he belonged at home. He hadn't been anxious to look for a job in Mesa Verde. What kind of work could he get there anyway? The good paying jobs were in Denver. He didn't have many friends outside of the military, and he was kind of a loner. When his Army buddy, Marty Ortega, suggested that they move to Las Vegas, he was all in. He had nothing to lose, except maybe a few bucks. Finally, near the end of summer in 1944, Paco got all packed and was ready to go.

When Marty picked him up at his house, Paco said some hurried goodbyes to his family. The two guys drove off quickly before one of them changed his mind.

Outside Mesa Verde, Paco thought they had missed the turnoff and were going toward Shiprock, New Mexico, in the wrong direction. Marty, who was driving his 1941 black Ford beater pickup with a cracked windshield, four bald tires, and a thousand dents, ensured him that they were on the right highway.

Twenty minutes later, Paco still had a puzzled look on his face. He saw that this road led to Farmington and that they had just crossed into New Mexico.

Paco reminded Marty that they were supposed to be going to Las Vegas.

Marty nonchalantly responded that Paco had assumed correctly. His Army buddy then chuckled and called him a fool. He couldn't believe that Paco thought they were going to Las Vegas, Nevada. The university was in Las Vegas, New Mexico.

Paco didn't know whether to shake his head "yes" and look like an idiot; or "no" and feel like an idiot.

Several hours later after an interim stop in Santa Fe, they reached their destination: Las Vegas, New Mexico. There was a shortage of school teachers due to the war and Marty had been promised a job as a History instructor at Robertson High School, if he completed his degree at New Mexico Highlands University. Additionally, the local high school offered him a sweetheart deal allowing Marty to be the assistant football coach of the Cardinals as he pursued his studies. Marty had mentioned all of this to Paco on several occasions, but his buddy hadn't been paying attention.

The two spent the night at a raunchy, cheap motel after eating greasy burgers at the local diner among the cowboys. Within the week Marty was signed up for the Fall 1944 classes at the college. He was going to take twelve units, the minimum required under the recently enacted G.I. bill.

Paco wasn't sure if he wanted to stay or go home.

"You mean that you can go to school and get paid at the same time?" Paco asked his friend incredulously.

"Yeah, man, you can do it too."

"You're kidding!"

"Come on, pendejo. Just do it."

Before the semester started, Paco had signed up for the gravy train, or so he thought. He enrolled in English 101, Art History, and Spanish. His thought was to skate through school and get paid for it. He laughed to himself. Since he needed twelve units, he had to add another class. The classes began to fill up, and suddenly he had a million scheduling conflicts. He wanted to bunch up his classes so that he only had to attend school on Mondays, Wednesday, and Fridays. He kept running into dead ends. Finally, the only class that worked for him was Entomology, that met on Wednesday nights from six to nine o'clock. He didn't know anything about the subject, but it made his schedule work.

School began for Paco and it was more taxing than he had imagined. For his English class, he had to turn in three hundred word essays every Friday on a variety of topics. Growing up he was never a great writer, but the professor for this class gave him some good tips.

In his Art class, all they did was watch photo slides of pieces of art. The teacher who seemed like a sissy to Paco, wore purple canvas slip-ons, and spoke Italian and gestured with his hands when he described the artistic works. The professor assumed that most of the students would never see such works at the Louvre, the Hermitage, or the Prado; they would be lucky enough to see real Native American art in Albuquerque. But what Paco liked most about this class was the overwhelming number of girls.

Then came his Spanish class. That was a joke. Paco was Mexican and fluent in Spanish. Most of the kids in class were native Spanish speakers. Everybody used this class to beef up their GPA (grade point average).

However, Paco's favorite class quickly became Entomology 101. It was a small class and the professor was very friendly with the students. Manny Brandon was a 36-year-old adjunct professor from Santa Fe. He was not tall, rather slender, and had curly dark hair. He was the CEO of Consumers First, an environmental protection advocacy fund.

Marty questioned Paco about why he was taking a stupid bug class. He accused Paco of having an affinity for creepy, crawly things.

Paco rolled his eyes and shook his head.

The two were living in a small two-bedroom, upstairs apartment close to the college campus. Very soon the pair became chick magnets. The young girls away from home for the first time were looking for excitement. A little flirtation and a little liquor were all that was needed. Since Paco and Marty were over twenty-one, they could buy booze legally. The mocoso college boys couldn't compete against these machos.

Paco was doing minimal homework for three of his classes, but he whole-heartedly dove into the Entomology class. What blew his mind was the first lecture by Professor Brandon. The instructor went to the blackboard, took his chalk, and wrote something down: "What is an insect?"

This simple term was discussed and dissected for the entire three-hour class. They took a ten-minute break at 7:30, but by then all the students were still engaged in the topic. The following weeks he learned about exoskeletons, thoraxes, and ocelli. Paco was a goner. *This is so cool!* He thought.

It was now late November in 1944, and Marty and Paco were thinking about driving back to Colorado for Christmas. The class schedule for the Spring semester had come out. Paco would, of course, take Spanish 102. He didn't want to take English 102, that would have required reading a new book each week. He was leaning toward Philosophy or maybe World Religions.

He was reviewing the class schedule after his last Entomology class, when Janet Tokarczuk approached Paco.

She asked him if he had turned in his term paper. The long-haired brunette was dressed in a pink parka with a white wool cap, leather gloves, and knee-high boots.

Paco responded in the affirmative.

She asked what his topic was, and he replied, "the unintended effects of pesticides and insecticides."

Janet's mouth opened wide in amazement.

He asked about her paper, just to be polite. He was freezing and all he wanted was to get back to his place and out of the inclement weather.

She replied that she had written hers on the advantages and disadvantages of fruit fly research.

Paco was impressed and asked if she was going to sign up for Entomology 102 for the Spring term.

She informed him that it was not being offered because Professor Brandon was not going to teach the next semester.

Oh, man! Paco panicked. *What class can I take to replace it? This was going to mess up my class schedule.*

But Janet hurriedly added that the professor, instead was going to offer a twelve-week practicum at his environmental defense fund office in Santa Fe for the Spring. She said that she was going to sign up.

Paco asked her how many units the course was worth. She replied that it was twelve, all in Santa Fe.

Paco bemoaned the fact that while his roommate Marty had a car, he didn't.

Janet replied that that was not a problem. Brandon had contracted a van to drive the student interns over to his Santa Fe Consumers First office one day a week and bring them back at night.

Paco wondered skeptically if there was going to be extra tuition or fees in taking the practicum.

Janet laughed. She told him that Brandon was a genius. This course was to be funded by a private grant. It would pay for their tuition, some expenses, and a stipend. *How cool was this?*

Paco was weighing his options. Less work and maybe more money. He would discuss it with Marty when he got home.

Janet gave him a hungry stare. She wanted a favor. Paco bit and asked her what the favor was.

She wanted an ice cream. Paco reacted negatively and told her that it was late, and the weather was really cold.

Janet told him that she would make it worth his while.

By the end of the week, Paco had signed up for Professor Brandon's spring semester practicum with Consumers First.

The following week, finals were over, and Paco found Marty moping around in their living room. The football season was finished, and the high school team had a five and five record. Marty was worried that he was going to lose his coaching job.

Paco asked Marty when they were leaving for Mesa Verde for the Christmas break. He wanted to see his family during the holidays.

Marty weakly begged off answering the question.

Paco pressed his roommate. He was excited about going home and thought Marty should be also. The sooner, the better, he thought.

Marty had a sullen look on his face. He reminded Paco that he had gone over to his girlfriend Imelda's house in Las Vegas for Thanksgiving. Paco laughed and taunted him about not bringing back any pumpkin pie.

Marty's hands were combing through his hair. He was sitting on the old hand-me-down sofa. His head was pointed downward. He confessed to Paco that he had a serious problem. He had discovered that Imelda was only seventeen!

Paco's head snapped back. His friend was in deep doo-doo. *Jail bait!*

The roommate continued his tale of woe. Imelda wanted to get married. She was the petite blonde freshman cheerleader for the university. She was very popular on campus. She knew everyone; and everyone knew her.

Paco nodded his head, as if he understood.

Then Marty dropped the bomb and told Paco that Imelda's uncle was the sheriff in town.

Paco did not know what all of this meant, but he knew it wasn't good.

Marty wanted to run away, even if he had to drop out of school. He wanted to go back to Mesa Verde for good at Christmas time. He would give Paco a ride home; however, he would not bring him back after the holidays.

A few months earlier, Paco would have been already packed, ready to go home for good with Marty. But now he liked his new lifestyle and independence. He and Marty finally agreed that they would have to give up the apartment immediately. Janet was more than willing to have Paco stay with her until classes resumed. But that was a non-starter for him. In the end, he cut a deal with the college to work as a temporary resident assistant (RA) at one of the college dormitories while the regular RA went home for Christmas. He got free lodging and meals and could store his meager possessions in the dorm lockers. He didn't get to go home for Christmas to see his family, but that was okay. Life was good.

In January Paco found a one-bedroom apartment and started the next academic term. Each Wednesday morning, the Consumers First van would pick up a handful of students and bring them back late at night. Janet had dropped out of the project at the last minute, when she hooked up with a student who was Music majors.

Paco was doing well in Professor Brandon's special class. He felt that he was serving a useful purpose in helping the environment. One day the instructor asked Paco if he would be willing to join him in a research project down in Mexico early the upcoming summer. The venture was a joint effort with the University of Minnesota's Monarch Butterfly Project, which monitored the migration of butterflies to and from Mexico and the United States. Paco's curiosity was piqued. Brandon explained that winters were too cold for the butterflies in the States and that the colonies had to spend the winter months in

Mexico where the climate was more moderate. The professor also amazed Paco by explaining that it took three to five butterfly cycles to make the trip one way. Paco was excited, but he didn't want to show it.

"What's the catch?" asked the cautious Paco. There was no free lunch in his mind.

The professor replied that it would be hard work, but the participants would receive course credit and another stipend. Paco was curious about why the professor wanted him.

"I need someone who is super-organized," Brandon stated and then paused for a second. "Besides I was a grunt a few years back too. I'm looking for a few good men . . . or women." They both smiled.

The spring semester flew by. There had been no further word from Marty. Paco made periodic phone calls home to check on his family. Meanwhile, Professor Brandon was finalizing his Mexico trip contingent. When the time came, he allowed everyone to store his or her personal possessions at his company's property. There were four volunteers. All male. *This will make life simpler,* Brandon thought.

On the first of June, the professor and four students climbed into the van and took off for Mexico City.

Suddenly, the Mexican bus lurched forward. The gears made awful grinding noises. Es' body jerked. They were on their way again. Es put her dad's journal away. *Hmm! I'm on the same journey as my father. Just twenty-five plus years later.* She looked at her watch. It was 10:25 a.m. The bus was already a couple of hours behind schedule. Xolo started to move around in his pouch. *Rats! I hope he doesn't have to go.* She reached into her backpack and grabbed a half handful of dog food. Her traveling companion went for it and was still licking her hand until she waved him off.

The older ladies in front of her resumed their chattering. Would they every stop? Somebody in the back of the bus had a chronic cough. The temperature in the bus was stifling. The air conditioning was off. At least this driver didn't play his crazy norteño music.

The bus started to climb up the hills. They stopped at a truck stop near Morelia. They could see Lake Cuitzeo from the side of the road. The body of water looked huge. Xolo was the happiest passenger to get off. He found a nice place to do his business underneath a scrub oak. The air was still, but fresh. Es gave Xolo some water. She hadn't eaten much in the last twenty-four hours and decided that she should try. She went to the truck stop restaurant that was filled with long haul drivers wearing threadbare tee shirts and grease-covered faces. *Poor guys!* She thought. She only had about forty-five minutes before she had to reboarded the bus. Esmeralda didn't want any more sopa de tortilla, so she ordered a soft-boiled egg with dry toast and manzanilla tea with lemon and honey. She also bought another bottle of water to go. The bus driver was smoking a cigarette three tables over and the two señoras were still talking close by. By a quarter to one everyone was back on the bus, with the addition of an indigenous family of seven that was toting several bulging burlap sacks.

As the bus lumbered up the grade through precarious curves that overlooked the valleys, the scenery became more pleasant and the skies seemed bluer. The hills seemed to be painted green. Xolo was sleeping. Soon Es joined him in a nap. She was a bit leery about getting motion sick on the winding roads. It was better if she slept, she thought.

She woke up later on as the bus now descended into an expansive valley. There was a purple haze in the air. The top of her head started to hurt. Her breathing became labored. She took a swig of water and gave one to Xolo. She looked at her watch. Must be Mexico City up ahead. As they approached the city over two hours late, the streets became more crowded with cars and pedestrians. It seemed that their bus was now competing with every type of transportation possible. There was a lot of horn-honking. The bus driver was constantly making right turns, then left turns, trying to get free of traffic jams.

At 3:25 in the afternoon they arrived at the gigantic bus terminal in Mexico City. Es got herself, Xolo, and their possessions off the bus. The terminal was like a city within a city. Es had to walk at least ten minutes to find a place of accommodation for Xolo. She returned to the terminal and used the services herself.

The depot was bustling with activity. Clouds of cigarette smoke bellowed everywhere. Every five minutes a loud speaker, complete with background static, announced departures and arrivals at the dozens of platforms. Baggage handlers were continuously loading and unloading luggage, boxes, and packages. Businessmen in suits were hustling here and there. Families with dozens of children were milling around. There were amputees and blind people asking for charity "¡Caridad!" Men with thin moustaches were selling every type of potion, perfume, and gizmo. There was a food stand or a wagon selling fruit at every corner.

Despite the noise and the turmoil, her headache finally went away. Es knew that she should probably call her aunt and uncle and let them know that she had arrived safely, but that would be really expensive. She wanted to go to the ticket office and find out how to get to Citlaltépetl. By chance, she spotted a little souvenir stand run by a short man with silver-white hair and a protruding gold front tooth. She bought a post card. He had stamps. She wrote a quick note to her godparents:

October 19, 1970

Dear tía and tío,

I just want to let you know that I am safe in Mexico City. Everything is fine.
Dad had a dog who is now my traveling companion. His name is Xolo.
You would like him.

Miss you.
Love,

Your favorite, Es

She handed the post card back to the vendor who promised that it would be mailed. *Okay! Now what?* Esmeralda looked at the directory and found directions to the ticket sales office. She walked over there. There were several people in front of her. One of them reeked of body odor. Es hoped that she wasn't ripe also. It had been a few days since she had properly bathed. *What I would give for a shower!*

When she got up to the ticket window, she tried to use her best Spanish.

"I want to go Citlaltépetl please."

The clerk was a young male with round-rimmed glasses and a black company logo tie. He looked bewildered at the request. He pulled out a couple of telephone book-sized tomes and thumbed through the indexes. Fortunately for the patrons behind Esmeralda, another ticket window opened. After a few minutes, the young man remarked:

"I can't find it," he seemed embarrassed. "Is there another name?"

"I don't know."

"Please wait a minute," the young clerk left the counter area.

Es was in a panic. *They couldn't find it! How could that be?* She wanted to scream.

A large bald-headed older man also wearing an open-collared white shirt came back to the window with the young man.

"Señorita, we think that the place you are looking for is Pico de Orizaba," the older gentleman said. The two ticket vendors tried to get detailed information from Esmeralda, but she didn't have any. They told her that Citlaltépetl was a volcano and

Mexico's highest mountain. *Was this where my father went? Why would he go there? But that was what his map indicated!* She knew that she should have researched the destination better, but she hadn't had time, she rationalized. *And if I screwed up, I will pay dearly.*

"Okay," she said to the gentlemen. "How do I get there?"

The young man started to explain that there was a bus that went northwards of Pico de Orizaba through Córdoba. It was about a seven or eight-hour journey. This bus left the next morning at five. *Rats! Why do all the buses leave in the middle of the night. Can I get a room?* Her right hand twisted the fire opal pendant around her neck. It was cool. *Great! I'll just sleep on one of the benches here.*

The older man interrupted. "But I think there is another bus that goes to Esperanza. It is a local bus and makes a lot of stops. Once you get to Esperanza, you can go north and get to Ciudad Serdán."

Esmeralda didn't understand. "What is Ciudad Sheraton?" She mispronounced the city's name, but nobody noticed.

"It's a little town that hikers use as a starting point to go into the mountain. The volcano."

"How far is Ciudad Sheraton to Citlaltépetl? Or Pico de Orizaba?"

"Close enough," the older man reasoned. In Mexico everything is relatively close, he thought.

Esmeralda was unsure about which bus to take.

"When does the bus to Esperanza leave?" she looked at her watch that read 5:05.

The older man looked through his timetables. "5:15. ¡Ahorita mismo!" Right now!

Rats. I hope I can make it! "Okay, I'll take a ticket to Esperanza," she said in a rushed tone. He gave her a paper ticket and a timetable for the Mexico City to Esperanza leg with all the designated stops. He had marked Ciudad Serdán as her next destination after Esperanza.

She paid the fare. "What platform?" she asked.

"Twelve," the older man yelled out. "¡Suerte!" Good luck!
"¡Gracias!"

At platform twelve, she found a small yellow bus that had a
sign that read "Esperanza" showing through the streaked front
windshield. She had three minutes to spare. She didn't know if
she had to go the bathroom, and there was no lavatory on this
vehicle. The van only had twenty-four seats with limited
overhead storage.

There were several indigenous passengers. She sat in front
of a middle-aged couple who were wearing Canadian flags on
their olive-green army jackets.

The bus was old and rickety. It seemed to have some sort of
leak that smelled like diesel.

She turned around to the Canadian couple. "Do you mind?"
she asked them politely as she opened her window. "Is this going
to bother you?"

They nodded their heads no and then slid their window open
also. Es found out that they were from Newfoundland.

For the next three hours they wound their way through every
pueblo and village east of Mexico City. They stopped for a half
hour break in Puebla. Es and Xolo took advantage of the stop.
The weather outside was relatively mild. There were outlines of
mountains and volcanoes similar to what her father's map had
indicated. Es bought another bottle of water and a cheese torta.
She talked to the Newfoundlanders who were celebrating their
tenth anniversary by climbing Citlaltépetl.

It was then that Es learned that if this bus did not arrive in
Esperanza by midnight, she would have to wait until Monday
morning for next one to her destination.

Back on the bus Es started to get another headache. She was
having trouble breathing. For the next three and a half hours she
suffered from nausea. She just wanted to die.

What am I doing here?

Chapter 10 – Esperanza

Tuesday, October 20, 1970

At just past midnight, Esperanza was waiting for the bus as it arrived at the town's only fueling station. There was no fancy bus terminal, just this station situated at a crossroads. The Newfies told Esmeralda that they were staying in the pueblo and said their good lucks and cheerios. The town looked deserted. Esmeralda quickly used the unisex outhouse in the back of the gasolinera. The bus to Ciudad Serdán had not yet arrived. She asked the dark-skinned, round-faced young service attendant when the bus would come.

"Ya mero." With an indigenous accent, he replied that bus would arrive fairly soon. She didn't understand what he said.

"¿No ha pasado por aquí todavía, verdad?" Es was worried that it might have already passed by.

The youngster shook his head "no," as he continued to sweep and pick up trash in the areas between the gas pumps.

It will get here, when it gets here, she thought. Es used this time to let Xolo out of his pouch for a while. She had noticed that Xolo had been more alert the last couple of days. He would stand, sniff the air, and look into the distance. Es wondered if he was sensing her dad's presence.

She looked both ways down the highway. It was a dark night and the stars were visible. She could see the Big Dipper. The air was crisp, and she rewrapped her scarf around her neck. There was the smell of firs in the air, mixed with diesel fuel. Finally, she saw a dim light approach. Next came a chugging sound. Es thought she was being attacked by ugly-personified. A noisy, canary yellow Ford Econoline with a white roof, one headlight out, and a tarped luggage rack pulled up. The side of the bus said "Tranportes de Lucero."

The obese driver exited from the van first and made his way straight to the head, leaving a half dozen passengers to fend for themselves. Nobody got off except an elderly gentleman who limped over to the nearest tree. Xolo barked at him.

"Shh!" Es reprimanded her traveling companion. She did not want to become a persona non grata because of the dog. Es waited for the driver to return to the van.

"Is this the bus to Ciudad Serdán, señor?" Esmeralda handed the driver the ticket receipt that she had received in Mexico City.

His plump fingers brought it up to his squinting eyes. "Sí," he nodded. "a San Andrés Chalchicomula." Es knew that he said "yes." What he said afterwards didn't mean anything to her anyway. *Maybe I should ask the gas station boy? Where did he go? They wouldn't have sold me a ticket to the wrong place . . . would they?* She climbed into the very back row of seats in the van. There an old couple with dry, walnut-wrinkled skin sat. She asked them if this was the van to Ciudad Serdán. The old man was silent and simply stared at her. His wife nodded "yes", very slowly.

There was the odor of warm bodies as the van swerved up and down the narrow highway. Her head start to ache again, and she was getting motion sick. *Rats! Not again!* She didn't remember if Araceli had given her any capsules to ward off the nausea. She closed her eyes and just tried to sleep. Her head felt like it was swimming. Es let Xolo out of his pouch and sat him on her lap. He looked up at her, and for a moment she thought that he was trying to tell her something.

Es nodded off to sleep and had a strange dream. Xolo had suddenly transformed himself into a powerful Aztec warrior who was defending her from giant tamales that were chasing her and smelled like diesel.

In less than an hour they arrived at their destination. The bus lurched to a stop and Es woke up.

Again, the driver escaped before anyone else. Es got off the bus and waited for him to return.

"Is this Ciudad Serdán?" she asked him again.

He shook his head "yes", quickly got back on the bus, and drove off with everyone else. This time she had been dropped off at the center plaza of a tiny pueblo. There was the sound of a howling coyote far away, but Xolo was napping and couldn't be bothered. She looked at her watch. It was two in the morning. The pueblo was partially lit by the moon. Otherwise, there were less than a dozen small lights hung from the power line to illuminate the small town. She saw no movement on the streets and all the storefronts were dark.

I'll do what my dad taught me. I will do a modified grid walk. A hundred steps to the left and then back here; and then a hundred steps to the right. She was tired and sick and wasn't sure that she could even count straight. But she had to find a place to crash. Es started her strategic trek. Near the end of the first leg, she found a cross street. Es could not spot any lights or buildings of interest as she looked both ways. She returned to the original starting point and then did another 100 paces in the opposite direction. There was another intersecting street. She looked to the right with squinting eyes and noticed a tiny light half way down the block. Es decided to take a chance and walk in that direction. She passed three stores and finally arrived at an iron-grilled door. The sign leading into the entrance said, "Hotel Las Vegas." She knocked on the solid oak door, but her knuckles hardly made a sound. She saw a little ceramic object hanging to the right of the door. She tugged at it a few times.

Moments later, the smallest, roundest cherub swung open the door.

"Juan Carlos Alberto Rios Nuñez Gonzalez para servirle." He greeted her politely. The clock behind him showed 2:30. *Oh, my God, it's still the middle of the night. I really need a bed.* She pressed her hand against the fire opal pendant.

"I need a room, please," Es could hardly talk. She felt like throwing up. "Do you have one?"

"Sí, señorita," he gave her a tired smile and asked what kind of room. "¿Qué clase?"

"No entiendo." She didn't understand what he had said. Her head was swimming and she was feeling dizzy.

"A big one for you," he attempted to speak English. "Or you sleep with another people. We have two."

Es just wanted to fall into any bed. "The cheapest!" she blurted out. The night clerk took her money and made her sign the registration book. Then he escorted her to a dorm room that had four bunk beds. There were three other guests who were not happy when the door creaked open and the light woke them. Someone muttered an expletive. Es found an empty bottom bunk and laid her backpack on the floor. She then ran to the bathroom and threw up.

At first light her "roommates" started to rise and shine. They all looked like climbers. Her nausea had subsided.

"Well, you came in a bit late last night," observed a tall young man who was dressed like he was going to climb Mount Everest.

Es nodded her head.

"Are you having a spot of breakfast with us?" he asked. She thought the guy sounded like he had an English accent. "It's included. Otherwise, it's difficult finding a decent meal around here."

Es took Xolo outside. There was a stiff breeze. She fed him his dog food. There wasn't too much left. She added a little peanut butter. Then she joined the other patrons. The young guy and his two friends turned out to be from New Zealand. Another couple was from Argentina and they spoke with German accents. The breakfast was hot porridge with sticks of cinnamon and sprinkled piloncillo [brown sugar] and pieces of dried fruit. In the middle of the table was a basket of bolillos. Hot herbal tea was poured for everyone. Es did not recognize the flavor.

Within the hour the four other travelers had left. They were going to take a two-hour ride via jeep to the western trailhead of Citlaltépetl. Es fell back to sleep on the bed. When she awoke, she was feeling better.

Es walked out the front door of the hotel and in less than twenty minutes had explored the whole pueblo. *Could my father have come here? But, I don't think he's here now. This is not looking so good,* she thought.

Back at the hotel, she went to the reception desk and asked the tall, slender man wearing spectacles if a Francisco Luna had checked in recently. She explained that she was his daughter and he was missing.

"Pues no sé," he empathized, but didn't know. He tried to find out some more details about her father. Physical description.

"Alto y muscular . . . Mexicano Norteaméricano." She told the man that her father was a tall and muscular Mexican from the States.

"Pues, la mitad de la gente que viene aquí son del otro lado." Half the people who come here are North Americans, he said.

"I think he drove," Es said in Spanish. "He had a VW van."

"Ah, sí," he rubbed his chin pensively. "Hace una semana había un hombre que quiso usar el telefono. Desafortunadamente no lo tenemos uno." He told her that a week prior, a man wanted to use a telephone. Unfortunately, they didn't have one.

"¿Cómo se llamaba?" Es asked what his name was.

"No sé," the clerk didn't know. "Déjame buscarlo en este registro." The clerk decided to look through the hotel register to find the name of the man. He flipped through the pages until he came to Tuesday, October 13. "Me imagíno que este séa." He thought that he had found the name.

Es leaned over the counter to look. The man turned the book to face her. Her eyes slid down the page. There it was! *Francisco Luna!* She recognized her dad's handwriting. *He has been here!* Upon further review of the hotel receipts, it looked like Francisco had spent two nights at the Hotel Las Vegas. The clerk did not recall seeing a VW van, though.

"Do you know where he went?" Es asked in Spanish.

"Lo siento no," he was sorry, but he didn't know. Then he explained that there were only two alternative routes to take from there. One was back to the Esperanza crossroads.

"¿Y la otra?" What was the other, she asked.

"Muchos viajeros van a Guadalupe Xochiloma," he added. He explained that this was one of the routes for the western trail head to Citlaltépetl." The name of the place seemed familiar to her, but her head was still not operating at 100%.

Es thanked him profusely and then asked how to get to Guadalupe Xochiloma. He explained that the daily jeep had already left that morning. He told her that a bus going in that direction would be stopping across from the plazita around 3:30, give or take fifteen minutes. She asked if she could wait in the office until the bus arrived. He nodded, "of course." Es went back to the dormitory, cleaned up a bit, and grabbed her backpack. She fed Xolo. They were both almost out of food. She then plunked herself in the office on a wooden chair retrieved from a torture chamber. The seat was hard on her butt.

She still had a half bottle of water left. Es pulled out her dad's journal and leaned back. It was going to be a long wait.

It was the beginning of June in 1945. Professor Brandon drove like a bat out of hell for three days. He would let Paco drive every once in a while, when he napped. There were potty stops and short meal breaks at the truck stations. The professor was a man on a mission.

"Enjoy these moments while you can, boys," Brandon smiled malevolently. "These are the good times."

Paco had served in the Aleutians during World War II. Compared to that experience, this was a piece a cake for him. Nobody was shooting at him or bombing their camp. The other students looked like they were still in junior high school. Two of them were from New Mexico. Joel Ferris, with his mop of curly brown hair, was the comedian in the group; he was from Silver City. He would try to tell jokes that went over like lead balloons. His major was "undeclared," but when asked by anyone, his response was "to get laid." Nobody thought that was funny either.

The kid with thick black eyebrows and dark skin was Xavier Baca from Mesilla. He was pre-law, but that might change. He didn't have enough money to transfer to a university and he might have to drop out and get a job. *Así es la vida*, Paco thought.

The third student was very reserved and serious. He looked Asian. His name was Benjamín "Benny" Chu. He spoke perfect Spanish because he was raised in Mexicali by his Mexican mother and Chinese-Mexican father. He was doing this field trip because it satisfied some of his science requirements.

Paco didn't share much with the others throughout the journey. He didn't participate in Joel's puerile joking or the melancholy discourse of Xavier or the pedantic observations of Benny. He wanted to work the project, earn a few bucks, and plot his next move.

Finally, they arrived in Morelia. They stayed in a cheap hotel in the historical center of town. The professor treated them to a fabulous dinner of enchiladas, tamales, and carne arrachera. They all drank beer even though only the professor and Paco were of legal age. They shared two rooms and took long showers.

The next day they set out for Angangueo, that was seventy-plus miles from Morelia. They arrived at the little village and found a camp that was consisted of several canvas-tented lodges and a main building. Professor Brandon shared a large lodge with Paco, and the three other youngsters had a small one. The showers, sinks, and outhouses were communal. There was also a common cooking area and tables with wooden benches. It was like Boy Scout camping.

Professor Brandon spent the first few days arranging the logistics for the group. He made arrangements with a local supplier to deliver groceries. He hired a local woman to cook breakfast and dinner; she was to make them sandwiches to take with them for lunch. She would also do their laundry.

Then the fun began. Brandon had set up command headquarters in the main building. He had butcher paper taped to a makeshift board and tripod. The briefings were held in the main common room.

Brandon began writing the objective of their project on the paper with a large black crayon. They were going to take inventory of the Monarch butterfly population at Sierra Chincua. He went on to explain that their project was funded to see if there was a correlation between the diminishing number of Monarch butterflies and the use of pesticides. His environmental protection defense fund knew that increasing amounts of pesticides and insecticides were being imported into Mexico by the Mexican subsidiary, Murciélago S.A., that had a black bat logo. The company was part of the multinational chemical conglomerate Nesplot Mondow. The increased use of these pesticides was having a deleterious effect on the Monarch butterfly population in Mexico. Brandon taped each finished page to the wooden supports of the lodge.

The professor asked if there were any questions.

Paco was hesitant at first. He wanted to lay back. He didn't want to be teacher's pet, but he was committed to the goals of their work. Presently, Paco addressed the professor respectfully, but incredulously, and asked if they planned to count every single one of the butterflies at Sierra Chincua.

Brandon smiled as he laid out the project's ground rules. The first rule was that he was to be addressed as Manny, not Professor Brandon. He liked the respect of the title, but this was a working group and they had to function as a team. Brandon told them that the simple answer was yes. Depending on how fast they could take the count, they might have to make adjustments in their date collection. One of the lessons that the professor wanted to teach the interns was that everything was flexible. They might have to revert to a sampling protocol if they couldn't make their timelines.

The four students nodded as if they understood.

The professor grinned at them as he spoke of their assignment. The project was planned to last until the middle of August. This would give them an opportunity to get a job or go back to school in the fall. Their first assignment would be to take an inventory of the Monarch butterflies. They would operate in teams of two. Each team would be responsible for specific territorial sectors.

Benny raised his hand. He needed clarification. Were they talking about butterflies in all of their various stages, like pupae? Benjamín had obviously done some preparation for this project. He seemed to be a detail guy.

The professor said yes. They would subdivide the tallies by stages, locations, . . .

Timelines were set for each phase of the project. They would go to Sierra Chincua and work five or six days a week. *It might as well be seven days,* thought Paco. *He's is not going to let us drive back to Morelia on Saturday or Sunday. Maybe Angangueo has a cantina. Otherwise, we're all are going to be bored to tears.*

The two-person teams were selected. Paco got Joel, and Xavier and Benny were a unit. Each team was given a multi-columned ledger, that they had to guard with their lives and came with the threat of death if it got lost. The professor laid out more ground rules ranging from being responsible for oneself to respect for others.

In addition to making the project a learning experience for them and doing valuable environmental research, the professor wanted them to have fun. He wanted this project to be one of the

best experiences of their lives. In conclusion, he told them to
meet him in them mess tent at 7 a.m. and warned them not to be
late. The students milled around for a few moments and
continued chattering about the orientation.

The next morning, promptly at seven, everyone was sitting
around a large wooden table. There were big bowls of scrambled
eggs, beans, and rice. The steaming hot tortillas were wrapped
in a multicolored cloth. An indigenous woman circled the table
pouring coffee in metal cups for everyone.

Joel asked the woman for milk in English.

The woman responded that there wasn't any.

He then requested sugar which the woman did bring him.

Brandon observed this little exchange. He felt bad for the
new cook for not introducing her right away to the boys. The
professor stood up and addressed the students. He introduced the
new cook, Adriana, to them. He gestured to her with his right
hand. The cook bowed. He reminded them that they were not in
a restaurant. He would do his best to feed them well and
plentifully (there was a little laughter by the group), but some
things just would not be available.

Joel made a crack about no hamburgers, but the others did
not laugh.

Brandon reminded them to always fill their canteens, as he
pointed to the corner where there was a common spigot for
water.

After breakfast, the contingent loaded themselves into the
van and drove a half hour to Sierra Chincua. The dirt road snaked
into a giant forest of sycamores and eucalyptus. At the end of
the road, there was a four-wheel drive vehicle parked in front of
three tents. A husband and wife team emerged to greet the new
arrivals. The 55-year-old silver-haired man had weather-beaten
skin that contrasted with his large handlebar moustache; the wife
had long black, white, and blonde-streaked hair that she wore
down. They both wore what could be best described as work
clothes covered by wind breakers. They were the permanent
staff for the project. Brandon introduced them as Lou and Sandra

Fisher from Connecticut. The professor turned the group over to the Fishers who gave a brief orientation and passed out assignments. The students were given sector maps and instructions. Lou led Paco and Joel to a southwest area, and Sandra took her group to the northeast corner. Everybody brought a package of two sandwiches that Adriana had prepared for them, along with canteens, toilet paper, and rain ponchos.

Lou dropped them off and left. Paco found the first day interesting, but a little monotonous. His partner, Joel, was not task-oriented. Instead, the youngster would just stare at the butterfly chrysalides attached to tiny branches and leaves.

Paco yelled out to Joel for some assistance. Paco was trying to be cool. He knew that Joel wouldn't have survived one day in the army.

Eventually, Joel came over and they started to work as a team. His partner was slower than Paco preferred, but those were the breaks. They took a ten-minute lunch just after noon. Paco thought this wasn't hard work, just tedious, but he was accustomed to being a worker bee.

The day dredged on, and around four Lou came back to retrieve them.

At dinner, after they had driven back to Angangueo, everybody shared their day's experiences. Brandon was paying close attention. This was like an informal debriefing. He would scribble down some notes for his project report.

The schedule was the same for the remainder of the week. Everybody was getting into the routine. There seemed to be harmony among the team members. The exception was when Joel would purposefully fart in the middle of the night, and that would throw Xavier and Benny into a lather. They would shout out "¡Pinche cabrón!" and other expletives.

Sunday finally came. It was their day off. Well, sort of. The professor spent the whole day collating and analyzing the week's data. Lou and Sandra had left early for a day trip to Morelia to buy supplies and to have some "alone time."

For the guys, it was a mixed bag. Paco wrote in his travel journal and then walked around the Angangueo pueblo. He thought he would ask Lou and Sandra for a ride to Morelia the next time they went or maybe he would take a local bus.

Benny had brought a couple of thick books. He was reading "Moby Dick." Nothing bothered him. He went with the flow.

And then there was Xavier. He had gone to mass in the village's tiny church on Sunday morning. There he had met some teenagers, just a little younger than himself. The next thing he knew he was playing in a pickup soccer game at the nearby park. The locals played every weekend and invited Xavier to play with them. When he saw one of his amigo's sisters, he definitely said that he would. After playing soccer, Xavier would go to the well-lit plazita with his new friends. There was usually a band playing music, taco stands, and a million vendors selling everything from balloons to perfume. Parents brought their families. Boys tried to pick up on girls. And the old men smoked and drank. The local atmosphere was festive and lasted until midnight.

Joel was a different story. He was bored to tears, especially when he did not have a captive audience. He tried to make friends with each new group of transitory visitors to the lodge, but with little success. While he didn't complain directly, he kept making snide remarks about how the project sucked. The other interns just ignored him.

The next few weeks went along fine. The interns were getting more efficient and more productive. Brandon was very content so far. One weekend, Paco hitched a ride to Morelia with the Fishers. Lou and Sandra dropped him off in the center of town and picked him up in the late afternoon. Paco had a great time exploring things alone. So many things to see, so little time. In his journal, he wrote a list of day trips to places that he wanted to visit. Ciudad Hidalgo, Pátzcuaro and its neighboring villages, Mexico City . . .

Paco was really surprised when he returned from Morelia and the professor met up with him to give him some unpleasant news. Brandon informed him that earlier that day, Joel had caught a local bus to begin his trip back home. He wouldn't be coming back.

Paco looked puzzled.

Brandon told him that Joel went back to Silver City, New Mexico. Still seeing the quizzical look on Paco's face, he elaborated in a hesitant manner. Joel had said that he had a girlfriend back home . . . and that she wanted to get married . . . and that he was lonely here.

They both really knew the truth. Joel was immature and he knew that he had made a big mistake coming on this project.

Brandon offered Paco the option to take Joel's bed with the other guys.

Paco declined. Why would he want to bunk with the other two?

Then the professor dropped the bomb. He told Paco that he would to have to do the data collection by himself. Brandon put his hand on Paco's arm. He smiled and told him that reinforcements were on the way.

Paco said that there wasn't any problem. He preferred working alone anyway. He didn't feel comfortable with someone looking over his shoulder.

Over the next few weeks, the project went along famously. Xavier was playing soccer non-stop and hooked up with Rodrigo's sister, Eva. Benny had finished all of his books and was reading Lou's "Don Quixote" in Spanish. Paco was taking Sunday trips around the Pátzcuaro area almost every Sunday. He loved the Mexican and indigenous culture and art. He also tried to learn a few words of local dialects, but he was lightly laughed at when he tried to pronounce some of the words. The end of the project was approaching, and Brandon invited Paco for a beer at the local cantina. Something that he had never done before. *Uh-oh!*

Brandon asked Paco how he was doing as he tipped back his Carta Blanca beer.

Paco replied "fine" in a neutral tone. He knew that when someone invites you for a lunch or a drink, it usually spells trouble.

The professor asked if Paco had any plans for the Fall.

Paco said that he would try to get a job when he got back. He was stretching the truth. He hadn't really thought about it. Maybe he would go back to Mesa Verde. Maybe he would go back to school. Paco took a swig of his cerveza.

Brandon said that they would be going back soon. Then he shifted into a serious tone and told him that Lou and Sandra wanted to take some time off. They had been working straight through for months. They needed a break.

The waitress came by and asked if they needed anything else. Brandon ordered them two more beers and an order of guacamole.

The professor continued his conversation. He had been impressed with Paco's labors and his work ethic during the project. He complemented Paco on doing such a great job working by himself. And then Manny made Paco an offer. He wanted Paco to supervise the Fall project. It would only last a month or so.

Paco's eyebrows furrowed just as the guacamole and chips were placed in front of them on the table. He wasn't sure if this sounded good. Paco knew that he was being schmoozed. He asked what the job entailed.

Brandon told him it would be more of the same. The things that he had been doing all these weeks. The professor was downplaying the commitment. Paco would be in charge. He could live at the Sierra Chincua Reserve or here in Angangueo.

Why would I do this? Live by myself? thought Paco.

Paco switched into his street wise, negotiation mode. He told the professor that he was barely surviving on the G.I. Bill and would lose his benefits and school credits if he dropped out of school for the fall. He needed some financial stability.

Brandon was ready to seal the deal. He told Paco that if he accepted the supervisorial role, he would get paid a stipend and at the same time earn twelve units of college credit. Paco wouldn't lose any G.I. benefits or school time.

Paco couldn't believe his ears. He didn't want to appear too excited, but he was. What a friggin' break!

Two more beers arrived at the table.

"Señorita, I think you should go to the bus stop now," the clerk said in Spanish waking Es up from her trance.

Rats! I was almost asleep. I'm so tired. She stashed the journal back into her backpack. She thanked the clerk and left. She walked over to the nondescript waiting place that had deep tire tread ruts cut into the dirt.

Twenty minutes later a tiny canary yellow school van pulled up.

"Buenos días," Es smiled at the very dark indigenous driver who wore a brown wool cap with ear flaps that had dangling strings at the end. "¿Guadalupe Xochiloma?"

He nodded yes, and she boarded with Xolo under her arm through the one and only side door. The van had a faded "Escuela de la Montaña" logo on its side. Es said good morning to the native passengers in Spanish. They were dressed in colorful costumes and seemed to converse in a non-Spanish dialect. She put her backpack on an empty seat in the back of the van. She settled herself and Xolo in, just as the van lurched forward. The road ahead was full of twists and turns and sloped upward. There were no guard rails on either side of the road. The drop-offs went down for hundreds of feet. Every once in a while, they passed patches of snow on the side. At one big bend, the driver slowed down to almost a crawl. The wheels of the van slid sideways a little until the driver regained control. Black ice! Outside it was getting chillier. The van heater was on. Its fan was whining. There was the obnoxious odor of carbon monoxide creeping in. Es cracked her window.

A few trucks were parked on the side of the road. One had an overheated radiator. Another driver, who was only wearing a plain wife beater tee shirt in spite of the cold weather, took a leak over the edge of the cliff.

The throbbing over her left eye gave Es a splitting head. She tried to sleep. She was oblivious to her fellow passengers. Xolo had also been quiet for hours. She had forgotten to feed him before they left. She gave him some water, and he seemed satisfied with that. He looked gratefully up at her and seemed to exude centuries of stoicism and the wisdom of the ages. Es felt a chill go up her spine as her pendant vibrated against her skin.

It was just before 5 p.m. when they reached Guadalupe Xochiloma. It was already dark, and things were relatively quiet except for a few people pushing carts down the dusty street. *It's a small town. Where could my dad have gone? I hope he stayed close by.*

She walked west for half a block. There was a two-story building with a handwritten sign that said, "No hay cuartos disponibles." *Oh, great! No rooms at the inn!* Esmeralda walked into the building anyway. A cloud of cigarette smoke engulfed her and almost made her choke. It exacerbated her headache. Es made her way to the counter where the culprit was inhaling the obnoxious tobacco product.

Before she could utter a word, the beer-gutted host preemptively yelled out, "¡No hay cuartos!" No rooms!

"I know," Es said in Spanish raising her hands in surrender. "I just wondered if a North American checked into this place this last week?"

The clerk took another drag on his cigarette and nodded no.

"Are you sure?" she pressed.

He nodded yes and resumed his smoking.

Esmeralda wasn't sure if he had understood her or if he even cared. *This didn't seem to be a place that my dad might pick. But who knows?*

She exited the place and walked back and forth for four more blocks. She found some wooden cabins called Las Casitas del Rey. She heard a group speaking English in the common room.

Es said hi and asked if anyone had seen an older gentleman, and she went on to describe her father. She didn't have any success.

Her head was throbbing. Someone in the group offered her a beer which she accepted. Within fifteen minutes she was eating some type of lentil soup with thick dark bread. Xolo was getting his share of attention and scraps of food. Some travelers, Sam and George, befriended her and Es gave them a brief summary of her quest to find her father. They suggested that because it was late, Es should get a room there. Heeding their advice, Es excused herself and successfully procured a bed in the dorm. She ditched her backpack in the common sleeping area and rejoined her two new friends from San Francisco. Samantha "Sam" was a registered nurse and her partner Georgina "George" was a bartender in North Beach. They were both avid hikers and planned to trek up to Pico de Orizaba on Thursday. They invited Esmeralda to join them if she wanted to. Sam suggested that the hike was mountainous and snowy and that she would need additional supplies. The big supplier in town was Suministros de José (hiking supplies), about two blocks away.

Esmeralda was taking it all in. *I can't find any trace of my Papá. He was supposed to have come here. Should I take a chance and go with these two women? They seem nice. Let me think about it.*

It was just eight o'clock when she found her cot and crashed. She would shower in the morning. The bus to the western trailhead for Pico de Orizaba left very early Thursday morning. If she was going to hang out with Sam and George, she would have to do a lot of preparation the following day.

She was asleep before her head hit the pillow.

Chapter 11 – Guadalupe Xochiloma

Wednesday, October 21, 1970

The rooster was the early bird that morning, and he insisted that everyone rise and shine with him. Esmeralda's eyes seemed to have gone cross-eyed. She blinked and closed them, and almost went back to sleep. However, the little yelp from Xolo forced her out of the warm horsehair blanket. She took the dog outside. There was no more dog food, so Es had to feed her little buddy some leftover beans. The Chihuahua did not complain. Es came back into the common room and sank her teeth into some hard toast and hot amaranth porridge plied thick with plumped raisins.

Sam and George were in an animated conversation when they joined Es. Xolo had switched his loyalty to Sam who constantly petted him and told him how cute he was. He was such a suck-up. Es liked the pair and thought that they would be great traveling partners. She told them that she was willing to go with them to Pico de Orizaba.

George told her that they would take the western trailhead up the mountain and that the trip would take at least two days. She conjectured that the weather would be cold, but not snowy. George also warned Es that it was a high altitude climb and that breathing would be exceptionally difficult. She told Es that she could back out at any time. George did not want her to feel obligated.

Es told them that she thought she would be okay. She did not tell the pair the maudlin details of trying to find her father. George highly recommended that Es go the outfitter's supply store, about two blocks down the road and next to the travelers' chapel, to get plenty of provisions. She suggested that Xolo could probably live off of sausage, if need be. George also told Es that she had to make travel arrangements with the outfitter in order to ride with them on Thursday morning and be dropped off at the trailhead. The outfitter ran a shuttle service to the trailheads a few times a week to drop off and pick up passengers and to deliver supplies along the way.

"And don't forget to tell her about the laundry," Sam interrupted.

"Oh, yeah, get your laundry done today. Ask Marta. She is the skinny, quiet one who works in the back. She does laundry for everyone," George advised. "And cheap too."

"But will my clothes be dry in time?" asked Es.

"I think so. I don't really know how, but people tell me yes."

After breakfast, Es asked Marta to do her laundry. Afterwards, Es put on her jacket and made her way to the outfitter's. The shop had a small wooden counter with goods stacked up behind and exposed electrical wires overhead.

"Buenos días," she greeted in Spanish. The long-haired clerk who wore a blue and red cowboy shirt looked up. "I need a few things. I'm going to Pico de Orizaba."

"Isn't everyone," the guy replied in English and smiled. "What can I get for you?"

In the States, everyone focuses on me being Mexican. Down here, everyone treats me like a gringa. Así es la vida, my Tío

Felipe would say. Geez! I miss them. I'm thinking I'm an idiot for being here!

She showed the clerk a list of items that she had scribbled down that morning. Sausage was number one. *How many?* She thought. *At least two, if not three. Cheese.* She also bought some non-food items like waterproof matches. The paramount concern was the weight of her backpack. She hadn't gotten rid of much, and hiking in the mountains was going to be taxing. She chatted with the clerk in English about the trek and received some useful information. He also recommended that she buy "palanqui."

"What's a 'palenque'?" Es questioned. *Isn't that a place down in Chiapas or somewhere?*

"You know, those palanquetas. Those little cakes made from amaranto, peanuts, pumpkin seeds, sesame seeds, and piloncillo [brown sugar]. Good energy." He pulled out some bars and cakes to show her.

Oh, those! She recognized them. *Tío Felipe sells these fah sung thong* [peanut brittle] *bars in his health store. There're good. And sweet!* She ordered six of them because they were light and inexpensive and then got carried away and order another half dozen. The clerk was happy as she paid for her purchases and exited through the front opening.

Esmeralda looked up and saw the travelers' chapel across the road. Curiosity made her cross the road. A small cemetery with a few dozen wooden crosses abutted the adobe chapel. There were no fresh flowers on any of the gravesites. As Es entered the chapel, she realized that it was the starting out point for many a journey to Orizaba. A couple of hikers were making the sign of the cross as they passed her. Es thought they looked like Germans or Aussies.

Inside the chapel she saw an ancient wooden retablo altar. To the sides were simple relics and the statues of a dark-skinned Virgin Mary and an indigenous looking Jesus Christ. She found a votive candle by the altar railing and lit it after depositing a few pesos into a tin box. She prayed for her success in finding her father and for the health of her aunt and uncle.

Back on the road Esmeralda met up with an older native woman in a reddish shawl that was draped over her whitish blouse and green skirt.

"Buenos días," Es spoke in Spanish straight away. "Has a North Americano been here within the last week?"

Either the poor woman didn't speak Spanish or didn't know the answer. She stared at Es with her black carbon eyes. The woman then lifted up her wrinkled hands and shrugged. Es thanked her. The old woman muttered something as Es left her. It sounded like "güera" [light-skinned Anglo] or "guerrera" [warrior] but Esmeralda did not understand her.

She put Xolo down because he needed a potty break. The dog suddenly bolted away and ran behind a travel lodge.

"Xolo, come back!" Es screamed as she tried to pursue him. She was panting. "Where are you going, you bad dog?"

As she rounded the corner, she saw it. It was her dad's 1965 mignonette two-tone brown and tan Volkswagen van with a thick layer of reddish clay dust on it. It had dirty louvered middle windows. She came closer and rubbed away some of the dirt. As she looked through the driver's window, the beige interior looked familiar. Es had been on several camping trips with her dad and thought for sure the VW was his. She tried the van door, but it was locked. She tried all other doors, but Es met with the same result.

Esmeralda raced to the travel lodge. As she entered, she saw a young boy, about 10 or 11 years old, standing behind the counter in front of her.

"Is my dad still here?" Es asked in Spanish.

"Sí," the boy replied.

"Where?" Es was getting excited. *She would get to see her father! Life was good again. Her quest was over.*

"Sí."

Suddenly, Es became very pale. This was the voice that she remembered from the week prior. The one that had hung up on her when she had called. This place was Posada Las Estrellas de Guadalupe Xochiloma! The brochure from her dad's house!

"Can you take me to where he is?" Es looked straight at the boy.

"Sí" the boy no effort to move.

"Do you speak Spanish?"

"Sí."

Es knew something was not right with this boy. "Do you speak English?"

"Si''

"How about French?"

"Sí."

Esmeralda was half-angry. *What was wrong with this kid?* An old woman came up behind the boy. She was the same woman that Es had just met on the street. The old woman was silent throughout Es' inquiry of the boy. Es abruptly turned to the old woman. "Where is my dad?" Es asked angrily again in Spanish.

The elderly woman stepped backwards. The kid repeated "sí," again.

"His van is here. Where is he?" Es pressed. The opal pendant felt hot against her chest.

After a few more minutes of a frustrating and fruitless attempt by Es to extract information from the pair, the old woman nudged the boy and spoke to him in an indigenous language. The boy stepped from behind the counter and grabbed Es' hand. Xolo growled. The boy escorted Es across the road back to the outfitter's. He walked with a limp. He had a club foot. His right foot was turned inward and downward. Esmeralda began to drop her attitude.

"Oh, yeah, I remember that guy," the clerk at the outfitter's said a few minutes later. "He stayed a few days at my aunt's." He pointed back to the Posada Las Estrellas.

"Did he say anything to you about where he was going?"

"I don't think so," the clerk rubbed his chin as if he was lost in thought. "But he gave me some things to hold onto until he got back." He went to the back of his store and brought out a canvas bag and dropped it in front of Es. Es unzipped it and started to pull things out. A few lightweight clothes, a book on Aztec legends, and a pair of black and white striped Adidas running shoes. Then she found what looked like a car key on a leather butterfly-embossed keychain. She grabbed the key ring and hurriedly ran out the door and back across the road until she reached the VW van. She unlocked the vehicle and discovered old, dirty food wrappers, two empty soda pop cans, and a "Grateful Dead Live at the Fillmore" tee shirt. There was a slight whiff of rancid greasy food within. There was nothing of import in the glove box, front seats, or back seats.

When Es and her dad went on overnight hiking trips, her father had taught her a trick. He always placed a map of their planned itinerary underneath the driver's seat. If they went missing, the map would, at least, assist any rescuers in tracking them down. Es, instinctively, reached under the seat. She found papers and within a minute, found a map. It was old, yellowed, and crumpled. There were places like Papalotepec and El Valle Escondido [The Hidden Valley] circled. *Where are these places?*

Es went back at the outfitter's. She asked about Papalotepec and the Hidden Valley.

"I think they're in Tamoanchan," he said.

"Where's that?"

"Don't know. Never been," the clerk said. "People take southern trailhead to go there."

Oh, my God! The southern trailhead. How I am going to get there? Es spent the next few minutes asking more questions and then changed her drop-off arrangement for the next day to the south trailhead location.

Es gathered up her dad's book and other belongings and as she was about to leave, the clerk unexpectedly handed her a bag.

"What's this?"

"Bolillos," he handed her bread rolls. "He bought a dozen before he left. Loved them. He will be happy when you bring him more."

The afternoon found Es in her cot picking up her dad's journal to read. She had finally run into George and Sam and explained the predicament. They were cool. There was no problem. However, Xolo did make a move to defect to Sam.

Es rearranged the contents of her backpack. There were a few things that she could leave behind e.g., lightweight clothes. Then she picked up her dad's journal and continued where she had left off.

On the fifteenth day of August in 1945, Professor Brandon, Lou, Sandra, and the students climbed into the van and departed for Mexico City. Paco was now alone. The new group of interns would be arriving hopefully within a week. Paco rearranged a few items in the large lodge room in Angangueo. He spent a few days studying the tallies, the maps, and timelines. He had a few ideas for how to adjust procedures in order to get better results for the project.

One of the benefits of his new position was that Paco now had access to the project's jeep. He was happy that he had wheels. He decided to drive down to the butterfly sanctuary.

Every day he would hike around the milkweed patches and the oyamel firs. One afternoon he wandered up to a wide open plain of painted ladies, marigolds, and tithonia. He sat himself against a fallen cypress tree trunk. The air had sort of a sandalwood scent. Dozens of bugs were buzzing around. He was relaxed. Paco was in paradise. He didn't have a care in the world. Life was good.

Paco's eyes felt heavy. He closed them for a moment. He took in a deep breath. Then he felt the slightest touch on his right forearm. This was followed by a tingle on his left cheek. Within a few minutes he felt hundreds and hundreds of tickles all over his body.

He opened his eyes and saw his body covered with hundreds of Monarch butterflies. He let out a sigh of astonishment and the butterflies flew off. The swarm took off in a vertical climb and then dived down and continued with a figure eight. Paco saw swirls of orange all around him. A small group flew toward him. The fluttering of their wings made an almost human sound.

Paco felt an affinity with them. Then his mind became filled with numbers. He couldn't figure out what was going on. The butterflies started to whirl around him. Faster and faster. He could see the image of a stellar comet spinning in his head. Paco was breathing in a relaxed state, but his heart was pounding. The comet started to change colors. It became all orange. Then suddenly it burst into a million pieces. The pieces started to fly. They sprouted wings. They morphed into butterflies.

Paco felt a spiritual connection with them. He had a premonition that he would see them again. He closed his eyes again.

The next thing he remembered was waking up from this mystical dream. Paco's eyes kept blinking. He looked around. The butterflies were gone. He hiked back to the camp trying to figure out his surreal experience that afternoon. It began to sprinkle before he got back to the sanctuary tent.

The following Saturday, he drove back to the Angangueo lodge to meet up with the new interns who had arrived a few days early. Before his departure, Professor Brandon had explained to Paco that the new interns had been recruited from various top-notch universities in the States in order to increase the project funding. The larger the national buy-in, the more money the project could attract.

There was a tall kid with brown wavy hair whose name was Walter "Walt" Brunt. He was a junior at the University of Minnesota. Walter was wearing a tan-colored sweater over his jeans and high hiking boots. He seemed fairly serious. David Roth wore a grey NYU sweatshirt. The sophomore sported a reddish-brown kinky beard. David was hyper and couldn't sit still. Angelo Esposito was a junior from Rutgers and spoke with the heaviest Jersey accent possible. Although Angelo spoke Spanish, Paco thought seriously about pairing him up with David, because of their similar accents; and besides everybody else would have a hard time understanding the two of them. The fourth and last intern was going to be a challenge. Veronica "Ronnie" Hardcastle, also a junior, had long blonde hair that came down to her curvaceous hips. The tanned, blue-eyed Berkeley coed was drop-dead gorgeous. Paco saw her as a challenge in oh-so many ways.

Paco gave them an orientation and afterwards took them to the loudest cantina in Angangueo. The students drank their brains out. Angelo tried to put the moves on Ronnie in a way that was obvious to everyone.

She told him haughtily that she didn't date "boys." Angelo grimaced weakly and slithered over to David.

The following morning, the group made the journey to Sierra Chincua. After another brief orientation on responsibilities, ground rules, and objectives, Paco asked them to form teams of two. He could see that the small group dynamics here were going to be problematic. For sure, Ronnie did not want to be with Angelo. That left Walt or David as her possible partner for the next few months. Who would get along with whom? In the end Angelo partnered up with Walt. That left David with Ronnie. *This works for me,* thought Paco.

After the orientation, Paco asked his crew if anyone had any questions. Ronnie asked him with a slightly suggestive smile where she was supposed to sleep at this camp. Paco, having dealt with every type of person in the service, recognized the set-up. It was a lose-lose situation for him.

Paco threw it back on her and asked where she wanted to sleep, knowing that this was a rudimentary campground, and no one was going to be comfortable.

Ronnie answered that she could sleep with the boys, without making any sexual innuendos. But she threw in a comment about them having to behave. Her three colleagues didn't know what to think. Angelo probably thought that she was going to be trouble the entire summer. David didn't care one way or the other, as long as she did her work. Walt's mouth contorted as he thought, *maybe I should go after her. I have nothing to lose and everything to gain.*

Ronnie then put everyone on notice with a stern look stating that she took her morning shower at 6 a.m.

So, the project began. All in all, the time went as planned with very little distraction. Angelo and Walt would somehow score liquor from whatever sources. Sometimes it was rum or tequila; other times it was local rotgut. They would get bombed on Saturday nights. David, however, was a good boy and always had a book in his hand.

And then there was Ronnie. On more than one occasion she had knocked on Paco's tent door and asked a seemingly innocent question. She would engage Paco in conversation as long as she could. Paco found her definitely attractive and desirable, but he didn't want to cross the line. He was making some money and did not want to jeopardize his future.

On Sundays, Paco would drive to Morelia for supplies or to just spend the day. His Spanish was constantly improving. He loved the culture and the food in the little towns. He always went alone.

For the most part, the students did excellent work, and Paco would write a weekly report to Professor Brandon and send it by mail. Paco posted it on Sundays when he was in a larger town. At the beginning of October, Brandon wrote back and notified Paco that Lou and Sandra were coming back to resume their positions. Brandon offered him an assistant directorship with a lesser stipend if he wished to stay.

Paco had loved the project objective of trying to protect Monarch butterflies from the evil pesticide and insecticide companies, but he was tired of the daily drudgery. He declined the offer. He had made some serious money. Professor Brandon had been depositing most of it, on his behalf, in a bank in Las Vegas. For the time being, Paco decided to drop out of the university and travel around the interiors of Mexico.

Paco submitted a very extensive report on the preliminary findings of the effects of pesticides on Monarch butterflies. He had worked on a draft of the Executive Summary for several weeks. The report was to be sent to the Monarch Joint Venture (MJV), one of the major sponsors of Brandon's Consumers First, an environmental protection advocacy fund.

THE MONARCH JOINT VENTURE
EFFECTS OF PESTICIDE USE

Impacts of Insecticide Use on Monarch Butterflies

The Mexican subsidiary, Murciélago S.A., of the multinational chemical conglomerate Nesplot Mondow is largest insecticide importer to Mexico, which uses them in agriculture. The widespread loss of milkweed due to insecticide applications in agricultural fields increases the mortality rate for immature monarchs (i.e., eggs, larvae, pupae). Additionally, adult monarch butterflies traveling across agricultural fields in search of milkweed or nectar during times of an insecticide application face a high risk of extermination. Insecticide use in agriculture is also a concern for other pollinators that forage for pollen and nectar in agricultural landscapes. Additionally, insecticides drift into ditches and field borders and can negatively affect monarchs. Insecticide use by commercial and government entities to control herbivores and pests often kills monarchs.

One group of insecticides that is raising particular concern is neonicotinoids, which are used on farms and around homes, schools, and city landscapes. While harm to humans and other mammals is minimal, these insecticides are extremely toxic to arthropods. They are systemic, meaning that when they are applied, plants absorb and distribute the compounds to all parts of the plant, making the leaves, nectar, pollen, and woody tissue toxic to insects and other arthropods that feed on them. A variety of application methods make neonicotinoids popular for use in pest control. Crop seeds can be treated before being planted, allowing uptake by the plant during growth, and thus protection from plant pests for a period of time while the chemical remains in the plant tissues. Neonicotinoids can also be applied topically on plant foliage or as drenches to the ground.

Pollinators exposed to neonicotinoids while foraging face lethal effects. As treated crop seeds are planted, particles of neonicotinoid compounds are often carried with dust and settle onto nearby vegetation. Additionally, pollinators can be directly exposed to these chemicals if they are foraging at the time when crops, garden plants, or natural areas are being sprayed with insecticide. Further concern with neonicotinoids arises because they persist in the soil and plants much longer than other compounds, making them dangerous to pollinators for a longer period of time after the initial application. Because they are systemic, nectar and pollen gathered from treated plants are contaminated. Compounds that are not absorbed by the plants remain in the soil for extended periods of time, and often leach into the groundwater or run-off into natural water bodies.

Neonicotinoids include imidacloprid, clothianidin, thiamethoxam, acetamiprid, and dinotefuran.

Es had fallen asleep and was awakened by Xolo around five o'clock that afternoon. She rushed to get some dinner. She chowed down on a thick maize gruel with chayote squash, chia, beans, tomatoes, and onions with a stack of tortillas hechas a mano. Es didn't try la salsa picante.

"You'd better enjoy your last night here." She stared at the Chihuahua. "Don't know what's going to happen next." Xolo looked back at her with a knowing glint in his eyes.

Chapter 12 – The Southern Trailhead

Thursday, October 22, 1970

It was pitch black when George shook Es and told her that it was time to get up. The chachalacas were making a racket outside. They even beat the rooster at his own game. Es slid off the hay-stuffed petate [the weaved mattress] and quickly got dressed. She took Xolo outside for a minute. She rushed into the dining room and saw that it was 4 a.m. There were several hikers that had already finished their breakfast. Es scored some beans and a flour tortilla for Xolo while she wolfed down some amaranth porridge, toast, and herbal tea.

At four-thirty an olive-green army surplus jeep pulled up in front of the lodging. Jaime, the younger brother of the outfitter José, operated the local shuttle service. George and Sam climbed into the mud-covered vehicle and positioned their backpacks on their laps. Two other Aussies hopped in behind them. Esmeralda was the fifth and last passenger. She was lucky and got the passenger seat. Jaime was of medium height and had a black goatee. He was a smoker who maneuvered the precipitous switchbacks with one hand and cigarette in the other. The scenery changed as they passed the timberline, and there were patches of snow off the highway. The weather was definitely colder.

It was still before dawn when they arrived at the western trailhead for Pico de Orizaba. At the trailhead, there was a large, dirt parking lot that housed several portable buildings plus a concrete outhouse. A few lights illuminated the forest ranger office, supply store, and private guide shack. All hikers were supposed to sign a big large registry in the ranger's office before they began their trek.

The supply store was owned by José's older brother, Oscar. Oscar charged three to five times more for items here at the trailhead. Next door, Oscar operated a separate business, providing private guides for hikers. Es could detect the braying (and the smell) of the mules stabled behind the store that were used for some of the trips. In front of the place was an ancient man with a grisly beard who wore a frayed straw sombrero. He was holding a cigarette in his boney hand as he talked to a seemingly imaginary person. His eyes were blood red. There was no one near him.

Outdoors, under a timber lean-to, was a braided, black-haired woman wearing a heavy reddish *quechquémitl* sarape who was constantly stirring a concoction of cuitlacoche (a type of corn fungus), chayote squash, some sorts of large insects, and chiles on her comal griddle. Two short indigenous men were eating her fare with homemade corn tortillas. It smelled wonderful. She was also offering a watery cacao froth drink. Es was tempted, but she didn't have time to experiment. She had a task or two to perform.

It took five minutes before the luggage was removed from the jeep. Final goodbyes and hugs took place among Sam, George, and Es. Sam snuck Xolo a farewell treat of a small piece of dried meat. Es sighed. Her chest heaved.

Es and Xolo both used the bathroom facilities in the primitive setting. Es looked around and found the ranger's office. She politely asked if she could look at the registry. The ranger gave her a friendly nod, and Es searched the last thirty days of hikers. *No dad!*

She went back to the jeep. Esmeralda was alone again. Well, not quite. A new passenger had joined them. He was a short, squat native whose face was weather-worn. Jaime and the new person, who sat in the back seat, chatted in what Esmeralda thought was a half-Spanish, half-indigenous language. She thought that the new passenger's name was Temo, a nickname for Cuauhtémoc. Es deduced that Temo was a guide who worked for Oscar and had just finished a climb with some travelers at the western trailhead. Temo had drooping eyes and elongated ears puffed with wiry black hairs. The threesome resumed their journey.

The narrow, rocky road was an endless series of switchbacks that twisted up and down the slopes. Es got nervous every time they drove mere inches from the edge of the highway that overlooked a steep cliff. The weather was overcast and misty. After a half hour of travel, they had to stop. Another van was coming in the opposite direction and the dirt road was not wide enough for both vehicles. After what seemed like a lifetime of back and forth moves by both vans, Jaime was able to proceed.

Es' head felt like she was being stabbed by an ice pick. She took deep breaths. Jaime and Temo had finally stopped talking. The visibility outside decreased as new cloud cover moved in. The van started bouncing up and down. Jaime slowed down a bit. The van started to wiggle. The road was uneven and craggy. Esmeralda's stomach wasn't happy.

Thump! Thump! Thump! The van grounded to a stop.

"¡Ay Dios Mio!" Jaime shouted along with a litany of expletives that Es didn't need any translations for. He put on his sweater and got out of the van to inspect it. "¡Un pinche pinchazo!" He had a flat tire. He kept swearing as he started to unload the back of the van. Es and Temo stood by the side of the road watching. The van was in a precarious situation with the low visibility and the constriction of the road.

Jaime tried to pull off the semi-bald tire. One of the wheel lugs was frozen. It wouldn't budge. More swearing by Jaime.

Es was dancing around on the cliff side shoulder trying to keep warm. Temo joined her. They both watched poor Jaime battling with the tire.

"Did you just finish a hike?" Es tried to make friendly conversation in Spanish with Temo while Xolo was lying on the suitcases.

"Si," he nodded. "Where you go?"

"To the south trail head," she replied. "Do you know it?"

"Tamoanchan? No. Only west," Temo answered. "My two friends know it. Very tricky."

"Do they take travelers on hikes there?" Her interest was aroused. "What or where is Tamoanchan?" she asked him. He didn't respond.

"Are your friends' guides like you?"

"Yes. But both die."

Es was shocked. *How dangerous was this trek? Why did her father choose this route?* She thought. "How?"

"Someone say fall off cliff. Other person say kill by jaguar."

She tried to get some more in-depth details of the route. Es wanted to assess the risk factor. *Papá! What were you thinking?*

"Señor, what's Tamoanchan?" she asked again. Esmeralda wanted to know what she was getting into.

"The people call it El Valle Escondido [the Hidden Valley]. Hard to find," he explained. "Very hard." Temo slowly began to narrate a Mexica legend in his broken Spanish. He told her that many, many years ago, the gods created human beings from the blood and bones of dead infants who passed into the Underworld. The human beings lived in Tamoanchan, a paradise ruled by the warrior goddess, Itzpapalotl, the obsidian bat. There was a legend . . .

"¡Ya, cabr*n!" Jaime shouted as he finally loosened the lug. Temo stopped his story and ran over to assist his friend. They succeeded in replacing one semi-bald tire with another. Es looked on with skepticism. *Will we ever make it to our destination?* She wondered.

Forty-five minutes later they hobbled into the small area that demarcated the southern trailhead entrance. Jaime parked the jeep in a muddy spot between two large trees. There was an old, rickety wooden-planked bridge over a raging creek that everyone had to cross. The clear water looked really cold.

This trailhead was much smaller than its western counterpart. Amidst the clearing was the tiny ranger's station and a supply store. Jaime toted a box full of food to the outfitter outpost and called for assistance to unload the rest of the provisions and inspect the tire. He needed another spare. Temo assisted the driver. Meanwhile, Es went over to the ranger's office after dealing with Xolo's needs. She saw the hiker registry. There were not many names on the list. She recognized the name on the fifth line down. It was Francisco Luna from the United States! She had found him! She bent over and gave Xolo a kiss. Upon further perusal, she noticed that all the hikers that had signed out after her father, had already signed in after their return. Only her father had not signed back in!

"Excuse me, señor, what happens when people don't sign the book or don't come back?" she asked the youngish ranger who had short black hair.

"Nothing," he gave the company answer. "They come back eventually."

"But what if they don't?"

The young man's body shrugged "who knows?" as he turned his back and picked up some paperwork.

Es was discouraged. She had to find her father now. He might be in trouble, and he might need her help. It was still before noon. She bought two tacos from an indigenous, silver-haired woman with a face of a thousand wrinkles. This woman, like the one at the other trailhead, squatted over a comal, heating tortillas and stirring a pot full of chayote squash, nopales, and some kind of sweet-smelling meat. Then Es walked over to the outfitter's store and bought some dried meat and bread which she shared with the Chihuahua. The two had a little picnic to themselves.

Esmeralda thought about camping outside of the ranger station and heading out the next morning, but then decided that she would be wasting precious time. Es decided to attempt the trail. She made a stop at the outhouse before she actually set out. *I can't believe that I'm going to miss outhouses for the next few days, if I make it that far.*

The quest had begun. There was a little shrine dedicated to La Virgin de Guadalupe. Some dead flowers were mixed in with plastic ones. There were three red votive candles. Two had buff-colored wax drippings on the outside of the glass containers; the third had a new unlit candle. Es stopped and said a little prayer. Xolo barked.

Esmeralda followed the walked-over footprints through the grassy meadow, hiking past small evergreen shrubs and over undulating dirt paths. Big rocks dotted the way. She felt no wind, nor did she see any fresh footprints. Nobody was on the trail.

Xolo walked in front of her. His little tail was wagging. He seemed excited. He also seemed to know the way. The temperature was in the low fifties. Es felt like she was properly attired. After the first half hour they took a break. Es gave the Chihuahua some water and then took a swig for herself. The two shared one of their palanquetes A rabbit gave them a furtive look and hopped quickly away. Xolo gave a protective bark. Esmeralda resumed the trek as the pine-needled and brown, yellow, and orange leaf-covered path became steeper and the bushes gave way to the occasional tree. Sometimes she saw a termite mud tube climbing up a trunk. Her breathing became more labored and her pace slackened. The sun was full overhead and the mist had disappeared. She looked back and could see the trailhead way down the cliff. Es resisted the urge to grab her camera and take a photo. Beads of sweat were on her forehead.

Esmeralda subconsciously looked at her watch. At least two hours had elapsed since she had started her trek. She looked above and saw an occasional patch of snow on the slopes. Es decided to plop herself down on a rock and take out some dried meat and trail mix. The two ate a little and drank more water. She took a sideways detour off the worn trail and scooped some snow into her canteen to replenish it. Overhead she could see a condor lazily soaring through the valley. Es continued until she spotted a navy-blue object just off the trail. It looked like a ski cap. *The poor hiker who lost it is probably is freezing his ears off.* Es examined the woolen head cover. *I have three choices: I can just leave the cap here and hope the owner eventually finds it. Not likely,* she thought. *I can pick it up and carry it. But why? Or I can put it to good use.* She shook off the dirt and bits of leaves from it.

"What do you think, Xolo? He gave an assertive bark. Within the next five minutes, Es had pulled out her hunting knife and cut five holes in the cap and with a little string, made Xolo a tiny snowsuit which he was more than happy to wear.

The pair continued for another forty-five minutes. They took a potty break. Es was already exhausted. The winds were picking up and the temperatures were dropping. The scent of pine permeated the pathway. As they continued, the trail in front seemed to disappear. She took out her compass and tried to get oriented. She didn't have a map and the terrain was getting more precipitous. She looked at her watch. *I need to set up a little camp an hour before sunset.*

Esmeralda labored for the next sixty minutes. She felt cold spray soaring over the slopes. She put on her rain poncho. The visibility was becoming impossible. She heard the sound of running water. She was unable to see any type of path. She slowly traversed the slope, the thunder of water growing louder and louder.

Panting harder and harder, she went around some large moss-covered rocks and finally saw a tall waterfall coming down the mountain. It looked like it came from hundreds of feet above her. Esmeralda stepped carefully, trying not to slide down the muddy, slippery hillside. Esmeralda was hiking free style. The skies were becoming darker and darker. She stopped within reach of the cataracts. A gust of wind ran toward Esmeralda, spraying the cold mist upon her. She almost lost her cap. She put Xolo down and turned her back away from the falls that were still seventy to eighty feet away. Es got wet anyway.

Es was cold and now was getting soaked. Her body started to shiver. She needed to find a place to hunker in before it got any darker. However, something inside her head said, *Keep moving!* Then Es decided that she needed to refill her canteen, but she didn't want to venture too close to the waterfalls. The rocks were slick. The ground was mucky. She maneuvered gingerly closer and closer to the falling waters. However, just in front of her, she spotted a sheer moss-covered rock around the curve where water trickled down. She held up her canteen and captured the dripping water. After she finished, she capped her canteen and fastened it back onto her belt. She looked at her watch and the luminescent hands showed three-thirty. It was later than she had assumed.

"Xolo!" Es called out. "Where are you?" The roar of the waterfalls made it nearly impossible to hear anything. Es looked around, but sadly could not find him. She was feeling chilled.

"Xolo!" she shouted louder, but without any results. She was worried that the powerful cascades might sweep the poor little thing down to the valley floor.

"Xolo!" Es pleaded as she took baby steps toward the falls. She was having difficulty seeing. Es started to inch her way uphill. The footing was tenuous, at best. Her face was getting wetter. She was breathing heavily. Then she noticed some movement above her and to the left. She barely heard the muffled bark. She turned to maneuver herself very carefully toward the grow

ling sound. Xolo appeared on the ledge above her.

"Xolo!" Esmeralda was unsure whether it was safer for the dog to come to her or to stay where he was. She used her hands to dig her way upwards. Es got closer and closer. Her hands felt the cold, lichen-covered rocks as she climbed upwards. Her glutes started to cramp. Finally, she was within three feet of him.

As she reached to grab him, he turned around and ran behind a big slab of rock.

"Xolo! You bad dog!" Es was irate. She tried clumsily to pursue him, forcing herself to take unnecessary risks. It was now dark and all she could see was a tall black monolith in front of her. *Where are you, Xolo?* She pulled off her backpack and sifted through it until she found her flashlight.

Es turned it on and aimed it toward the slab. She could make out the dog's tiny face peeking out from behind it. Xolo looked like he had something in his mouth.

"Are you a bad dog?" she struggled to grab him as she bent over. She took a hard, brownish object from his mouth. It looked like a petrified piece of bread. He licked her hand.

"Okay! Okay!" Es sighed. "I know you're hungry. Let's find a place for us." She shone her flashlight straight ahead. There was a narrow, pebbled pathway between the two walls of mountain. The sides were black, but splotched with white gunk. Bird poop? Bat guano? She couldn't tell. In front there was a sharp bend to the left that went about twenty paces, and then another acute bend to the right. The whistling of the wind had subsided. She pointed her flashlight upwards. She couldn't see much, except maybe a star or two.

A cloud of warm air hit her as she came upon an opening in the rock. It looked like a cavernous room. The visibility was still bad, but Es thought she discerned a ring of small stones in the middle of the room. *Could this have been used as a fire pit?* she wondered. The place was covered with lichen and smelled moldy.

Esmeralda took off her backpack and wet poncho. She rubbed her hands together for a few moments. Finally, she found a flat, and fairly smooth, place to roll out her sleeping bag. The luminescent hands on her watch now said 4:25, but she felt like it was midnight. She ate a bolillo and some trail mix, that she washed down with her water. She cut up some sausage for Xolo which he inhaled. Afterwards, Es swished water in her mouth. So much for brushing her teeth. She went over to the other side of the cave and pooped. She had not packed a shovel, so she had to kick small stones over the damage. Not to be outdone, Xolo added his contribution close to hers.

The temperature in the cavern was cool, but not cold. Es could not have built her own fire even if she wanted to because she had nothing to burn. Es took off her boots and crawled halfway into her sleeping bag. She removed Xolo's makeshift cap sweater. He snuggled up to her in the sleeping bag.

The two immediately fell asleep. Es had unsettling dreams. She thought that she saw the walls move and little eyes staring at her. She heard the fluttering of a thousand wings overhead. Xolo gave a puny yelp as he cuddled up next to her.

The opal pendant on Esmeralda's chest seemed to come alive and flared for a brief moment before it faded.

PART III

TAMOANCHAN

THE HIDDEN VALLEY

Citlatépetl

Citlaltépetl is the highest mountain in Mexico, located 120 miles east of Mexico City on the border of the Mexican states of Puebla and Vera Cruz. It is a dormant volcano that last erupted in the 16th century. Citlaltépetl comes from the Náhuatl citlalli (star) and tepētl (mountain) and thus means "Star Mountain." Its Spanish name is Pico de Orizaba. It peaks at an altitude of around 17 thousand feet and has nine glaciers.

Chapter 13 – El Valle Escondido

Friday, October 23, 1970

A hazy light descended on Esmeralda and Xolo from a narrow slit in the cliffs above. There were hints of blue sky. Es opened her eyes slowly. They were itchy. She rolled over in her sleeping bag. Es' left hand moved to her cheek where she felt a small scratch. She looked at her fingers and saw a few smudges of blood. *Hmm?* Her brain tried to wake up. Her body ached all over from the previous day's exertion. She rubbed her eyes. She was still exhausted.

Damn dog! Es got up and checked her poncho. It was dry, but her boots were still a little damp. She changed into some clean dry socks.

Xolo was already up and had gone over to the other side of the cave to poop in the same place as the night before. Esmeralda's head turned to the walls. She noticed some drawings on the black stone that were partially covered up by muck (bat or bird) and soot. Then her stomach growled. She needed to ingest more calories if she wanted to survive the elements and rigor of this quest. Es and Xolo shared some cheese, sausage, and a bolillo. The dog continued to lick her hand after everything was eaten.

"Xolo!" Es petted him. "You're such a little piglet!" As she stroked the dog's head, she suddenly realized how fond she had become of him. It was comforting to have him along on this lonely journey.

He gave her a happy wag of the tail. She repacked her things and folded up her poncho. She didn't know if she was going to need it later. Es started to exit the same way that they had entered into the cavern the night before. There was enough ambient light to guide her back through the zigzag path. However, Xolo had a mind of his own and didn't want to follow her. He kept growling and darting in the other direction, toward the back of the cave.

Great! Es thought. *I have Lassie as my traveling companion.* She could only see the back black wall in the dim area of the cave. It looked like there may have been a borderline of pictographs along the top of the cave once upon a time. *Jaguars or eagles, maybe?* She surmised.

Esmeralda's eyes popped open when she saw Xolo disappear into the obscurity. Instinctively, she pulled out her flashlight. What seemed to be a solid black wall was an optical illusion. As she approached, she saw that there were overlapping slabs of rock that led to yet another path. Es continued forward. This track also zigzagged until it opened up into a fissure onto the side of the mountain. The air was now a little steamy and more temperate. In front of her, there seemed to be a long corridor. It was shadowy. She could faintly make out a jaguar relief on each side of the aperture to the passageway. It looked ancient and part of it had crumpled away.

Esmeralda took a few more steps forward. Her boots started to make a crunching sound. She pointed her flashlight downward and slowly creeped forward. The beam shone on tiny, greyish and brownish twigs. There were pieces of broken ceramics. *Oh, sh*t!* Her eyes tried to adjust. *Ugh! They're bones! What kind of small . . . oh, sh*t! These are human! Little babies! Holy sh*t!*

Her chest was heaving. She stopped. *This is crazy! I gotta get out of here!* There were beads of sweat dotting her forehead. *My aunt and uncle were right! I screwed up! I'm in over my head! Sh*t!* She took a deep breath. *Breathe. Breathe. Try to relax. This is probably the place that my dad was looking for. But I haven't seen any sign of him! I hope he's all right. I miss him!* Her face furrowed. A tear trailed down her cheek. *And Xolo, you're no help! Getting us lost! What a pain!*

Xolo seemed to ignore her. He was sniffing and pawing among the bones. Es was grateful that he was not trying to chew on any baby bones. Ick! *If we leave right now,* she thought, *we can make it down the southern trailhead by nightfall.* Es tried to recall when the next drop off/pickup would be. Xolo snarled as he snuck up next to Es. *Sh*t! He has something in his mouth!*

"Ugh!" she was afraid of what he might be eating. "Xolo, drop it!" Well, he didn't. So, she grabbed for it. After a brief tug of war, she snatched what looked like another petrified piece of bread. *What in the heck is this? Where did it come from?* Xolo shamelessly came over to her and started to lick her fingers again.

"You're still a piglet!" she exclaimed and then the light bulb came on. Was this hard thing a leftover bolillo? The ones that the outfitter said her dad had bought from him? Esmeralda thought. *Why would her dad leave bread crumbs . . . or pieces of bolillo? Was he leaving a trail like Hansel and Gretel? I hope not!* she thought. *The ending of that story was not a happy one.*

What then? she ruminated. *If these are signs from my Papá, I have to go on. Oh, great!* She blew out a breath. "Okay, Xolo, let's go!" Esmeralda led him forward to the corridor. Es thought for a moment. Her father had taught her several hiking tricks. One was to leave trail markings e.g., rocks. She could grab a handful of baby bones and drop one every 300 paces. *Ugh! I don't think so.* "Let's go, Xolo."

The dog barked. Esmeralda was sure to step carefully as she marched onward. She walked slowly on the winding path that snaked through the crack into the mountain. There were more reliefs of animals scattered seemingly randomly on the walls as she advanced. She had enough light to navigate most of the way without a hitch. Most of the time, she could see either cloud cover above her or blue skies when she looked overhead. When there was an overhanging cliff that cast deep shadows onto their pathway, she utilized her flashlight. Now, to the right, she found a niche in the wall that housed a broken terra cotta statue. Es couldn't make out if it was a person or an animal. The air had the ammonia smell of bat guano.

Finally, the path opened up and Es turned off her flashlight. Es was on high alert, her head moving from one side to the other. Xolo sprinted forward and found another discarded bolillo. *My Papá is pretty smart. I hope he kept it up. Why didn't he hire a guide? I know why; he's too stubborn.* Es smiled to herself. *And I take after him!* She continued forward another twenty minutes. The temperature was getting more moderate and the wind had ceased to blow.

The ground became gravel-covered dirt. Single plants started to spot the walls above her. There was a wet earthly smell that greeted her. Es did not recognize any of the species of the growth. She let out a breath. *How much further?* she thought. *Be patient!* Es told herself. She looked at her watch. It was still early.

Suddenly, she tripped. "Sh*t!" she screamed out as she fell hard on one knee. She had scraped her right palm as she tried to break her fall. "Ow!" She spied a protruding basalt rock that had caused the slip. Es inhaled deeply and poured water from her canteen onto the scratches, wiping the loose gravel away from her pants. She was mad at herself for not being more careful.

As Esmeralda continued, she found a few more bolillos on the path and additional pictographs on the walls. Finally, she came upon a fork in the trail. She stopped and tried to figure out which way to proceed. Unfortunately, there were no more bolillos or any footprints to give her a clue. If her father had passed this way, he would have left a marker. Es observed that no rocks were piled up. There were no knife markings. Her father would always advise her to take the path most traveled and if that didn't work, go to the right. *It takes the stress of deciding out of the picture,* he would say with a big grin.

Esmeralda took the challenge and went to the right. It was a true cave and she had to turn her flashlight back on. The path was dirt-packed. Blackened tree branches were found scattered haphazardly on the ground. She thought that they may have been old torches. The air seemed stagnant with an acrid odor.

Xolo jetted forward. Esmeralda followed. The tunnel opened up into a chamber with some type of stone altar toward the back. There were several skulls on the ground, but there were no signs of skeletons. She stepped on something that crunched. She picked it up. It looked like the remnant of an ear plug or nose plug. *Ick!* Her eyes bulged with a combination of fear and disgust. Es found piles of ashes and footprints around the rust-colored, splotched altar. The prints seemed to be adolescent-sized. *Who were these people? Were they sacrificed here? When did all this happen? I don't like this place.* Her armpits dripped with sweat. She smelled of fear. She wanted to get out of there as fast as she could.

"Xolo, come on," Es turned around and quickly exited the chamber. In a few minutes, she was back at the fork in the cave. This time they went to the left. Xolo barked. He had found another bolillo. *Way to go, Papá! You could have left it at the fork. Urr!*

The path continued to snake around for several more minutes. Suddenly, Esmeralda made out a blinding light way ahead of them. She felt relieved and she stopped, clenching her teeth. She began to pick up her pace. *Finally! We're almost out of here!* Xolo dashed ahead of her. The light became brighter and brighter. Es was going forward blindly.

"Sh*t!" All of a sudden, Es felt something biting her right ankle. It was clinging to her and growling. "What in the heck are you doing, Xolo?" Es was mad and was now out of patience with this dog. She was tired and stressed and didn't need this type of nonsense. She roughly pulled him off. He kept snarling. She tried to pick him up, but he kept out of her reach. When she tried to proceed, he barked loudly and snapped at her heels. "What in the heck is wrong with you, Xolo?"

As she tried to take a step forward, he snapped at her and blocked her way. As she peered down at him, Xolo's eyes began to glow red. She was startled and stopped dead in her tracks. Her eyes had been blinded by the glare at the end of the tunnel, but then she noticed something dark in front of her. She bent over and felt around with her hand. It seemed to be a hole. Her hand pushed out in front of her, in a sweeping motion. She couldn't feel anything. She carefully pulled out her flashlight. *Frig! Is this a mine shaft?* Slowly she leaned over and shined the light into it. She couldn't see the bottom of the abyss that was only inches away from her.

"Poor Xolo," Esmeralda felt bad for verbally abusing him. "You saved us." Minutes later they were on the opposite side of the hole, having cautiously traversed around the void. She reached into her mochila and pulled out a piece of dried meat. She gave it to him. He was more than happy to gulp it down. They continued a few paces when Esmeralda had a terrible thought. *What if my dad fell into the pit?!* She returned to the void and shone the flashlight downward for a few minutes without any luck. She picked up a couple of small stray rocks. She dropped the first one. She didn't hear anything. No splash or clunk. *How deep is this hole?* She dropped the second rock. Again, there was no sound. She didn't like this situation. "Okay, Xolo, let's get out of here and find out what's at the end of this tunnel."

A moment later Xolo barked. He had found another bolillo. *Thanks, Papá. You could have given us a warning sooner! We almost got killed. Urr!*

They were about fifty yards from the opening of the cave. A wind gusted in with wet showers. *Of course, it would be raining!* Es sighed to herself. She pulled out her poncho and put it on. She struggled forward toward the entrance. Her head jerked to the side. She was blinded by the sudden brightness. She blinked several times. She stopped and after a few minutes her sight gradually became adjusted to the light. But now all she could see was a mist. *Too dangerous to try to leave this protected area,* she thought. *Besides, it's dry here.* She remembered what her father had taught her about traveling: to look beyond one's field of vision. She decided that the end of the tunnel could wait.

Es and Xolo spent the next few hours eating and taking a nap in the cave. By late afternoon the wind had died down and the rains had disappeared. The weather was pleasantly cool. There was the smell of damp earth. Es and Xolo made their way to the entrance of the cave. In front of them was a misty valley with a tall volcano in the distance, surrounded by puffs of clouds. She didn't remember packing any binoculars; they would have added unnecessary weight anyway.

Maybe this is Tamoanchan, she surmised. *El Valle Escondido! The legendary hidden valley that the goddess Itzpapalotl ruled over.* She vaguely remembered the legend from her father's possessions. *Why was my Papá crazy enough to come here?* Just below the entrance of the cave, they discovered a series of narrow stone steps descending the steep cliff. *A couple hundred feet?* Es thought she might be on top of a Mexica pyramid or something. There were scores of block-like stairs filled with little puddles of water from the last shower. "Xolo, do you want to give it a try?" Es said as she looked down the vertical face. The dog barked. She picked him up and put him in his pouch. *I could wait a little while until some of the water evaporates from the stairs,* she thought. *But by then, it might get dark and I won't be able to see. Too dangerous! Besides, I want to get away from these creepy caves. Be patient!* She told herself.

The stones stairs were cold and slippery as she slowly climbed down. Her gloves got wet immediately as she steadied herself on the stones. She would have preferred to butt-walk, but the steps were too steep. They came up half way to her calf. At first, she started the descent looking outward toward the valley. Her toes hung over the step tread by almost a half inch. But she didn't like the feeling of not being able to see the nuances in the stairs. Es turned to face the steps just as one of her feet slid in some wet gravel. She froze and held on tight to the steps just above her. She looked down. *One step at a time,* she told herself. *Pasito a pasito.* She could see better now. On those steps that had a lot of water or were eroded, she moved more slowly. It took her almost twenty minutes to hit terra firma or, rather, a muddy ground. She sat on one of the bottom stairs and let Xolo out. He ran off for a minute. She took a swig from her canteen and gave one to the dog when he returned.

She noticed several weather-worn skeletons on both sides of her. They had probably fallen, or were they pushed down the stairs? She recalled going to the pyramids at Chichen Itza with her father when she was younger and seeing young boys in leather shoes fearlessly racing up and down the pyramids. These people had not been so fortunate.

Esmeralda thought that from the tunnel entrance above, she had seen a large lake ahead. Now, it looked like it was about a mile away. She needed to reach this destination and set up camp before dusk came upon them. She took out her little compass. Es remembered that the volcano lay north by northeast from the tunnel entrance. She would reckon her path in that direction. Pico de Orizaba should be the ultimate destination for her father, Es thought. *I could wait for him here. This seems the most likely place he would return to. I could set up camp here and it would make things easier.* But there was something in her, pushing her forward. Right now, she could feel the heat of the opal pendant on her chest.

"Okay, Xolo," Esmeralda commanded. "Let's go." For the next hour she crossed a tall grassy meadow. There were no signs that anyone else had traveled by here. When she approached some pine trees, she stooped over to collect a few cones. The ground was becoming softer. Up ahead, Esmeralda found the bank that bordered a large lake that was located in this part of the valley. She guessed that the water was runoff from the volcanic mountain. She gave a quick look into the water. She pulled off her glove and stuck her hand in. The iciness sent pangs of cold throughout her body. She shivered. The water looked fairly clear. Es didn't know if there were any fish swimming in it, but thought she needed to refill her canteen.

Within the next thirty minutes, Es had set up a makeshift camp. She hung her backpack on a tree limb, as her father had taught her, to protect it against any scavenging nocturnal critters. Her sleeping bag was on the bank. She built a little fire using the pine cones as kindling and dead branches that she found close by. It would sure be nice to have some food that was heated. Xolo agreed and chomped down on the roasted sausage.

Esmeralda did her best to clean herself up before retiring. The weather was a little cool. She brushed her teeth in the mountain lake. Going to sleep was no problem. The canopy of stars shown over their heads. There was a waning crescent moon whose light shimmered off the lake. Es smiled and closed her eyes. Xolo followed suit.

A howling wind picked up. And then came a croaking sound. And then another. Within minutes there was a symphony of glottal cries. Xolo half-heartedly woke up and started to bark.

"What is it, boy?" Es asked with her eyes still closed, as she reached for the dog that had been sleeping on top of her sleeping bag.

Xolo started growling. Es sat up with a start. She was now fully awake.

There were rivulets of some slimy foam engulfing them.

Chapter 14 – Cueyatlatezcatl - Frog Lake

Saturday, October 24, 1970

Daybreak found Esmeralda sleeping painfully in the lower branches of an aromatic pine tree, with burls poking her in the back and her mouth open. Xolo was in his pouch, strapped to her lap. The pair had been immersed in some type of slimy, silvery bubbles in the middle of the night. Es had immediately abandoned everything and scrambled up a nearby flame tree. For the next few hours she was vigilant of everything. One hand was on her knife. Eventually, her eyes started to droop. The boughs of the tree were uncomfortable, but she hadn't wanted to climb down. In the wee hours of the morning she had finally fallen asleep.

She looked around in the morning light and everything seemed safe. The aromatic red flowers on the flame tree were beautiful. There was no sign of the attacking slime or creatures. Es and Xolo gingerly made their way back to last night's camp. "Sh*t!" The sleeping bag and abandoned backpack were covered by a green mucousy film. "Gross! It was a friggin' frog orgy!" She pulled out her bandanna and dipped it into the water that was close by. She started to wipe off the spirulina-like secretions from her sleeping bag. The exterior of her bag was now wet. The last thing she wanted to do was to haul around a wet sleeping bag. After a half hour of rubbing and rinsing, the sleep sack was almost good to go. She would let it sit out in the cold sunshine to dry for a while.

Now for the backpack that also was coated with slime. As she lifted the knapsack off the ground, something flew up at her. Esmeralda screamed and instinctively swatted the object with all her might. The unfortunate bullfrog landed about fifty feet away. Xolo growled, ran to the stunned amphibian and sank his little pointed teeth into the neck of the creature.

Afterwards, Esmeralda moved her campsite about a hundred feet away from the lake to ensure that they didn't meet with any other surprises. Their breakfast of roasted frog was the morning's highlight. It tasted like chicken. "You did well, my friend," Es thanked her dog. She ambled back to her backpack and went through the same routine cleaning it up. She made sure that there were no other critters around. She brought the sleeping bag and backpack back to the campsite where the fire was still going. She threw on some more dead branches. She positioned the sleeping bag and backpack fairly close to the fire to help them dry faster.

The weather was fluctuating between cool and temperate. She now had a difficult choice to make. She hadn't showered in a few days and she had some dirty clothes. It probably was too cold to bathe and to wash clothes. On the other hand, she wouldn't get another opportunity with a lake so close. *It's too cold!* Screamed her body. *Suck it up!* Countered her mind *Urr! I'm going to die!* Her hands were sticky from the funky frog foam and the flame tree tar. She pulled out a small towel, a small bar of soap, and a tiny shampoo bottle. She removed her boots and tiptoed barefoot to the edge of the lake. Es cussed as she stepped on little pebbles. *Should have brought my flip-flops. Whatever!*

She dropped the towel on the ground. *Sh*t! Here goes nothing!* She splashed into the water with her clothes on. Her eyeballs froze in place. A sharp pain hit her in the middle of the forehead. *Sh*t! It's friggin' freezing.* Quickly she squirted some shampoo onto her head and threw the bottle back to the shore. Faster and faster her hands massaged her scalp. Xolo stared at her and barked. She pulled off her top. Then she had to submerge completely under the icy water to pull off her pants, underwear, and socks. *Sh*t! Sh*t! Sh*t!* She had to pee really bad now. Xolo ran to and fro on the bank. Es used the little bar of soap to lather up herself and the clothes. She got up quickly and then dove back in. She spent several seconds under water trying to rinse off.

Five minutes later she was back in front of the fire naked, trying to dry herself off and get warm. *Forget the deodorant,* she thought. She towel-dried her hair, even though the rag was now soaking wet despite the repeated wringing out. She grabbed a pair of clean socks from her knapsack and put them on. Esmeralda knew that her greatest threat now was exposure.

She couldn't risk the danger of hypothermia. She spread her wet clothes next to the knapsack. Her mind hesitated and then she made a split-second decision. She chose to crawl into the sleeping bag that had several spots that were warm from being close to the fire. She pulled the top of the bag over her head. Xolo was more than happy to snake in with her. Es just wanted to get warm. Her body was shivering. She put her frozen hands under her armpits. *Sh*t!* She tried to calm herself. Her teeth started to chatter. Es closed her eyes. All of sudden she noticed that it was deathly silent around her. *What's going on?* She was confused. Within a few minutes she fell into a somnolent trance. She moaned and groaned. Her breathing was shallow. She pictured dozens and dozens of skeletons surrounding her, just staring at her.

Xolo seemed to be snoring. Es was in a deep sleep, but she had to take a pee. "Okay, boy. Out!" She tiptoed over to a bush about twenty feet away. Her brain was fuzzy. Instinctively, she went to her knapsack and grabbed some clean clothes to put on.

Es then put on her boots. She tried to collect her thoughts, but she was disoriented. "Okay, let's get some food," she slurred her words. "We need some food."

Es scrounged around the campsite for more dead branches. The fire was almost extinguished. She needed some sustenance. She grabbed a palanqueta. With some difficulty, she made herself some of the native herbal tea that she had purchased from the post. She burned her hand in the process. Her bones started to thaw out. Es looked at her watch. It was past three o'clock in the afternoon. She had slept for a long time. Es and Xolo stuffed themselves on sausage, bolillos, and cheese. She was feeling better.

Her compulsive personality wanted to push forward. She could probably accomplish a mile, or maybe two miles of hiking, if she left right now. But her opal pendant seemed to tell her to be patient. She had been traumatized and needed to recuperate. She still had a long way to go. Es checked the clothes that had been drying. The jacket was dry, as was her top. Her pants were still a little damp, and her socks were still wet, so she nudged them closer to the fire. She took her boots off and crawled back into the sleeping bag and stared up at the cloudy sky. It was calm and there was still plenty of ambient light.

"Sorry, mi amigo," her speech had been restored. "We're just going to rest up today." He woofed. She reached for her jacket and folded it up to make a pillow. She rummaged around her knapsack until she found her dad's diary. Although she could have fallen back to sleep quiet easily at that moment, she was afraid that she would be awake all night if she took another nap. She resumed reading Paco's journal.

Chapter 15 – Cuitláhuac - La Brea Tar Pits

Sunday, October 25, 1970

Dawn found Esmeralda rolling up her sleeping bag. Her head felt like it had cracked in half. Her face felt flushed and she felt scratch marks on her neck. Es wasn't that fond of spiders. She had slept deeply, even if her dreams were filled with strange creatures. At least, she didn't remember any croaking. She rearranged the items in her backpack. Es made sure that nothing was leaking or smelling bad. The temperature was cool. When Es looked up into the cloud-streaked skies, she thought she saw a lone star, or maybe Venus. Her dad had tried to encourage her to learn more about astronomy, but she had blown it off. *Why did he ruin my life? He can't expect me to forgive him for abandoning me. Okay, I understand that mom's death was bad for him. But what about me? He should have manned-up. I don't know why I'm trying to find his sorry butt.*

Es fixed Xolo and herself a little breakfast and she went back to the lake to top off her canteen. Her plan was to hug the shore of the lake in the direction of El Pico de Orizaba. Her watch said 7:14. She looked at her compass to get her bearings.

"Okay, Xolo, let's go," Es pointed in front of her. He barked. For the next half-hour they hiked through mud, ground cover, and grass with the lake on their left. There was an herbal marshy smell permeating the air. The trek was fairly easy, and Es finally started to relax. Then it started to drizzle. She pulled out her poncho. Es' mind went into oblivion in order to avoid thinking about the rain. *Well, there's no question that my Papá really loved my mom.* In her mind she started to replay the part of her dad's journal that she had read the night before. There were some things that she didn't understand. She wanted to figure out exactly what she had read.

Paco had picked up Lou and Sandra Fisher in Morelia, the first week in October, 1945. The couple thanked Paco profusely for holding down the fort while they went on a brief vacation. The couple had glowing smiles on their faces. The trio drove back to Angangueo, where Paco debriefed the couple and told them of the procedural changes that he had made to increase the productivity in data collection. The Fishers were impressed. Leaving Sandra alone to meet the arriving students, Lou drove Paco and his one duffle bag back to Morelia. Lou had a colleague there who allowed Paco to stay at his house for a week. Lou also handed Paco an envelope with $500 in U.S. dollars per the agreement with Professor Brandon.

The first few days in Morelia were relaxing and rewarding for Paco. He was able to explore the colonial city better than on his prior little visits. Morelia was the capital of the state of Michoacán. All its narrow streets seemed to lead to the baroque cathedral with its twin towers. The old buildings were made of local pink cantera stone. He enjoyed eating the local food and talking to the locals. However, he had been cooped up in Sierra Chincua for weeks and weeks and now wanted to get out to explore more of Mexico. He thanked his host after only a few days and wandered off to new places. He wanted to make sure that his money lasted, so he hitchhiked to the various sites rather than take the bus. He picked the cheapest places in which to lodge and ate from the street food vendors.

Going north, he arrived in Salamanca in the state of Guanajuato. The town was simple and had been built up by the oil industry. Murciélago S.A. and the petroleum companies from here had been at the top of Professor Brandon's corporate polluters list. Their pesticide products had been injurious to the butterfly migrations. After his second day there, Paco decided to move on and went back to thumbing for rides.

To the east, in Celaya, Paco learned that this was the site of two famous battles in the Mexican Revolution. In one of the battles, Mexican President Obregón and the Constitutionalistas defeated Pancho Villa. Paco splurged and bought a book on the local history. He was fairly proficient in reading Spanish. He loved the free spirit of the people here, and the women were beautiful. He longed to learn more about Mexico and his own cultural heritage.

After a few days he hitchhiked over to Querétaro, which seemed like a simple, undeveloped location compared to the larger cities. He then decided to take the local bus to Toluca, another charming colonial city. He could live here, he thought. He started inquiring about places to live. The problem was that he had no job. He thought about trying to fight the corporate polluter or maybe he could teach English someplace. Things didn't seem too promising. Time to move on. So, the next thing he did was to hitch a ride with a cement company truck driver who was going to Mexico City. He found some cheap lodging at the Hotel Geneva. He spent the next few days exploring the National Museum of Anthropology and Chapultepec Castle. He was in heaven. He spent the evenings in the Zona Rosa drinking and flirting with the local Chilangas (Mexico City women). He heard that the Pyramids were a must-see during the upcoming Día de Los Muertos. Francisco decided that since these Days of the Dead were a cousin to Halloween, that he should check it out. He took the local bus to Teotihuacan and entered the archaeological complex. In front of him were the Pyramids of the Sun and the Moon. He was awestruck. The information board said that the site was over two thousand years old. Francisco hiked up the 248 steps, resting a couple of times. The view was spectacular. Unfortunately, he didn't have a camera.

There were several organized tour groups at the top of the pyramid milling around. Close by to Paco, there was an English-speaking guide giving a description of the pyramid to a bunch of students. Suddenly, he saw her in their midst. She was about 5'4" with long brown hair and dark eyes. She wore no make-up, but the woman was naturally gorgeous. She was wearing a tie-dyed top with bell bottom jeans. Large gold hooped earrings complemented her face. She was such a fox!

Paco walked over to her and politely asked if the structure they were on top of was the Pyramid of the Sun. It was the "playing dumb" approach that normally worked with unsuspecting young women.

The young woman's brow furled. She said "yes" with a puzzled look on her face. She thought the intruder's question was rather strange.

Paco then pressed her, putting on his best poor-me pleading impression with his hands. He needed a favor. He needed a camera. He wanted a photo of himself on the pyramid. Paco wanted to borrow her camera.

Her group had moved on, but she stayed behind with Paco. The woman said that indeed she had a camera, but she wondered if he was really serious about borrowing it.

Paco nodded yes. He knew that once he got her talking, he had a chance (on romance).

But then she asked him what he was going to use for film.

He feigned ignorance. Now he felt stupid. He hadn't thought the ploy through. He told her that he could buy some film or pay her for some.

She blurted out incredulously questioning why anyone would want to buy a whole roll of film just for a few photos. She made him feel like an idiot. Then she eviscerated him, telling him that she knew that he surely didn't want to borrow the camera for the whole day.

Paco needed to quickly regroup. He proposed that she take the photos and then mail them to him. He would give her a few bucks. Paco said this with a smug grin.

She stared sternly into his brown eyes and made a counter offer. She would in fact take photos of him, and then he had to treat her to lunch when they climbed down the pyramid.

Paco was shocked by her offer. He nodded okay. Within the next few minutes, she lined him up with the sun behind her and took a few photos. Her group had long since disappeared. Then she put up the palm of her hand for Paco not to move. She walked over to a tour guide who was with another group and spoke to him. Paco did not hear what was said. The young woman handed her camera over to the guide and then walked back to Paco and took his arm. A number of photos were taken of both of them.

Paco's eyes were about to pop out of his head. He mumbled a weak thank you.

Then she smiled and brazenly asked him where they were going for lunch.

Esmeralda had passed several bottlebrush shrubs with their red flower spikes. A couple of squirrels scurried by while scrub jays squawked. The mountains in front of her were snow-covered and now there was an easterly breeze blowing in more moisture. At her two o'clock she observed an inactive volcano.

The vegetation by the lake had turned from grasses to marsh reeds as she walked further along. The little raindrops were showering the top of the water. A flock of quacking mallards skimmed the surface as they took off. Then the ground around the path turned murky and muddy. Es had to detour to the east. They had now walked several hundred yards off course. The small trees became black and barren. It looked like they had been burned by a fire or lightning. Her boots were getting sooty. Xolo started barking. Es noticed movement in the tall grass ahead of her. Animals? Birds? She put her right hand on her knife. She started to smell something pungent.

Xolo ran behind a small cluster of emaciated oak trees. Es could not see him. "Come back, boy!" she cried out. Silence. Then she heard yelping. She started to run toward the little grove. She looked around for the source of the sound. Then she saw her dog in the middle of a pool of black liquid. As she approached, she realized that Xolo was stuck in a tar pit. Es was afraid of stepping in the viscous liquid and getting stuck in it. Or even worse, losing her boots. She retreated and tried to find a long branch to try to retrieve the dog. She couldn't find one. Meanwhile, Xolo was wailing in pain from the intense heat of the tar pit. Es was in desperation mode. She looked into her backpack and found a cord. She tied a loop at the end of it. She threw one end of the rope toward Xolo, who was less than ten feet away. She came up short. Xolo's eyes looked worried. She thought that there were tears in his eyes. Es threw the cord a second time and it landed next to Xolo.

"Grab it, Xolo!" she shouted. "Grab it, boy!" But he didn't attempt to grab it. Es was frustrated. She retracted the tar-covered cord and threw it again. Miraculously, it went around Xolo's head. Carefully, she made the rope taut and started to pull. He yelped and dug his feet into the tar which made him cry louder. She could feel his pain. Finally, after several failed attempts, she succeeded in pulling him clear of the pit. Xolo crumpled into a small ball and panted heavily. Esmeralda poured water from her canteen onto her bandanna and tried to wipe away as much tar as she could. Xolo wailed every time she touched him. She reached into her backpack and pulled out her shampoo. She poured a little of it onto her bandanna and tried to wash the tar from Xolo's paws. Es did this at least four times. She was successful in getting most of it off, but the dog was still in pain. After doing her best to clean the cord, she put Xolo in the pouch and continued onward.

After a quarter mile, the murky tar pit ended, and Esmeralda veered northwest trying to find the lake again. The light rain had stopped. The terrain became more like high desert with succulents and agave plants. Es took out her knife and cut off some aloe vera leaves from a plant by the side of the path. She put them into her pockets. The traveling pair finally found the headwaters that fed the lake. It was a narrow stream that was about twenty feet across. Large granite boulders rimmed the edges of its waters. Es climbed on top of one of the large rocks and pulled out the aloe vera leaves and set them down in front of her. She cut off the ends and scraped out the gel from the leaves. She gently stirred it, making it into a kind of salve. She found her bandanna that was still sticky from the shampoo and dipped it into the ointment. Carefully, she cupped each of Xolo's tiny paws into her hands and wiped them with the aloe vera salve. At first Xolo cried out, but then he started to settle down. He licked her hand.

"Is that better, boy?" Esmeralda asked. She pulled out some peanut butter and they ate an early lunch. Xolo's feet may have hurt, but his appetite was still healthy.

They resumed their journey, with Xolo still being carried in the pouch. Es had to climb carefully over the rocks that were smooth and slippery. She wondered if she should go back east of the trail to hopefully avoid the rocks. She went over to a little pool in the stream. Es tried to wash off the residue soot and tar from her arms and hands. Finally, she dipped her canteen into the water, after using her hand to spoon some of the refreshing liquid into her mouth.

She walked slightly east where she encountered swamps with high reeds. The waters were stagnant and slimy. There was a foul odor as if something had died there. Esmeralda was forced to go further east. Finally, after two more hours of hiking, she decided to set up camp in a little clearing. She collected some dead branches from nearby shrubs. She would use these later to build a fire. Since it was still light, she read more of her dad's journal and then made a little dinner for Xolo and herself.

Chapter 16 – Moyotlachahuitl - Mosquito Coast

Monday, October 26, 1970

Es was in a deep sleep, before she had to get up to go to the bathroom. She heard buzzing by her left ear. And then at her right ear. She felt little pricks on her arms and face. She instinctively started scratching the back of her hands. *Sh*t! Friggin' mosquitoes!* She cussed. Es tried to swat them away, but she knew it was futile. She hastily took a pee close by and then jumped back into her sleeping bag, pulling the end part over her head. *How many of these little boogers are in here with me?* Es tried to pull down her sleeves. *Ugh!*

She couldn't sleep for the remainder of the night, disturbed by the unwanted guests. As soon as it became light, she took inventory of herself and the surroundings. She knew that she should have known better than to camp by a swamp. She saw the welts on the back of her hands. Her face and arms also felt irritated. *Ugh!* She looked into the horse pouch and found Xolo scratching. Es didn't see any of the critters flying around, so she wanted to act quickly. She had fortunately packed a small tube of calamine lotion. She rubbed it on herself and then on Xolo.

Within a quarter of an hour they had hightailed it out of the area. Es now had to make a strategic decision. Should she backtrack to the lake, even if it meant climbing big rocks and exerting lots of energy? Then all of a sudden, Es noticed a stream that seemed to be coming from some foothills in front of them. These foothills would be difficult to negotiate, she thought. The other option was to head toward the inactive volcano to the east and then swing northwest, hugging the cliffs until she reached the base of El Pico de Orizaba. Es thought the odds were better making the foothill detour. The walk now was a gradual sloped climb. The area ahead again appeared to be more like high desert terrain. The air seemed drier. A few pine trees appeared. The leaves on the ground were magenta, brown, and yellow. Xolo had finally calmed down after his scratching fit. Es' mind started to drift into thought. She thought how helpless she felt alone in a strange place by herself. *Am I just stupid? I'm so unprepared for all of this. Why am I making everybody suffer because I can't get my act together? Papá, why did you love mom so much? How did you guys fall in love?*

Paco and the woman took their time climbing down the Pyramid of the Sun. He had to make good with the agreement to buy her lunch. His initial inclination was to buy a torta from a little stand in the plaza. But he thought he would have to do better than that.

Paco asked the young woman if she had a name. She gave him a devilish response, "of course."

He asked her name. He could play the game too.

She replied "Kelly."

Paco was now playing "twenty questions" with her. Next, he asked where she was from, putting on a charming smile with his ivories.

Kelly said that she was from Eugene, Oregon.

He told her in a suave manner that he was Francisco Luna, but his family and friends called him "Paco."

When she asked where he lived, Paco was genuinely stymied. The truth of the matter was that he didn't know. He was between abodes. Then he mumbled that he was originally from Mesa Verde, Colorado.

That seemed to intrigue her. They had finally exited the pyramids and found an eating place that consisted of a metal awning that hung over eight wooden tables and accompanying benches. An indigenous woman with coarse black hair and only half of her teeth was cooking some kind of stew in a big pot. It smelled delicious. The two sat down and ordered the potage. They also asked for some jamaica (hibiscus) agua fresca.

Paco inquired about Kelly's tour group. He didn't want them to leave without her.

She didn't care, she said nonchalantly.

Paco was surprised at her cavalier attitude and asked who her group was.

Kelly told him that they were her classmates. Her group was on a two-week field trip to study Mesoamerican art and architecture.

This piqued Paco's interest. He wondered if she was some type of art major.

After hemming and hawing, she gave an equivocation. She had her elbow on the table and her chin supported by the palm of her hand. Finally, she qualified her response with "Ceramics."

Paco couldn't believe that they taught ceramics in college. Probably even had basket weaving. He laughed.

She told him that the University of Oregon where she was enrolled had a good program.

So now he knew she was a college girl. He found out that she was a junior. He figured she must be around 20 or 21.

The food arrived, steaming hot. The brownish meaty broth was loaded with chayote squash, tomatoes, avocadoes, rice, and beans. A multicolored striped cloth napkin filled with steaming corn tortillas was placed between them. Both of them dove in. It was several minutes before either spoke, the food was that good. He looked up at her and smiled. She reciprocated the gesture.

Kelly turned the tables on him. She gave him the third degree on his work, school, and life. She wanted to know who Paco was and what his story was.

He gave her a nervous laugh. Paco told her about studying Entomology at New Mexico Highlands University in Las Vegas, New Mexico, and that he had just finished working on a project dealing with the deleterious effects of pesticides on the populations of the Monarch butterflies. Paco surprised himself by vocalizing that he wanted to find a way to fight the big pesticide companies and save the Monarch butterflies. He was making a semi-commitment, something that was rare in his DNA.

Kelly seemed genuinely interested. He could feel her spirit. She was unique. She was simple, but complex. He definitely wanted to get to know her better.

Suddenly, Kelly stood up. She had to catch her ride back to town.

Paco was devastated. *Why was she leaving?* He couldn't open his mouth.

She started to walk away. Kelly turned her head and yelled out that she would meet him back there at three o'clock the next day.

Paco tried to hedge and said he wasn't sure he could make it.

Kelly replied smugly that, for sure, he would be there. Or he wouldn't get his photos.

Esmeralda noticed that she was walking more and more at a steep incline. The footing was getting slippery. She figured that she was at least a half mile from the stream, and according to her latest compass reckoning at the moment she was going northeast. The clouds were covering up the sun. Es crossed into a forest that was stocked with evergreens that had a wonderful conifer smell. She saw stellar jays, sparrows, and orioles. The floor was covered with needles and cones. She heard the melodious songs of a mockingbird.

Es continued walking for the better part of the afternoon. As she approached an area that was riddled with large rocks and boulders, she decided that this would be a good place to camp for the night.

She debated whether to sleep on top of a large boulder or on the ground. But the coldness of the stone might leach off her body heat, she thought. There also seemed to be a pictograph etched onto the big rock, but it had been rendered indiscernible by time. She chose the earthen floor that abutted a big rock to lay out her sleeping bag. This would offer her protection and she could build a nice fire there. She scanned the surroundings for potential threats e.g., friggin' mosquitoes.

Es pulled out some stuff from her backpack and laid out some traps for some possible food. Their provisions were running low and she wanted to take advantage of the possibility of snagging something edible.

She built a nice fire after finding dozens of small branches in the area. The flames crackled with delight. After a quick dinner, Esmeralda retired into her sleeping bag. She read a little more by fire light. Xolo started to bark as he looked up to the rocks above. Some movement had also caught Esmeralda's eye. Something felt strange. Were there dozens of eyes staring at her or was she dreaming?

Chapter 17 – Tláloc - God of Rain and Thunder

Tuesday, October 27, 1970

The sounds of honking Canadian geese flying overhead in a southerly direction woke up Esmeralda. She noticed more scratch marks on her arms. They seemed deep and had drawn beads of blood. The red irritation on her arms was pronounced. Es applied more calamine lotion to her mosquito bites. After putting on her boots, she went to check out her snares. One out of two. Not bad. There was a tiny rabbit caught in her trap. It was cute, but here it was survival of the fittest. Es picked up a sharp stone nearby and with a sweeping motion came down hard on the bunny's head, killing it instantaneously. She threw the carcass down on the flat surface of a boulder by her side. She made a tiny slit in the back of the rabbit's neck and spent the next five minutes removing the fur and gutting it. Es threw a cut-off leg to Xolo who sniffed it. Within seconds he was furiously licking the morsel. He got the lucky (or unlucky) rabbit's foot.

Es made a little fire and the two enjoyed a roasted rabbit breakfast. Xolo struggled to eat the tough and rubbery meat.

Okay, so it's a bit chewy, Es thought. *But today is going to be a good day*. The hike up to the top of the ridge took longer than she anticipated. *I should have made a walking stick,* she grumbled to herself. She looked ahead and saw another hilly ridge in front of her, blocking most of the view of El Pico de Orizaba. There seemed to be an endless series of hills that she would have climb up and down. A turkey buzzard soared in circles above her. *A sign?* Carefully, she descended the rocks, hopping here, and sliding on her butt there. Es decided to take a break at the bottom, grabbing water for both of them.

Es then resumed the climb up to the volcanic rock plateau, noticing that a mist was blowing in. Although she was wearing her gloves, the sharp edges of the magma coral-like formations kept scraping her skin. She stopped on a little ledge and donned her poncho. Finally, she got to the crest of the mesa. She could see that a black sea of igneous basalt, obsidian, and pumice rocks stretched up the slope toward the inactive volcano. A moist, warmish wind was coming from the east. Cumulus clouds started to form. Es was hungry, and she knew that Xolo always had an appetite. But she knew that the weather was starting to turn. Her lunch would have to wait. Es put Xolo back into the pouch and began her way downward. Rain started to fall slowly. Drip . . . drip . . . drip . . . In a moment's time there was a downpour! *Xolo, I hope the rain gods are going to be good to us,* Esmeralda thought.

The footing became slippery and slimy. Esmeralda was having trouble keeping her balance on the path. She was getting drenched. However, she knew that she couldn't rush. The good news was that the rain was not cold. A clap of thunder crashed over her head. She climbed down, one crag at a time. She spotted a stand of madrona trees down the hill to her left. She veered in that direction. Es finally reached the bottom and hurried underneath the canopy of the trees. Her cap was soaked, but the poncho had done a good job of keeping the rest of her body and Xolo fairly dry. The little grove abutted a white-stained rocky cliff that had an overhang. She moved toward the cliff, trying to get out of the spray of the rain. Xolo yapped, so she put him down, so he could do his business. She had to take a pee herself, so she followed him to the bluff. He went potty by a pink-flowered oleander bush. As she squatted, she thought that she saw an opening in the rock. She pulled up her pants and made her way over to it. Xolo barked and wagged his tail.

The aperture seemed natural and was a little over five feet in height. She bent over and peered in. It was dark. She grabbed her flashlight and pointed it inward. It was a little grotto. The walls that lined it had small blackish figures painted on them. *At least, the ground is dry*, she thought. She pulled off her poncho and wet cap. Es placed her backpack on a flat rock in the middle of the cave. She dashed outside and picked up some fallen madrona bark, making four trips in all. She dumped some of the kindling in the middle of the cavern floor and started a fire.

As an afterthought she ran back outside with her canteen and caught rain water to fill in up. She also was able to wash out her bandanna that was the worse for wear. She made some cheese sandwiches with the bolillos that had hardened. Es had actually held them out in the falling rain for a few seconds to moisten and soften them.

The deluge lasted all afternoon and Es made occasional dashes outside to grab more bark to maintain the fire. On her last foray, she discovered some grubs churning themselves in and out of the wet soil. She scooped up about a half dozen of them to roast for Xolo and herself.

"Hey, bud," she threw down a freshly-cooked critter in front of him. "This is a gourmet meal."

Xolo barked and then sunk his tiny, sharp teeth into the morsel.

"You'd pay big bucks for this in a fancy restaurant," she smiled. *It tastes like chicken. Papá, you created a monster. I don't know why I am so mad at you. You taught me to be independent. You taught me that I didn't have to depend on others. You taught me how to hunt and fish and how to survive*

*in this crazy world. I should be more understanding. I think I'm
just projecting my frustration over mom's death and losing you.*

She laid down on her sleeping bag and thought about the
latest entry she had read in her dad's journal.

October of 1945 ended, and Paco was excited about
spending El Día de Los Muertos in Mexico City. His mother had
told him that the Day of the Dead was special because the souls
of the deceased returned to visit their relatives, arriving on
November 1 of each year. This date mysteriously coincided with
the migration of the Monarch butterflies that arrived into Mexico
during the week of The Day of the Dead. According to legend,
the Monarch butterflies were believed, to hold the spirits of the
departed.

Paco took the bus back to his hotel after he met Kelly.
Something is different about that woman, he thought. She is her
own person. She seemed to be a free spirit. He wondered if he
should return to the pyramids the next day. He knew that it was
the second day of El Día de los Muertos. He had originally
thought about hitchhiking down to Acapulco as soon as the
festivities were over. He had heard about the beautiful bay and
crazy nightlife. He was tempted. Back at the hotel he counted
his cash. He barely had enough to last one more week on the
road.

The next day it rained a little in the morning. The air was
smelling cool and fresh. Instantly, Paco made his decision and
hurried to the bus station. In the afternoon, he found Kelly
standing facing the Pyramid of the Sun, still as a statue.

"Excuse me, miss," his voice beckoned. "Can you please
turn around? I want to take your picture."

Kelly spun around with a quizzical look on her face. "I
thought you said that you didn't own a camera."

"What I actually said was that I didn't have a camera at the
moment," he was seeking his revenge on her. "And this one, I
don't actually own. It belongs to the project that I was working
for."

She took him by the arm and they walked north down the Avenue of the Dead toward the Pyramid of the Moon. He told her about how he had recently spent almost every day with the Monarch butterflies in the sanctuary. He felt an affinity with them and wanted to save them. She laughed when he told her stories about the other students. "Yeah, I have a couple of those in my group, too."

Paco also shared his mother's legend about El Día de Los Muertos with Kelly. This was supplemented by telling her about the stages of Monarch butterfly migration from the United States and Canada into Mexico. The Monarchs could travel up to three thousand miles, averaging between fifty and a hundred miles a day. It could take up to two months and a few generations of butterflies to make the journey.

Paco and Kelly finally stopped and read the information kiosk at the Pyramid of the Moon. It said that this was the site where the ancients conducted rituals to worship the goddess of water and fertility. The two climbed up the steep stairs. They were fortunate that this temple was smaller than the Pyramid of the Sun. At the summit they took pictures of each other and asked a few bystanders to photograph them together. They both had big smiles during these shoots. They sat on the top stone step and chatted about life, beauty, and adventure. When there was a lull in the conversation, Paco pulled out a paper bag and handed it to Kelly.

"What's this?" she asked with raised eyebrows.

"Lunch, of course," he smirked. He had given her roasted chile-powdered peanuts.

"You really know how to treat a girl," she retorted. They continued chatting while they ate the peanuts.

After a while, they descended from the top, with Kelly grabbing onto Paco's arm. At the bottom she told him that she was thirsty. They found a bottled water vendor not far away at the Plaza of the Moon. Dusk was approaching, and people were setting up ofrendas (altars) at the Palace of Quetzalpapálotl in the southwest corner of the plaza.

"Wow! Paco, look at what a magnificent building this is!" Her finger outlined the paintings and reliefs. The inner courtyard had stone columns with reliefs of birds. The rafters were decorated in geometric designs.

Mexican families and friends started to arrive to celebrate El Día de Los Muertos. They came to pray for those who had died and to honor them in the spiritual world. There were dozens of ofrendas [altars] in the plaza decorated with skulls, orange marigold flowers, cigarettes, food, and beer. Mothers tried to control their children who wanted to touch everything. Their husbands smoked and drank. Soon the music started. There were drums, chanting, dancing, and the light of hundreds of candles.

Kelly and Paco ate some tamales from a little stand close to the entrance of the palace. Suddenly, seemingly out of nowhere, a wizened elderly lady with long silver-grey hair intertwined with red, white, and green ribbons approached the couple and held out pieces of jewelry to Kelly and Paco.

"Para proteger del mal," the old woman offered Kelly protection from evil spirits. Paco intervened and said "no."

But the indigenous woman pressed the orange fire opal into Kelly's hand. Kelly's eyes dilated as she felt the heat from the stone. A moment later Kelly said "no." The old woman came closer and said something to her that was incomprehensible. This time, Kelly nodded "yes." Then the woman looked at Paco and stared at him. He said nothing.

"Paco, I want it," Kelly said excitedly. "I need a souvenir from here." To Paco, it sounded like a payback for his ploy the prior day to gain a photo. He examined the opal pendant closely without saying a word. It was in the shape of a butterfly.

"Es destino," *It is Fate,* the old woman said softly, barely discernible about all the noise and music.

"Paco, I can't buy it for myself. It's bad luck."

She's good. Really good, he thought as he smiled.

Paco took out his coin purse and bought the orange butterfly fire opal pendant for her. He and Kelly started to walk away, but the shaman lady blocked their way and said in Spanish, "It has a twin soulmate. You are the chosen ones." He was shocked. It reminded him of the Navajo K'aalógii butterfly legend that he learned growing up in Mesa Verde.

Kelly interrupted, "Fair is fair." She then bought the second orange fire opal butterfly pendant for Paco. They both laughed.

"Paco, my personal mantra is '25 minutes or 25 years.' We don't know how much time we have in this world. We need to live now. For the moment. Life is too short."

Esmeralda got up and went out one more time to grab more bark for the fire. She needed her flashlight because it was already dark. Es returned to the cave, and above her she heard loud flutters and high-pitched squeals. Es shone her flashlight upwards, but she couldn't see anything. There was an unpleasant ammonia smell penetrating their cavern. Es subconsciously touched her opal pendant as she crawled back into the sleeping bag.

"Xolo, pleasant dreams," Es signed off for the night. Her skin started to fell clammy. She felt a mysterious presence in the grotto. As she slept, a drop of blood appeared on her cheek.

Chapter 18 – Tletepetl - The Lava Beds

Wednesday, October 28, 1970

Esmeralda woke up and wondered how she had gotten still another scratch on her face. At least the itching on her arms had subsided. And this morning Xolo was in good spirits running in and out of the grotto. She looked outside and the sky was blue. Steam was rising from the volcanic rocks to the north of her.

She took inventory of their provisions. For the moment, they had enough water. But she still had to be vigilant about water sources. Their food was getting a little low. They had almost finished the sausage and a third of the cheese. The bolillos were as hard as rocks. Es was holding the palanquetas in reserve. *I think I need to do a little more foraging.* With this thought in mind, she harvested some grubs from the wet soil and cooked them. They had some for breakfast and she saved some for the day's journey.

Her bandanna was finally dry, even though it smelled of mildew. She rolled up her sleeping bag, wiping away the clinging debris. She didn't need her poncho anymore. They were good to go. As they left, Es looked up and saw the underside of the cliff overhang. There seemed to be a large black mass gyrating above. *They are probably just bats,* she thought.

Xolo barked and ran forward a little, down the sandy path. *Maybe he saw a rabbit or squirrel.* "Xolo, you need to pull your weight around here." She shouted. Es shook her head as she started to venture onto the lava field. Xolo barked again, with his tail wagging.

After about ten minutes of trekking upwards, Esmeralda climbed onto a large igneous rock. She took out her compass and took a bearing on El Pico de Orizaba. She needed to proceed in a west-northwest direction. She could see the snowy slopes of the majestic mountain. *Why is my Papá going there?* There seemed to be a large grove of trees hugging the incline, about a mile up. However, her immediate challenge was this ancient lava bed that had once spewed from the now inactive volcano.

She continued slowly. Her breathing was labored. Es did not seem to be getting enough oxygen. As she proceeded, she detected the heavy smell of sulfur that came drifting down toward her. The crags turned into rocks and then the ground became relatively flat. Her steps seemed to be falling onto a softer surface, almost like asphalt. Es thought the air was getting a little warmer and smelled like rotten eggs, but she wasn't sure. Then she came across a narrow fissure that had raised edges and contained what looked like hot ashes. *Was this magma from the volcano? I thought it was inactive.* She stepped over it. About twenty paces later, she encountered another slit in the lava field. She repeated her little ballet leap. Since the ground in front of her was black and auburn-colored, she was unable to discern what the lay of the land was in front of her. Es continued at a slower pace. She did not want a repeat of Xolo's misadventure in the tar pit. The brimstone smell was getting stronger and making her nauseous. She snatched up Xolo and quickly put him in his pouch.

Esmeralda arrived at a river of lava bubbling up in front of her. It was about twelve feet wide and there was no way she could get across it safely. Es decided that she had to retreat. An insight hit her. If the lava flows downhill, then it spreads as it descends. That would mean that the lava field should be narrower uphill. Es wasn't sure of this theory, but she chose to pursue the upward course. This trek was steeper, and luckily, she had gloves on to protect her hands as she supported herself. She climbed up about two hundred feet. Es was now exhausted and sick to her stomach from the smell. The magma river to her left was still too wide to traverse and what appeared as a narrow fissure way below was also much wider up here. The ground seemed hot to her. She sat on a pock-surfaced rock trying to catch her breath while she let Xolo out of this pouch for a while. Then she heard a noise above her. It sounded like a gurgle. She saw a small geyser of lava erupting halfway up the volcano. *This can't be good!* The ground shook beneath her. She snatched up Xolo and started to retrace her steps. She did not want to get trapped between the two magma streams. The dog sensed that something was amiss. He yelped.

Es couldn't find the spot where she had initiated her upward climb. Instead, she took a diagonal path. *Where were the narrow splits?* The fissures seemed to have expanded. Now they were a foot wide. She leaped over the first one. The second one was a little broader. And the next one more so, and the lava was starting to flow faster. "Don't panic, boy! We're almost there," she said trying to convince herself.

Her head jerked when the second explosion occurred. It seemed to have erupted near the first one. This one spouted magma about twenty feet into the air. The earth beneath her feet trembled. She had trouble keeping her balance. Smoky vapors started to vent from the fissures. There was now a deeper, acrid sulfuric smell. She hurdled another fissure. The lava seemed to be flowing quicker down the slope. Es was starting to panic. She felt trapped.

Xolo started to bark. He was fidgeting inside the pouch. He wanted out. Esmeralda, for some reason, put him down. Xolo started to sniff the air. He sensed something. He took off. Es tried to pursue him. She lost sight of him and then found him hindered by a lava streamlet. She picked him up. He barked again. She set him down. He ran off again in a circuitous route. A hundred yards later and totally out of breath, she found him in front of a rocky passageway, safe from the lava. It was the entrance to a tunnel that was bored underneath the lava field. The magma was starting to expand as it gained momentum going down the slope. Xolo started to enter the passageway, even though it was dark. Es flipped on her flashlight. Xolo was in front of her, running in the dark. As she beamed her flashlight forward, she could have sworn that she saw a small creature, or a young boy, running away from her.

For the next twenty or so minutes, she was in the sweaty environment of a lava tunnel. She surmised that she was directly underneath the lava field. Every once in a while, small drops of magma would ooze down from the ceiling. Her flashlight flickered. The batteries were low. Several times, Es ran into the walls that showed different levels of sediment. Maybe this was an old lava tunnel. She didn't see any pictographs or writing. Finally, she reached the exit. In front of her was a ridge, just this side of a forest. Es breathed a sigh of relief. She tried to catch her breath. She had miraculously arrived at the other side of the lava field. She was near the base of El Pico de Orizaba. She took a swig of water from her canteen.

Out of the corner of her eye, Es saw movement. *Was this what Xolo was chasing? She saw a small boy. What's he doing here? No wait, it's a skeleton! What!* The creature turned back toward her. It was half human, half skeleton! *"Holy friggin' sh*t!"* she screamed.

The human hybrid ran off. Esmeralda couldn't decide if she should follow. Xolo tried to give chase up the ridge. Es pursued him. Minutes later Es found herself in front of a small ancient temple. She walked up the twenty chiseled rock stairs of the carved pyramid. Es entered the chamber. There was a large stone table in the middle. *Was this for sacrifices?* She wondered. She swept the darkness with her flashlight.

There were drawings on the wall. The colors were faded, but still discernible. She saw a pictograph with a black bat battling with butterflies. There was also a warrior. It was a woman. Esmeralda looked carefully at the warrior. *Oh, my God!* she exclaimed. *The warrior has green hair!*

Chapter 19 – Itzcaqui Glacier

Thursday, October 29, 1970

Esmeralda and Xolo spent the night in the little temple. She tossed and turned all night. Es was too freaked out to think clearly. *What do these drawings mean? Why did my dad lead me here? I still haven't seen hide nor hair of my father. I'm really tired. I don't have enough food to last much longer. Why do I have to prove my loyalty when he didn't? Why do I have to prove my love when he didn't?*

They had a sparse breakfast. She looked at the food supply. Even if she returned now, she would barely make it back to the trailhead with enough rations. Grubs and roots. Her favorite things. "What do you think, Xolo?" she said as she rubbed him under his chin. "Are we ready to go back?" She sighed. She was exhausted. Es was ready. Xolo barked and bolted to a dark corner of the temple. He was sniffing something. This time he howled. He had found something.

Esmeralda went over to examine what all the commotion was about. It looked like a little sack with a broken strap. She picked up the fawn-colored leather pouch. She recognized it. It was her dad's medicine bag! Es knew that he always carried a medicine pouch. It was part of his upbringing, having been raised near the Pueblo reservation. She dumped out its contents onto the dirt floor of the pyramid. There was a tied bundle of sage, some loose juniper berries, a bundle of greenthread stems and flowers, a baby tooth, a conch shell disk, and a lock of hair. She assumed that the tiny tooth was hers. She looked at the brown hair braided with red, white, and green ribbon. It appeared to be her mother's. Es became emotional and tears welled up in her eyes. She pulled on the fire opal pendant that felt warm next to her heart. "This is the sign, Xolo!" Es proclaimed. "This is what I've been looking for!" *Oh, Papá, I'm coming! We need to be together again!* With renewed energy, she threw everything back into her dad's medicine bag. She packed up the rest of her things and started out to the west from the small pyramid. The route seemed more like a deer path and the foliage consisted of small shrubs and succulents. A doe was startled by their presence and skipped away. Es exhaled slowly. *I could have had some fresh deer meat!* Es had missed an opportunity, but she hoped that there would be others. On the other hand, she couldn't have killed the doe, because that would mean that her baby deer would not survive. And she certainly couldn't kill a fawn – so that's that.

The new trail seemed well trodden. There seemed to be some fresh human footprints. Finally, Esmeralda came to a three-way juncture. There was a well-worn path that seemed to go downhill, that looked fairly innocuous. *This is the path more traveled,* she concluded. *My Papá would tell me to take this one.* The middle route aimed directly toward a forest, about a quarter of a mile straight ahead. To Es, this way made the most sense and was the most practicable. She started in this direction, Xolo barked. He didn't want to go this way. *Was it dangerous?* She wondered. She picked him up and held him chest high. He sniffed at the medicine bag. *Do Chihuahuas have a sense of smell? That is, besides for food?* She parenthetically thought. Es put him down and he started toward the uphill path. "Oh, Xolo!"

Es was not happy. "Why do you have to make it so hard?" Es thought that this was the way to one of the glaciers of El Pico de Orizaba. Her left hand rubbed the back of her neck. It was stiff and painful. Stress!

About a hundred and fifty feet up, there was a sprinkling of snow and ice. She put on her gloves and put the ersatz vest on Xolo. She wanted to be prepared for the cold. It was hard to discern if there were footprints in the white ice. Es picked up Xolo and put him into his pouch. "You picked this way," she looked at him unappreciatively, "and now I have to carry you! Something is wrong with this picture." They climbed higher and higher. It was getting harder and harder for her to breathe. She thought that she saw imprints in the snow. They were not animal prints. They were small footprints, like those of children. *This doesn't make sense.* She was getting confused. *I need to stop and catch my breath.* She was gasping for air. Finally, Es plopped her butt onto the snow and looked back over the valley that seemed to be split in two. She had come up the eastern section. Es could almost make out the pyramid cliff on the south side of the valley where the passageway was miles away. But she wasn't sure. She put pieces of snow into her canteen to replenish it. Es threw a small handful of trail mix into her mouth. She gave the last piece of sausage to Xolo who gulped it down in a nanosecond.

Es saw what seemed to be more footprints in the snow as she traversed the glacier. She was now half way across. She wasn't sure what there was after the glacier. She stopped and rested. She put Xolo down and took off her backpack to look for her compass. Es wanted to do a reckoning. She held the apparatus in both hands and took a step to the side to get a better angle.

Suddenly the snow sank underneath her! Her body started to drop. Es tried to stretch out her arms. The ice beneath her broke and she was hurled down a crevasse, bouncing off the icy walls on her way down. She had fallen at least twenty feet. Her left shoulder was writhing in pain. She winced as she tried to stand up. Her right ankle was killing her. She struggled to take a few deep breaths in an attempt to recover the wind knocked out of her. "Holy frig!" escaped through her lips. She rested for a minute and then tried to climb out of the glacial fissure. She noticed that there was a rip in her parka. There were no handholds on the walls, and she had no success in trying to make some with her knife. Fortunately, (or unfortunately), her backpack was at the top of the crevasse, as was Xolo, who was now incessantly barking. Her rope was packed inside her rucksack. Es rested and then attempted to climb out several more times without success. Everything that could save her was up on top. Xolo kept barking.

Esmeralda sat down on the icy floor and tried to think of a solution. Take deep breaths. *Let's inventory the situation. I'm really okay even with the shoulder and ankle. No bleeding. Have water. Have no food. Reminder to self: should have a protein bar on person at all times. But how would that really help? I have to relax and remain calm. Breathe. Breathe deeply.*

She looked at her watch. There was still ambient light. Sh*t! She didn't have her flashlight. It was just past noon. Es tried to rest. She made a few futile attempts to climb out again. *What can I do to get out of here? It's my own dumb fault! I screwed up again. My aunt and uncle were right. Have I really ever thanked them for everything they have done for me?*

Es got out her knife and started to try to dig a hole. She needed a shelter if she was going to spend the night there. The ice would act as insulation. Her feet started to feel numb. She wiggled her toes. She blew into her hands and pulled the cap down over her ears. It was going to be a long afternoon.

The hours went by slowly. Xolo kept up his howling. Finally, total darkness encompassed her. *Have I ever really forgiven my Papá? Yes, he has been weak and non-committal, but who am I to judge. He lost his wife. I lost my mother.* Her eyes closed.

Twenty-five minutes or twenty-five years. Paco knew exactly what Kelly was suggesting as they kissed in one of the dark corners in the Palace of Quetzalpapálotl. The couple did not see the dark shadow that was lurking behind them, seething with anger and jealousy. The two bodies pressed against each other. They did not hear the hissing. The music outside was getting to be louder and more high-pitched.

Paco asked her, "Another half hour?"

"Why wait?" she responded. "¡Vámonos!" *Let's go now!*

The drums beat louder. Then the fireworks exploded.

Kelly and Paco spent the next three days in his hotel room. They barely came up for air.

Finally, they left their little love nest. They spent the next two weeks going to Eugene, Oregon, by bus with intermittent layovers on the way.

"Twenty-five minutes or twenty-five years," Kelly kept repeating.

Chapter 20 – The Temple of Lost Souls

Friday, October 30, 1970

Esmeralda stretched out her arms as she tried to wake up. Her entire body was stiff and in pain. She yawned. Es winced as she slowly opened her eyes. Her skin felt chafed and her lips were chapped.

Suddenly, she screamed so loud she could have woken up the dead. She was frightened! There were hundreds of eyes staring down at her. *These are those same creatures that I've seen before!* After her initial shock, she tried to sit up. She was naked except for her fire opal pendant. She felt that some type of parchment was adhered to her right ankle, left shoulder and forehead. She was submerged in multicolored maple leaves. The room smelled of copal incense.

A wizened figure approached her waving a sahumedo, an incense burner, in circles over her. Half of his body was a brownish-grey skeleton. The left side of the skull had no eye and was punctuated with large yellow teeth. The ribs, the arm bones, pelvic area, and foot bones on the left side were visible. *What in the heck is this? I can't believe it's alive!* Es was mesmerized.

The right side of his body was intact with dark skin and coarse black hair. The creature had indigenous features. It grabbed her left arm and started to rub an ointment on it. It smelled like tobacco. Es wanted to pull away, but as he massaged the forearm, she started to relax. Her body felt no pain. Not even her ankle or shoulder hurt. The figure wore a white head band with three feathers. Es guessed that he was some sort of shaman.

Another withered figure scooted forward and said something to the shaman in Nahuatl. This second person then turned to Es and asked, "Cuautemoc cíhuatl huēyi?" He pointed to her with his rattle. "Cuautemoc cíhuatl huēyi tzontli xoxoctic?"

Es responded, "I don't understand." *I haven't got a clue what he is saying. Obviously, he doesn't speak English or Spanish.*

"Cuautemoc cíhuatl huēyi tzontli xoxoctic?" he repeated a little more forcefully.

Why is he talking louder? I'm not deaf! I just don't understand. Who are these creatures? She looked behind the two aged figures. There were hundreds of half-human, half-skeleton beings behind them. *They all seem so sad.*

How did I get here? she tried to recall. The afternoon before, she had tried every conceivable way to escape from the glacial crevasse that she had fallen into. Xolo had howled for hours, probably waking up the dead. *This might be too close to the truth,* she suddenly thought. She had tried to climb up the icy walls with her legs spread to each side, but her right ankle could not sustain her weight. Finally, she bundled up, making sure that none of her body was touching the ice. She didn't want frostbite. *Breathe. Relax. Think warm.* The opal pendant began to radiate heat for Es. She fell asleep.

It was dark when something suddenly touched her. Es had jerked back subconsciously. *Was it some kind of rodent?* She felt like her body was frozen solid. She ached all over. Es thought that she felt a paw on her. *Did Xolo fall down too!?* No, it was more like a small hand. No, wait! Two small hands. And then there were four. Es could not tell if it was daybreak. In the pale light, she thought she made out two small figures. There was something strange about them. She couldn't see them clearly. Did she see skeletons? Es felt a cord being wrapped around her. The two creatures lifted her up. The cord became taut. They guided her off the ground and turned her body as she started to be pulled up. Several times she collided with the side walls. Es did not scream out. She felt faint and her body was clammy. She fell in and out of consciousness. Es didn't know what was going on.

Finally, her body was flopped onto the glacier, above the crevasse. Es thought that she saw dozens of half-human creatures huddled around her in the darkness. *What are these things?* Her head went from side to side. Xolo jumped up on her and started to lick her face.

"Cuautemoc cíhuatl huēyi tzontli xoxoctic?" the chief asked more than once, several hours later.

Esmeralda was trying to make sense of the situation. Her mind was in a trance. *What is he trying to say?* "No entiendo," popped out of her mouth. *What am I doing here?*

The shaman gave her a gourd filled with a yellowish mush. Es put the bowl up to her mouth and drank it all. It tasted like unsweetened tapioca pudding. *Where is Xolo?* She was used to eating with him. He wasn't around.

"¿Dónde está mi perrito?" Es blurted out. *Where is my little dog?*

The old man and the shaman spoke to each other. The old man wore a golden multi-feathered headdress. *Is he a chief or something?* she wondered.

The shaman responded in broken Spanish to Esmeralda that the dog was outside. He spoke slowly with a strange enunciation. He was very difficult to understand. Then he asked, "¿Es uste la guerrera con el cabello verde?" Are you the green-haired warrior?

What is he talking about? Then she vaguely recalled the pictographs on the walls of the temple where they had spent the night a few days before. That stuff was a myth, she thought.

"No. Not me," she replied in Spanish as she shook her head.

"Tien el cabello verde," the shaman declared. *You have green hair.*

"Is that important?" she again asked in Spanish.

The high priest and medicine man conferred again. The shaman moved closer to her. Another creature came over and gave them both some herbal tea. Es was really thirsty. She hadn't urinated in over a day.

The shaman spoke very slowly and deliberately. He had a raspy voice. He began to explain that they were the Toltec people from many eons ago. They worshipped Quetzalcoatl [the feathered serpent god]. In those ancient times, Itzpapalotl [the obsidian bat] was an evil goddess. She was the mistress of disguise and deceit. Itzpapalotl turned herself into a beautiful maiden and tried to seduce the chief of the Toltecs. However, some member of their tribe stole the invisibility cloak belonging to the goddess. When she found out that her cloak had been stolen, she placed a powerful curse on the whole tribe by striking every member with her obsidian claws leaving them half-dead. They could never go into the afterlife because they were not entirely dead. They could never live in Teotihuacan because they were also not alive. They were banished to El Valle Escondido (Hidden Valley) of Citlaltepetl (Star Mountain). For centuries they had been exiled to these surroundings and to the Temple of Lost Souls.

"But what does this have to do with me?" Es inquired. She reached for her backpack and tried to grab some clothes to cover herself. Xolo with his sharp ears came barreling in. She could read his little mind. *I heard some racket. Does this mean food?* She pulled out a piece of cheese that had started to mold. He didn't care and went for it.

The high priest put his hand on the shaman's shoulder and whispered something into his ear.

"You save us," declared the shaman in Spanish.

"What are you talking about? How?" Es had a bewildered look on her face. "Why me?"

"You girl with green hair. You warrior from Quetzalcoatl. You save us. Our souls go to afterlife. You save us."

Esmeralda remembered the name of Quetzalcoatl from one of her history classes. She didn't know if it was in high school or college. She thought that he had something to do with the Mexicas or Mayans. She had barely gotten a C in that class anyway.

"How do you know it's me?' Es couldn't imagine any other person with green hair, but this was so strange.

The shaman pointed to the pictograph on the wall. He described Itzpapalotl, the evil black butterfly with claws. He sometimes referred to her as *"el murciélago negro"* or black bat, and more precisely in this case, *"una hembra mala,"* an evil female bat. The pictograph had Itzpapalotl battling with Chilcozlicpapalotl, the valiant orange butterfly. A feathered serpent and a dog hovered around in the background. And then there was the green-haired warrior woman. Es was frightened. She was no Joan of Arc.

"You Ixzonxoxoctic," the shaman replied. "Green-Haired Warrior."

"How can you be sure that I am the one?" Es nervously challenged.

"You wear sacred opal."

Chapter 21 – Papalotepec - The Temple on Butterfly Hill

Saturday, October 31, 1970

Esmeralda and Xolo marched down a path with six of the Toltec creatures leading the way and six trailing behind. Rows and rows of maize covered the acreage below the Temple of Lost Souls. The Toltecs had loaded her backpack with a dozen stalks of corn for her travels. She was ambivalent about continuing her journey that day. She would have preferred to rest and recuperate and eat some more before venturing out again. The weather looked cool but not like it was going to rain so Es donned her jacket, scarf, and cap. Her face was just a slit. Her cheeks and hands were still numb because of the exposure to cold in the crevasse.

On the prior afternoon, after having the conversation with the shaman and high priest, Esmeralda fell into a delirium. She was suffering from hypoxic shock from lack of oxygen and exposure to the elements. One of the Toltecs gave her a liquid mushroom potion that put her into a deep sleep. It also, unfortunately, gave her disturbing dreams. She felt death and danger lurking about her in her unconscious state. Blood pouring from sacrificed babies. Flesh falling off bodies. Animals altering their shapes into humans.

Before she fell asleep, however, Es was able to get a little more information. The medicine man kept stroking her left arm, applying more of the ointment.

"He gone," the shaman told her in broken Spanish.

"Who?" Es was still dizzy and didn't understand.

"The man you look for."

Esmeralda was not grasping what this person was saying. "How do you know?"

"You do not come here for nothing," he replied. "This person important for you."

"I am looking for my father," she blurted out.

"What he look like?"

"About this tall," Es lifted her right hand up. "Has long black hair in a ponytail. Big build. Skin like yours." She didn't know how well he was understanding her Spanish or explanation. "He has a fire opal pendant like mine." She pulled up her locket to show him.

"Don't know. Don't see opal."

Maybe it wasn't my dad. "Did you talk to him?"

"Yes."

"What did he say?"

"He go to Citlaltépetl," the shaman answered. "He go to Papaloteopan."

"What's a Papaloteopan?" *This is crazy,* she thought. *What is going on?*

"Holy place. Holy temple," the shaman's head bowed. "Temple of the Butterflies. Papaloteopan."

"Did he say why?" Es pressed on.

"To find someone," the medicine man said. "Maybe lost soul."

"When was he here?"

"Three suns," he used his fingers to show her.

Another Toltec came into the room and the shaman and high priest left. The new person appeared to be a woman, at least half of her. Esmeralda was given another gourd of liquid. It tasted like plain atole. Es fell back to sleep a few times before dusk. Her bladder hurt, and she needed to urinate. There were still dozens of Toltec spectators around her. She was embarrassed, so she held it. Finally, the pain was uncomfortable, and she got up. It was dark. She felt two thin arms grasp her. Es was led to a dark corner where she squatted.

I want to go home. I want to go back. Es was trying to hold back the tears. *But I know that my dad was here just a few days ago. I just have to find him. He's my dad!*

She went back to the primitive bedding. *Where was Xolo?* Then she fell into a deep sleep.

The next day she was feeling better and was ready to continue. She and Xolo were led to Papalotepec [Butterfly Hill] by the Toltecs. At the end of the maize acreage, the Toltecs stopped.

"What's wrong?" Es asked.

"We can't go more." The shaman said. "Bad curse."

Now their green-haired warrior was leaving. There were no farewells, just sullen half-faces. But the shaman surreptitiously slipped a small obsidian blade into Esmeralda's hand. She tacitly gave him a nod of thanks, wondering why this gift.

The trail was discernible, and the traveling pair had no trouble continuing. Manzanita bushes bordered the path. They found a little rivulet and filled up the canteen. Xolo barked. "No, my little friend," she looked sternly at him. "Too early to eat." She knew that the Toltecs had probably been spoiling the guy. *What a little suck-up!*

There were low flowering buddleia lining the way as they trucked on, keeping the little stream to their left. They spotted a deer that darted off as they came close. The pair went around a bend and in the distance saw a giant orange-colored field. Es thought it looked like a marigold patch. Es tried to smell the air, but she didn't succeed in identifying anything. As they got closer, Es realized that these were not flowers. They were Monarch butterflies, hovering over milkweed plants, marigolds, asters, and coneflowers. At first, the butterflies veered off, but as Esmeralda reached the center of the orange plot, they startled to swirl around her. Her eyes grew wide. *This is so cool!* She stopped. Some of the Monarchs landed on her, on her head, arms, and chest. They fluttered to and fro. Finally, Es resumed the trip with a big smile on her face.

Es felt a slight breeze coming from the mist-covered summit in front of them. Xolo was sniffing excitedly on both sides of the path. He was yapping loudly. As they approached the bottom of what appeared to be a small pyramid, the nebula dissolved. There were narrow stone steps that led upward. Es picked up Xolo and held him as she climbed. He was barking. He was excited. After climbing about a hundred steps, they reached a platform. In front of them was a large temple that was open faced with stone columns and painted rafters. The cross beams had drawings of jaguars, serpents, butterflies, and bats. The floor was made of stone and slanted upward. There was a narrow rust-colored culvert etched in the middle that ran out to the stairs. Es put Xolo down. He took off in a split second to an opening at the back.

"Xolo, get back here!" Es yelled.

Xolo scampered into the next room. Es heard a muffled human voice. She entered the passageway. The opal pendant on her chest throbbed.

"Hey, boy!" someone said. "What are you doing here?"

Es observed the scene and was thunderstruck. Xolo was jumping up onto the legs of her father, Paco! The bad news was that her dad was tied to a rock pillar in the open room. The rope that bound his hands was looped through some stone rings that protruded from the pillar. Behind him was another pillar and what looked like an altar in the middle of the space. He was naked down to his waist.

"¡Papá!" she rushed forward.

"Es!"

She broke into tears. "What are you doing here?" Es rushed to embrace him. "Are you all right?"

"It's kind of a long story," he gasped. He looked forsaken. "It's all my fault."

"I've been so worried! We all have!"

Es took off her backpack and threw it onto the sacrificial altar. Her dad's eyes were sunken and bloodshot. He had at least a week's worth of a stubby beard.

"Water!" he beseeched her. "Give me water!"

Es grabbed her canteen and opened it. She put it up to her dad's parched lips. He tried to guzzle it, but she kept the canteen fairly level. "Papá, are you okay?" Her eyes betrayed her feelings. She thought he was dying.

Paco almost choked as he drank. He spat up the liquid.

"You probably need some food," she became task-oriented. "First, let's get you out of all of these ropes." She started to take things out of her backpack and separate them. She found an old piece of dried meat in a little packet. She cut a piece and fed it to her father.

She examined the ties that bound her father to the rock column. This was not a rope binding. Instead it was more of a silk gossamer. Her knife had difficulty cutting into it.

"What is this stuff, Papá?" she cried out.

"It's a long story."

The large black pictograph of an Aztec figure in the wall behind the altar started to quiver. It slowly started to take on a different shape.

"Well, we have plenty of time now," Es was exasperated trying to sever the bindings on her father with little success. She gave up on the arms and was now trying to saw the ties around his legs.

There were squealing noises from the high vaulted ceiling. Xolo barked.

"How did you get here?" she asked as she continued to slice at the strings. She pulled off her gloves to get a better grip on the knife.

"Well, your mother and I made a pact many years back," Paco paused to recount. "You remember how she always used to say twenty-five minutes or twenty-five years? Well, we agreed that we would celebrate the twenty-fifth anniversary of the day we met by coming here. The date coincides with your birthday. Kinda cool, huh!? That was the plan, anyway." He started to get sullen. "And then she passed."

"Oh, sh•t!" Es remarked. "Today's my birthday!"

"Twenty-five years after we met," he said dejectedly. "Twenty-two years since you were born."

"But why did you come here? You could . . ."

There was a high squealing sound. A black massive form descended. A hundred bats pounced on Esmeralda, knocking her down. The knife flew across the floor. Xolo tried to defend himself, but he was being attacked by dozens of bellicose bats. He retreated towards the opening of the temple, yelping all the way.

"Esmeralda!"

Chapter 22 – Itzpapalotl - The Obsidian Bat

Sunday, November 1, 1970 morning

The next morning Esmeralda found herself bound to the other rock pillar, facing away from the altar. She could not see her father. She had been knocked unconscious by the colony of bats the night before as she was trying to free her dad. Now Francisco and Esmeralda were both in the same dire predicament. She did not understand what was going on. Es had goosebumps because she had been stripped naked down to her waist also. The fire opal pendant hung from her neck.

Es surmised that it was dawn or at least very early morning. It was very quiet. Nobody seemed to be around.

"Papá!" she called out. "Are you here?"

"I'm behind you," he answered somberly. "Are you okay?"

"Guess so. Tied up like you. What's happening?"

"It's a long story."

Paco began to share what had happened to him in the past few months. He had promised to bring Esmeralda to Mexico for El Día de Los Muertos this year, but he had flaked out on her.

He knew that for the last ten or so years of his daughter's life he had been irresponsible. Sometimes they would spend quality time together and get close; other times, he just disappeared from her life. He was sorry. He apologized. He always was repentant. His only excuse was that after Kelly had died, he found himself totally lost and unable to function.

Several months earlier, Paco had been rummaging through some of Kelly's belongings that he still kept with him, especially her poems and bookmarkers. He had found a 1950 photo of Kelly, baby Esmeralda, and himself at his mom's house in Mesa Verde. He recalled that they had left Es with his mother while he and Kelly went into the mountains around Halloween time to celebrate their "anniversary." They had vowed that they would get together twenty-five years after their first meeting at Teotihuacan. Over the years, they had planned to celebrate their 25th anniversary in Mexico. He had forgotten all about this since his wife had passed, but the orange fire opal pendant on his chest awakened his obsession for Kelly. He had to see her again, to feel her, to be with her. He researched El Día de Los Muertos and found several places where people had seen the souls of their deceased loved ones. He then recalled that he and Kelly had talked about going to Citlaltépetl in their future plans.

Paco began reading books on numerology, astronomy, and mythology, but still felt himself at a loss. He made a trip up north to see his family in Mesa Verde. His mother Lulu fed him his favorite foods and they spent hours conversing in Spanish. Little by little, Paco shared his feelings with his mother and told her how his life had fallen apart. He still didn't know how to deal with Kelly's death.

Mama Lulu shared with Paco stories of her childhood that he had never heard before. How she was brought up in Morenci, in southern Arizona, and how she had met Paco's father when she was only fourteen. He had worked in a copper mine with his father and brothers.

Paco told her about his plans to go to Mexico with Kelly this year, but now that was not possible.

"Mijo, you are destined to go to Citlaltépetl," she interrupted gently.

Paco was shocked at what she had just said. He had never told his mom where exactly they were planning to go.

"Mom, why do you say that?"

"Because that is where our roots are from," his mother began to elaborate. She traced her ancestors to the Nahuas around Puebla, Mexico. These indigenous peoples were bound by culture, religion, and customs to Citlaltépetl, the Mountain of the Stars. She told him about legends that predicted a battle between a warrior and the Aztec goddess, who ruled over Tamoanchan, around Citlaltépetl.

Paco could not believe what his mother had told him. His opal pendant warmed up as she spoke. He trusted his mother, so he decided to pursue his ill-conceived journey. He left his family a few days later, not saying anything about his future plans.

The only person that he told about his trip to Mexico was his neighbor lady, Magdalena, back in Tubac. She was supposed to take care of his dog. He had planned to take off the entire month of October for this endeavor.

"But Papá you forgot to pay the rent!" Es was used to his woeful stories and how he always expressed regret for his bad decisions. "If I hadn't gotten that stupid phone call from your landlady, I wouldn't be in this mess!"

"You are right, mija. I'm sorry," he said contritely. "But then I wouldn't have been able to see you again."

"See me? There's some crazy stuff going on! What if something bad is going to happen?"

There was silence. "Where's Xolo?" Es yelled out. "Xolo! That friggin' dog!"

The only sound now was a soft wind that entered from the front of the temple. The silence lasted a while until Paco resumed his narrative.

During his recent research and inquiries in preparation for the trip, Paco had received several brochures for treks to El Pico de Orizaba (Citlaltépetl). There was a Sierra Club expedition that was leaving in early October. Initially, he was going to sign up for it, but it was too touristy. The Automobile Club gave him road maps for Mexico, and the next thing he knew he was driving to Mexico City. Paco was fairly familiar with the Mexican highways and even made some quick stops to see friends along the way. He liked the food down here better anyway. Things got dicey when he arrived at Guadalupe Xochiloma. He knew that he had reached the end of the driving portion of his trip. He talked to an outfitter in town that told him what his options were. The supplier knew very little about El Valle Escondido, the Hidden Valley. Paco bought some provisions and decided first to try the southern trailhead, a path less traveled.

"But you bought some bolillos," Es interrupted.

"How did you know?" her father asked in amazement. Then he continued his story. He was becoming hoarser and Es had a difficult time hearing him, especially since they were back-to-back, secured to the rock pillars. It seemed like Paco was mumbling. Then his narrative stopped. Es started to worry that he might not be all right. She assumed that he had not eaten in a while. Maybe he was too weak from the deprivation.

"Papá!" She shouted, but there was no response. Es closed her eyes. Her knees were sagging. She fell asleep.

Es woke up when she heard a bleating sound coming from behind her.

"Papá!" he did not respond. Instead, Es heard a snort. *What in the heck was that?* "Papá!" she called out again. Then she heard what sounded like hooves coming in her direction. Out of the corner of her eye she saw what looked like a doe. It approached Es and came face-to-face with her. Its nose touched the orange fire opal on her chest. Then the deer withdrew and escaped out the opening.

"That was her!" Es heard her father yell. "It was her!"

"Who, Papá? Are you all right?" *Is he going crazy on me?* She wondered.

"No," he responded despondently. "She tricked me."

"Who?"

Paco began to say something incomprehensible.

"Papá, I don't understand!"

"It's the story," he began. "The long story."

Paco resumed his tale starting when he was dropped off at the southern trailhead.

"Why didn't you do the western route?" Es interrupted.

"Too many people," he continued. He had registered at the southern trailhead like he was supposed to.

"Yeah, I found your name in the register."

"Smart girl," he replied. Paco had hired a local native guide who took him up to the waterfalls and to the entrance of the passageway. But the guide would not go any farther. He said that the Hidden Valley was cursed by the obsidian bat. Paco just shook his head in disbelief and told himself "ni modo." Whatever. Francisco paid him, and the fellow took off. Cautiously, Paco maneuvered through the tunnel, dropping old bolillos on the way.

"Why bolillos?" Es asked curiously. "We found some."

"An old army trick so I could find my way back."

When Paco exited the tunnel, he saw a deer nearby. He decided to follow its path, hoping for either a clue to Papalotepec, the butterfly mountain, or at least some deer meat. While he filled up his canteen at the lake, he lost sight of the deer. But it was no big deal.

"Were you on the west side or east side of the lake?" Es probed.

"The west," he answered. "I went left because I was following the deer."

Es thought, *no wonder I didn't see his tracks. He was on the other side of the water. So much for going to the right if one doesn't know the exact direction.*

Paco continued his journey toward Citlaltépetl for two days. He caught a few squirrels and ate some berries, but he could not find the deer again. Finally, he found a temple with about sixty steps that had wall paintings of a deer and black figures. A whole colony of bats lived in the high ceiling. There he met a young native woman dressed in huipil style clothing. Her large brown eyes sparkled at him. She spoke broken Spanish, but he could understand her telepathically. She questioned him about where he was going, and he replied that he was searching for the Valley of the Monarchs. She then asked why? He told her openly an abbreviated version of the story about Kelly and himself. About their marriage. Their child. Their matching fire opal pendants. Their plan to rendezvous during El Día de Los Muertos.

The woman said she knew where the place was, and she would take him there, if he liked. He was overjoyed and readily agreed. The next day they arrived here at this place. Then suddenly the woman sprouted giant black wings and her hands turned into claws. She morphed into a gigantic bat which the natives sometimes described as a black butterfly.

"What!?" Es exclaimed.

"The next thing I knew I was tied up. With no food or water."

"Papá, the legend must be true. She's Itzpapalotl, the Obsidian Bat, isn't she?" Esmeralda exclaimed incredulously. "Isn't she the friggin' evil goddess?! And isn't this her paradise, Tamoanchan?! We're so up sh*t creek!"

Chapter 23 – Chilcozlicpapalotl - The Monarch Butterfly

Sunday, November 1, 1970 night

Night started to fall, and darkness entered their prison. Paco and Es had been sharing stories for hours, with both dozing off for periods of time. Her father had shared that on her deathbed, Kelly had made him promise that he would continue to fight for the preservation of the Monarch butterflies. She knew that it had been his passion when they first met. Kelly had always regretted taking Paco away from his work. His mission. His crusade. But they were young and in love, and it seemed that there would always be time to do it all. First, they would get married, and then they would get back to Paco's project.

But things did not work out that way. Soon afterwards, Esmeralda came along and they needed to settle down and create a stable home for her. They were no longer free to roam around Mexico and the world.

As she was dying, Kelly confessed to Paco that on the day that Esmeralda was born, she secretly made a wish that their child would someday continue the work her father had begun.

Kelly's dying desire for Esmeralda was that their daughter would grow up to be a strong and committed warrior in the battle to protect and preserve nature.

Kelly also made Paco promise to take good care of Esmeralda and help her grow up. Paco now apologized to Esmeralda for failing to do either. He was now trying to atone for his sins by seeking out Kelly's spirit on this volcano.

The acoustics in this room were not wonderful, so neither of them heard the cloven hooves of the deer return. The deer sniffed the air. The deer went over to Paco, who was now asleep, and put its nose on his chest.

Suddenly the feet of the deer seemed to melt into the ground as the animal materialized into a beautiful woman with native features, big black eyes, and long black hair. She looked like she wore a black leather indigenous tunic dress. The woman walked over to Paco and grabbed his opal pendant. She examined it carefully. Then she walked over to Esmeralda who was awake, but who had not heard the commotion. Es gave a surprised look. "Can you help us?" Es cried out.

The native woman gave a scornful laugh and came over and licked Es' upper chest. She grabbed her opal pendant and looked at it also.

"Who are you?" demanded Es in a frightened tone.

The carbon-eyed woman swayed side-to-side in a figure eight. It looked like she was trying to size Es up. She said nothing.

"What do you want?" Es was trying to sound brave, but she was frightened. "We came here by mistake. Just let us leave, please," Es pleaded as her eyes held back tears.

A sound came from the woman who was the transformation of the evil goddess, Itzpapalotl. It was not a human voice, but the sound seemed to communicate telepathically. Es understood. "This was not an accident," the apparition said. "This is my celestial destiny. It is the time for my regeneration. He will be my catalyst." She looked over to Paco. "Tonight, we will unite."

"But what does that mean?" Es said, straining to turn her head around as the woman walked back toward Paco. "What does this have to do with us?"

Itzpapalotl sneered. "Do you think the two of you could come into my lands and desecrate them with your human passions? He belongs to me!"

"I don't understand," Es was confused. "I came here to look for someone."

"You came here to copulate in the human way."

"No! No!" Es tried to explain. "What makes you say that?"

"Both of you are wearing the sacred opal pendants," the woman smirked. "They signify celestial union. They are the symbol of rebirth."

"You're Itzpapalotl!" Es screamed out. "Wait! You don't understand!"

"He and I will mate tonight," Itzpapalotl said defiantly. "And then we will drink your blood." The woman looked to the side at the sacrificial altar.

"Es! What is happening?" her father yelled out. The commotion had woken him up.

Itzpapalotl left Es who was trembling. Esmeralda tried to maneuver her body to loosen her ties. Her knife was God knew where. And where was Xolo? Es knew that her backpack should still be on the sacrificial altar, but she couldn't think of anything there that could help her.

Meanwhile, Itzpapalotl had returned to Paco and pressed herself next to him. "I'm ready," she suggested to him lasciviously. When he cringed, she mockingly cackled, "You need to be purified. You are not acceptable the way you are now."

Itzpapalotl reached under her tunic top and pulled out a tied bundle of rosemary and another of lavender. She held them over her head as the she recited a monosyllabic chant. She broke the herbs in two and started to rub her hands together, forming a lather. The aroma of copal incense slowly drifted into the area. She then rubbed Paco's chest slowly, in circles as she spoke more unintelligible words. Her hands went down his back, moving sensually. Her face drew closer to his. Then she rubbed her body against his face forcefully, standing intimately close to him. Paco moaned. He went up on his tip toes, as he tried to avoid her advances.

"We are almost ready," proclaimed Itzpapalotl as she stepped back. Her feet spread apart. Her form began to morph. Her arms started to elongate, and her hands became claws. She grew taller . . . one foot . . . two feet . . . three feet, until she was towering over Paco. Her face darkened, and her eyes became bigger and bigger. Her body became semi-skeletal and her wing extensions unfolded from her back. Paco was horrified at the monstrosity that was evolving before his eyes, something between a humanoid butterfly and a giant bat.

With one of her obsidian claws, Itzpapalotl made a swift motion toward Paco. Swoosh! She had effortlessly severed the ties on Paco's feet that had bound him to the stone pillar. His upper torso and hands were still tied. Paco tried in desperation to avoid the black creature as it came closer to him. She laughed as she leaned forward, her long pointed purple proboscis tasting Paco's neck.

"¡Mija!" Paco screamed. "I love you! I'm so sorry!"

"Papá!" Es screamed, panic-stricken. "What's wrong?" There was no response. "Papá! Talk to me! Pleeease!'

Instantly, the large black half-skeletal creature was standing in front of Es. She made a lightning fast movement. Es felt a faint trickle of warm liquid on her right cheek. At first there was no pain, but soon a sharp throbbing set in. A streak of warm liquid trailed down her face.

Itzpapalotl's countenance approached Es and sniffed her. Then she withdrew. The figure started to rub the captive Esmeralda's semi-naked body with the edges of her talons leaving little scratch marks. The creature drew its arms overhead and brought them crashing down. Within seconds, Es was thrown on top of the sacrificial altar. All her bindings had been cut away except for her hands. She was lying supine on the table.

Her eyes were inches away from a trail of blood that was slowly dripping toward the narrowly-carved slot that ran the width of the altar. She had the wind knocked out of her and could hardly move. She winced in pain.

"Your sacrifice will be finished by dawn," laughed the creature as she moved away from Es.

Itzpapalotl now stood again in front of Paco. She leaned her body forward. She pushed and swayed sensually against Paco. Her spiny figure pricked his naked torso. He groaned. Tiny droplets of blood erupted on his chest. He felt agitated. She continued to press harder against him. The fire opal pendant started to heat up against his chest. It started to glow. Paco cried out in pain.

At the same time, the opal pendant on Es' chest started to pulsate. It became more and more agitated. Es could feel energy pulsating throughout her body. Her face contorted, tightening. Her shoulder muscles started to constrict, getting harder. Her veins popped out like a Da Vinci sculpture. Her teeth were clenched. Es' body was transforming.

A that moment, a blast of wind exploded into the room. There was an invasion of thousands of orange Monarch butterflies. The swarm of butterflies circled around Itzpapalotl and Paco. The black creature instantly retreated and closely observed the intruders. Then Itzpapalotl rushed forward, slashing out with both obsidian claws, but the butterflies easily eluded her. The orange swarm came together and swirled and swirled until they were transformed into a giant Monarch butterfly with a human face . . . Kelly's face, in a fiery orange-feathered headdress.

"You're too late!" the black figure admonished. "They're both destined to die."

"What do you want?" asked Chilcozlicpapalotl, the Monarch butterfly.

"His body," the bat creature said brazenly. "and her blood. And I shall have both!"

"Let them go right now and I will give you whatever you want,"

"You're just a dead soul," mocked Itzpapalotl. "You offer nothing." The creature made a sudden slashing sweep with her right arm. Chilcozlicpapalotl gracefully spun counterclockwise. Itzpapalotl then charged forward and lashed out with her left hand. The corpus of the Monarch butterfly rose effortlessly until it was flat and parallel to the ground. The claw missed her by less than an inch.

Itzpapalotl cried out in frustration. "You may be safe for the moment," Itzpapalotl slithered over to the altar, "but she is not." The black creature was back in front of Es. The chamber suddenly darkened. There was a rushing sound coming from the front of the temple. An ominous shadow advanced.

"What?" shouted Itzpapalotl in amazement. Facing off against Itzpapalotl was Xolo. He had returned. His sharp teeth showed as he growled at Itzpapalotl. He charged forward to within three feet of the black creature and then he retreated. She lunged at him and he took off behind Paco's stone pillar. She snickered.

"Good boy!" Paco shouted coming back to life. Xolo looked at him for only a split second, but it was all Itzpapalotl needed to flick the dog off the ground with the sweep of her left wing. She caught him in mid-air and now clutched the dog tightly in her left claw.

Chilcozlicpapalotl came forward, but she seemed powerless to do anything. "Sorry, Es," Kelly said to her daughter. The fire opal pendant around Esmeralda's neck started to heat up. Es' blood started to boil. She had beads of sweat all over her upper body. She felt the Monarch butterfly communicating with her through the opal. Es saw her mother's face and then realized that the Monarch was her mother's soul.

Itzpapalotl squeezed the dog. Xolo yelped. The black creature slowly raised the dog over her head as she leaned back. Esmeralda screamed. Itzpapalotl drew Xolo up to her mouth. "Papá!" Es cried out with all of her might.

"Es!" cried out Paco. "What's happening?"

"A little pre-sacrificial ritual," Itzpapalotl cackled as she opened up her mouth, posed to sink her fangs into Xolo. The dog tried to squirm free, but it was no match for the iron grip of the Obsidian Bat.

With a sudden burst of energy, Es had catapulted off the altar. In her hand she held the obsidian blade that the shaman had given her. She had freed herself surreptitiously from her bondage with the blade. Es rushed forward to attack the evil goddess. Es had to save Xolo from being devoured by the horrible black creature.

Instantly, there was a shriek of pain. "Aaay!" The sound shot through the room.

Dark red pus and blood splattered everywhere.

"Es!" Her father was in a panic.

"Aaay!" Again, there was the sound of agony coming from Itzpapalotl. She was crumpled up, on the floor, writhing in pain, and holding what was left of her limb. Nearby Xolo was on the floor licking the blood off the severed claw. Four talons were still intact and the fifth one was dangling.

Es automatically inventoried the scene. Itzpapalotl started to wail and curse. Her form slowly started to quiver. Esmeralda moved quickly to her father. She cut his ties with the obsidian blade. The Monarch butterfly, Chilcozlicpapalotl, flew over to Paco and Es and embraced them as all three felt a totality with the universe.

Itzpapalotl started to hiss as her body rose from the ground. Her eyes were flames of red and yellow. Yellow pus was oozing out of her severed limb. "This is not over!" she cursed out loudly. Black sulfuric vapors started to exude from the creature. The form started to shrink in size. Within moments Itzpapalotl had reverted back to her deer nagual, minus one fore hoof. The creature hobbled out of the temple, leaving a path of bloody prints.

Es took charge. She found her backpack and took out a long-sleeved Levi shirt to wear. She also had packed one of her dad's thermal shirts and brought it out for her father. She used another shirt to clean up the blood and then she applied some antibacterial ointment on both of them. After a brief search she found her knife and cut up some cobs of cooked maize for her dad, Xolo, and herself to eat. They washed it down with water from her canteen. Her body was returning to its normal slender form.

Telepathically, Kelly, in the form of Chilcozlicpapalotl, the Monarch butterfly, led them out of the temple, to the upper platform. The air was crisp. Here they all sat, huddled together. A comet in the sky glittered, looking for the new dawn. Venus had disappeared from its cosmic setting.

Paco could feel the Fifth Dimension. The Universe was more than length and width and depth. Time was being warped. Electrons on the other side of space were syncopated. He knew that Kelly had safely made the transition from this world to the universe of souls. There were tears in his eyes. He had failed Kelly, Esmeralda, and the Monarch butterflies. He had broken his commitments. However, through this supernatural reunion with Kelly's spirit, Paco was beginning to better to understand himself. He had lacked the courage and discipline to do the right thing. Francisco held the opal pendant and made a promise to do better. He knew that Kelly had forgiven him.

As for Kelly's soul, she had actualized a spiritual connection to her husband and daughter. She felt their love across the cosmos. She had the best of all worlds.

And for Esmeralda, the experience made her realize how much she loved her mother and her father. However, she did not understand what had just happened and had no idea of what was yet to come. For her the quest had just begun.

Chapter 24 – Quetzalcoatl

Monday morning, November 2, 1970

There was a hoary frost encircling Paco, Es, and Xolo when they woke up from their "totality with the universe" trance.

"Where's mom?" Es called out in a yawn.

"She's gone," Paco's face radiated happiness. "Let's get warm." They retreated into the temple chamber. Es pulled out her sleeping bag and the three crawled into it, crammed together for warmth.

It was mid-morning when they finally awoke and began preparing to leave. Paco's backpack was nowhere to be found, but Es still had his medicine bag. She quickly stuffed the severed claw of Itzpapalotl into it. Es noticed that Paco's eyes were glazed. She checked the cut marks on her father and herself. She wanted to reapply some ointment, but Es saw that her father was in some sort of daze. Es didn't panic. She realized that she would have to take charge and figure out the return route. The chamber seemed dark and the wind outside was howling. There was very little food, just some maize. They were getting low on water also.

The ground started to tremble. Es and Paco tried to recover their balance.

"We need to get out of here!" Es commanded. She put Xolo into his pouch. As they started to exit, black clouds shrouded the mountain above them. Hail showers started to fall upon them. "New plan!" Es called out. They retreated back into the temple. Paco was only wearing a thin shirt. Es removed her poncho and made her father put it on. Since it was not form fitting, it did not provide a lot of warmth, but he made due with it. Es retrieved her jacket and adjusted the cap on her head. They set out again. The steps were slippery from the mud. The hail had turned into cold rain which was falling down hard at an angle. Visibility was becoming an issue. Their path zigged and zagged with puddles of water popping up all over the place. At one bend in the path there was a little shelter where they stopped for a breather. Es grabbed her canteen and refilled it with rain water after everyone had a swallow.

What are we going to do for food? Es was in planning mode in her head. She was thinking that her father was still looking spaced-out. The storm subsided. They resumed their journey. A rainbow appeared over a gigantic field of milkweed with hordes of Monarch butterflies feasting on nectar flowers. Although the rain had stopped, Es and her traveling partners were soaking wet and cold. The group slowly moved forward.

In the early afternoon, there were puffs of clouds surrounding Citlaltépetl. Es followed the little rivulet and a few hair pin turns until she found the trail back to the Temple of Lost Souls. As they approached the temple, they found that the stairs were decorated with marigold petals and stacks of maize cobs. The first to greet the tired travelers were the Toltec chief and the shaman. The remainder of the half-human, half-skeleton beings drew close around the travelers. The shaman led the trio to the center of the temple where there were several pitch fires blazing. The heat felt good. Xolo escaped to look for handouts. Es and Paco were separated and stripped of their wet clothes. Colorful garments of tree bark were given to them. The humanoids gave an inaudible sigh when Es' cap was removed, and her tangled green hair was exposed. Everybody looked at the wall mural that showed the green-haired woman warrior battling Itzpapalotl. Finally, Xolo returned to Es and Paco. Xolo was wearing a wind jewel, a spirally-twisted conch around his neck.

The trio was then herded around a large fire with the chief, shaman, and other elders. Communication was difficult, but it was established that Itzpapalotl had attempted to seduce Paco and sacrifice Es (and Xolo). The priest announced the victory to his followers and everyone jumped up and down making strange noises, clapping their hands (one flesh hand, the other skeletal). Es went over to her backpack and withdrew her father's medicine bag. She emptied the contents in front of the shaman. The shaman grabbed the severed four-talon claw of Itzpapalotl and went over to another fire pit where there was a large pot of boiling liquid. He raised the claw to the heavens and chanted a sacred song and then dropped it into the pot. Gradually, he added spices, chocolate, chile, and some magical potions to the cauldron, stirring it with a jaguar leg bone.

Meanwhile, Es, Paco, and Xolo were given gourds of a liquid chocolate atole known as champurrado which they inhaled. Es kept drinking the atole. The chocolate flavor was a little bitter and spicy, but she couldn't stop ingesting it.

Xolo kept running back and forth between the fire and Paco's medicine bag. The shaman and some of the elders were in a deep discussion. From what Es could ascertain, something was not right about the restorative elixir that was supposed to break Itzpapalotl's curse over the half-souls. The shaman came over to the chief and tried to explain something. The chief did not seem too pleased. They both walked over to Paco's medicine bag. Es went over to both of them and tried to ascertain what the problem was.

The severed claw of Itzpapalotl was not dissolving as per the recipe of the spell. Instead it was turning into mercury, that was potentially highly toxic. No one knew what it would do to the half-souls. Paco was full of drinking the champurrado and seemed to have awoken from his catatonic trance. He came over to his daughter's side. He looked at the contents in his medicine bag. No help there.

"Hey, Papá, didn't Tío Felipe tell us about some kind of cure against the amalgam in dental fillings?" Es was trying to think.

"Yeah. That was a while back," Paco scratched his head. "I think it was some type of food. He's always something about everything." For the next half-hour Es and Paco tried to recall the antidote to mercury.

The shaman sent several natives to bring cinnamon sticks, coriander, and cumin. Someone brought him some Mexican parsley. "I keep coming up with some type of Chinese food," Paco was exhausted. "I need to lie down. I'm so tired."

Then he remembered. "Chinese parsley!" Paco blurted out. "Cilantro!" Within the hour the sacred brew was reconstituted into the proper potion.

The shaman brought a gourd half full of the concoction to where Es was sitting and dipped his thumb in it. He anointed Es on her head and arms. He uttered incantations. The pounding of drums began. The half-souls started to encircle Es and the shaman. Xolo went over to Paco's medicine bag and with his tiny teeth retrieved the conch shell that Esmeralda had discovered several days before. He dropped it in front of the high priest. The shaman dipped the shell into the gourd and raised his eyes to the heavens. The half-souls started humming. The drum beats got louder. The shell became elongated and emitted green vapors. It curled, and its skin became feathered.

"Oh, great Quetzalcoatl, high god of the heavens," the shaman lifted up the conch shell. "We beseech you to break the curse of Itzpapalotl on our souls." Es and Paco stood in shock as a gigantic feathered serpent slowly uncoiled itself from the shell while the entire assemblage prayed.

Drums sounded in the background. A heavy chant permeated the air. Foot stomping began.

"Oh, great Kukulcan, the Morning Star, the Evening Star, and Venus," the shaman touched his head to the shell. "Let these half-souls travel into the afterlife to complete their stellar journeys." The drums were beating at a fever pitch.

The feathered serpent lifted Xolo up with one arm and touched the conch shell to his chest with the other and in a thunderous voice proclaimed, "By the power of the Precious Twins, I declare your curse broken!" Lightning shot from the god and hit the brew that had been boiling. Sparks flew from the pot. Quetzalcoatl stood aside, and the shaman went over to the magical concoction. The shaman summoned a half-soul toward him and splashed a little of the liquid onto the creature as he mouthed another incantation. Within a few seconds the half-soul started to bubble and turned into a clear gel figure. Then it morphed into a Monarch butterfly and stuck itself to the wall with the pictograph of the green-haired warrior. This ritual was repeated for each of the half-souls and lasted almost two hours. At the end, the walls of the Temple of Lost Souls were surfeited with Monarch butterflies.

The chief and shaman were the last to be transformed. In departing they expressed their gratitude for the bravery of Esmeralda. Quetzalcoatl attached the conch shell to his breast plate. He gave Es the fifth talon of Itzpapalotl for the medicine bag.

"Thank you for saving my people," the Aztec god said in a hissing tone (that everyone somehow understood). "You are a brave warrior."

Esmeralda face drew a blank. "But I didn't do anything."

"My brother, Xolotl, tells me otherwise," Quetzalcoatl looked at Xolo and then continued. "You forsook your own life and safety to find your father. You overcame innumerable dangers in the hidden valley with bravery and determination. And you defeated our nemesis Itzpapalotl. Indeed, you are the green-haired warrior."

Xolo barked. There was a mass fluttering from the butterflies on the walls. In human terms, it would have been deemed applause. Quetzalcoatl placed his hand on top of Es' head and smiled.

Then he stepped back. Xolo jumped into his arms. Quetzalcoatl's body started to coil up.

"Xolo, come back!" Es yelled after the dog. Fumes were emitted, and a gust of wind dispersed the vapors. Quetzalcoatl and Xolo disappeared. Es shook her head in disbelief. She could barely comprehend the truth. Xolo was Quetzalcoatl's brother! And therefore, also a god!

The butterflies started to peel themselves off the walls and flew out the front of the temple.

Minutes later, Es quietly called out. "Papá, we're all alone." The father and daughter were filled with sorrow at losing their companion and savior and the butterfly people.

Paco was silent. The ground started to quake. "Papá, let's grab our stuff and get out of here. Throw all that maize into my backpack."

There was a loud explosion that emanated from the top of the mountain. The air smelled of sulphur as ashes started to fill the sky.

Chapter 25 – The Exodus

Monday afternoon - Tuesday, November 2-3, 1970

Es figured that there was no time to waste. She emptied out her entire backpack onto the floor. The ceremonial garb they were wearing didn't have any value in the outdoors. Her dad still did not have real clothes. Hopefully, he could squeeze into something of hers. All of Xolo's items would have to be discarded, like his pouch and sweater vest. He had eaten every last bit of his food and then some.

Paco could wear the poncho because it was large and loose. He tied his medicine bag around his waist. Paco did not have his own backpack, so he volunteered to carry hers. Es thought that was a great idea. They would have to share her canteen between them.

The Temple of the Butterflies was getting darker and darker. They had to leave as soon as possible. They could not risk being trapped inside. The tremors became stronger and the walls shook and creaked.

Paco scrounged around and found a sack. He and Es shucked a few more ears of maize and threw them into the bag. That would save them weight and volume.

"What are we forgetting?" Es muttered out loud. Her dad said nothing. They walked to the front of the temple and Es took a reckoning with her compass. They needed to go west along the northern section of the valley. This was the way that Paco had come.

"Papá! How many days did it take you to get here from the crack in the mountain?"

Paco hemmed and hawed. "I don't really remember." Es was getting the sense that her father was not fully recovered. He seemed a bit confused. Paco was unable to concentrate. He didn't know his whereabouts.

The pair started down what looked like a path, with Es in the lead. Misty clouds clung to the northern hills. Again, the downpours began. It was difficult to see any type of trail or any prints. Es knew that they only had one or two hours of traveling before nightfall would be upon them. They could not rest or eat until they found shelter for the night. Es, however, did stop occasionally to catch rain water in her canteen. Her father drank ten times more water than Xolo. As they proceeded, they kept silent. The sound of the rain was loud, and they did not want to be distracted in such adverse conditions. Raindrops bombarded the mud puddles in front of them.

Dusk was upon them when they spied a small eucalyptus glen to the right of the trail. Es noticed that butterfly pupae were exposed on the long, fingerlike leaves of the trees. The pair set their provisions on some beds of discolored tan and yellow leaves. Above them, there was a granite overhang that would protect them from the wind and rain. A narrow spurt of water cascaded next to the clearing.

"Papá!" she yelled over the loud sounds of the elements. "We should build a fire." Paco went out to scour the area for some dried branches.

Within the hour they were drying themselves off. Paco seemed better and more lucid now. He had devised a way of baking the maize on the large rocks. Es ate three and her father had two. They sat and talked about the last few days. Paco was both sad and happy. On the one hand he wanted to see Kelly again. Maybe on the Day of the Dead next year? But he knew that it was not a certainty. He told Es again of his promises to Kelly on her deathbed: to take care of Es and to continue his crusade to explore, enjoy, and protect Nature. Es did not respond.

Paco left the premises to urinate. When he came back, it was Es' turn to go.

Afterwards Es and her father resumed talking. Paco reminisced about his life with Kelly back in Eugene. He told his daughter that he would probably have to close up his shop in Tubac. He owed more money than he was making.

"Yeah!" Es tactlessly jumped in. "And now you owe more rent."

"I'm thinking about moving back to Mesa Verde," he said slowly. "I need to be around family." Es took that to mean not her or her aunt and uncle. She knew that he wanted someone to take care of him. Paco promised that he would come to visit her around Christmas after he spent some time with his mother in Mesa Verde. He was a lost soul. Es was not taking the bait. She had drawn the line on pity parties for her dad. She was the kid and he was the adult; not the other way around.

"Papá," Es threw another few twigs into the fire. "I think I'm going back to school. I think I'll give Entomology a go. I need to protect Nature." Paco nodded.

Esmeralda was physically and emotionally exhausted. She had forsaken the love and counsel of her aunt and uncle. She had hurt them and put them in harm's way. But on the hand, she had reconnected with her father, even if it was for a little while. Es was also elated that she had crossed over into the spiritual world and had seen her mother's spirit. And then there was the mystical journey to the Hidden Valley. *You're lucky to have survived, girl,* she said to herself. *I feel rejuvenated, and I have a purpose in life!* The final challenge was her father.

They talked and talked. "I finally finished your diary," Es told her father. "I have a question. Why did you guys name me Esmeralda?"

"Because the name Quasimodo was already taken," he tried to keep a straight face, but then the two of them started laughing.

But then Es got serious. "Papá, one thing that has always bothered me," Es' heart was heavy, but she needed an answer. "Why did you abandon me?"

At first Paco did not answer. "You read my diary. I had promised your mother that I would meet her twenty-five years after we first met. Your grandma verified that. I had to see Kelly."

"But what about me?" Es was perplexed.

"Your Uncle Felipe and I became very good compadres. We were two Mexicanos who had the good fortune to find two smart and beautiful girls. When Kelly started to grow weaker and weaker, Felipe promised that he and Chlora would make sure that you would be taken care of. He knew that I was irresponsible, but he made it easy for me. I had no direction. Kelly had been my compass. I know what I promised her, but I couldn't do it. I was a lost soul." Tears were pouring down in his cheeks as he slobbered through his explanation. "If I had to do it over again, I would not have left you. But I am so proud of the way you turned out. I love you!"

Es' opal pendant tugged at her. Her eyes started to water. She was ready to forgive her father.

There was a fluttering sound that slowly approached them. Es turned her head and noticed that a horde of Monarch butterflies was approaching and hovering overhead. Within ten minutes, thousands of butterflies were circling Es and Paco. Paco's wrinkled face beamed. Es' heart and soul were at ease. She had finally made peace with her Papá.

The pair sighed. They were exhausted. Es and Paco snuggled close to each other to stay warm during the night. The butterflies fell upon them and shielded them for the night. There was a collective heart beat emitting from the horde.

The storms came in and out all night. There was the smell of wet eucalyptus in the air. As the dawn broke, Es noticed that the Monarchs had disappeared. Her eyelids felt sticky as she tried to open them.

"Did you think that we were finished?" a cackling voice cried out. The large black form of Itzpapalotl appeared in front of the sleeping pair. Itzpapalotl glared at her withered hand. "I want my revenge!"

Paco awoke from all the commotion. He unsheathed his daughter's hunting knife. Es still had her obsidian blade. The two rose to their feet. Es placed her body between Itzpapalotl and her father. The black figure leaned forward and grabbed Paco by the arm. Paco was shocked and was not able to pull away.

"Looking for this?" Es held the fifth and missing talon that Itzpapalotl had lost. Es had surreptitiously retrieved it from the cauldron after the transformation ritual.

"Give it back!" In a rage, Itzpapalotl lurched forward releasing Paco as she tried to snatch the talon from Es. In a sweeping motion Es slashed the obsidian blade across the body of Itzpapalotl. There was a howling scream that emanated from the black she-demon. Boiling pitch erupted from the creature who was now writhing in pain. The figure started to shrink and mutate. A putrid odor invaded the air. On the ground, a black beetle missing its two front legs scurried away.

Es rushed to her father. He seemed okay. "We need to get out of here right now." They put on their boots and grabbed their outerwear. But before they could resume their travel, buzzing sounds approached. Little flying creatures started to attack them.

"Papá! They're wasps!" Es screamed. She didn't know what the natural protection against wasps was. Probably fire, but their fire had gone out a few hours before. The wasps attacked Paco as he covered his face. The poncho was doing a fair job of blocking the stings. Es was not as fortunate. She ran back and forth, throwing up leaves as a diversion.

The wasps were gaining on her. Her face started to welt up. She felt the fire opal pendant on her chest begin to feel warm. Es was getting exhausted trying to swing a shirt at the intruders. She began to weaken.

"Es!" her father cried out.

Her eyes closed. She started to fall backwards. The pricks were replaced by a gentle breeze. She felt weightless. She opened her eyes. Es saw her father being held up by a kaleidoscope of Monarch butterflies. She realized that she was floating next to him. Some of the Monarchs were fighting off the wasps while Es and Paco were being rescued.

Es closed her eyes. It seemed that the hours went by quickly as the Monarch butterflies delivered the pair to the mountain tunnel where they had initially entered the hidden valley several days before.

Chapter 26 – Epilogue

May 1, 1971

Seven months later, Es was studying for finals back at the University of Oregon in Eugene. She was working on a master's degree in Entomology. She wanted to carry on the crusade that her father had started.

The skin treatments to her face and body had been quite successful. She had suffered over two hundred wasp stings. Es had almost drifted into toxic shock. Her Uncle Felipe's knowledge of natural herbs and spices had been invaluable. She had rubbed so much avocado on her body that her uncle called her "Miss Guacamole." But a strange physiologic phenomenon happened to Esmeralda during her trip back to Eugene. Her hair turned dark brown, her natural color. Es didn't know if she liked it or not.

Esmeralda put down her textbook and walked to the kitchen of her off-campus apartment. She inhaled a glass of orange juice. Es had put on a few pounds since returning to Eugene. She still had flashbacks of their exodus from the Hidden Valley.

The hordes of Monarch butterflies had stayed with them for a few days after that dreadful attack. Paco had taken over the guide duties and helped them navigate their way through the tunnel. He had not been aware of the dangerous abyss in the shaft, but they did find the petrified bolillos. The batteries in their flashlight were on their last legs. The pair traveled slowly, taking their time. Most of the maize had been consumed and the body weights of Es and Paco were dropping. The butterflies swarmed slowly in front and in back of them.

Es had no idea what the date was when they reached the secret entryway to the tunnel from the waterfall side. They had two cobs left. They replenished their water. The Monarch butterflies flew together and went straight up into the skies. They made several figure eights and dived close to Paco and Es. They spread out and came back together again. Then they rose and flew to the north, leaving the father and daughter sitting on the rocks.

Paco and Es needed to resume the trek. Es was concerned about getting hypothermia and running out of food on their descent down the trail.

"Papá!" Es was unsure of herself. "Should we try to make it down the mountain or stay the night in the tunnel?"

"What do you think?" Paco threw it back to the warrior guide.

Erring on the side of caution and good hiking practices, they spent one last night in the mouth of the tunnel. The next day the weather coming down the mountain was agreeable, and by the afternoon they reached the southern trailhead. They both signed out at the little hiker station, to the surprise of the park ranger. The smell of burnt tortillas and sight of the molcajete were nostalgic moments for the pair as they entered the supply office. The outfitter stocked them with new clothes and plenty of food. This had cost a dear amount, and Es was almost out of funds. Paco only had a modest amount of money.

The next day they were given a shuttle ride to Posada Las Estrellas in Guadalupe Xochiloma. Paco had hidden a hundred dollars in his car, so they were able to stay there for a few days before driving back. Es recuperated nicely on the drive back to Tubac. She had not been strong enough to drive, so Paco did the whole trek by himself. He seemed to have changed and mellowed out. He was singing and laughing. He was in good spirits.

When they arrived in Tubac, they gorged themselves on Mexican food for the next few days. Paco scraped together some money for back rent and gave his landlady notice that he was going to vacate. Paco said goodbye to his daughter as she loaded up her Pinto to drive back to Eugene. They both promised to keep in touch, although both knew that it might not happen. Paco was going to move back in with his family in Mesa Verde. Es made sure that she gave him back the travel journals and his other important papers. In return, Paco handed her an item wrapped in brown paper that he made her promise not to open until she got home.

A week later Esmeralda was back home giving her aunt and uncle the sanitized version of her adventures. Aunt Chlora realized that Es was now grown up and was elated that her niece was going to become a teacher. Uncle Felipe's business was expanding. He now offered whole wheat tortillas and several types of homemade salsa.

Esmeralda was going to register for Entomology classes starting the first of the year. Christmas was filled with gratitude for Es and her aunt and uncle. Her father called her at least once a week. Their relationship was getting better. The conversations were light and humorous. A week before Christmas, Paco had left a cryptic telephone message that he would not be coming to Eugene for the holidays. Es hadn't really counted on him joining her any time soon. She just sighed. She was used to that.

The bad news came the day after Christmas when Esmeralda's grandma Lulu called her and notified her that Paco had passed away. The coroner had said that the cause of death was some type of heavy metal poisoning. Es, however, thought it was from heartbreak. Paco had been separated from his one true love, Kelly, for too long. Es was not sad. She knew that their souls were united in the Fifth Dimension, another stage of life in the universe.

It was at that moment that she knew she was doing the right thing by pursuing her father's dream (and also her mother's), to take up the fight to protect Nature. She would follow in her father's footsteps and study Entomology.

Es walked over to the wall of her apartment where photos and her mother's poems were mounted. She grabbed the wooden frame that her father had given her when she had left him in Tubac. The framed poem had been written by her mother and Paco had cherished it. It was his parting gift to Esmeralda. She started to softly read the words:

THE PRESSED FLOWER

A red rose in my garden grew,
It was beautiful, just like you,
Should I pick it and enjoy the instance?
Or let it seek its own existence?

Does the beginning of summer bring the threat of fall?
Does a first bite mean an end to all?
The child is born and then it dies.
Is life just a dream, laden with lies?

Can I press the flower into my book,
To enjoy at my leisure when I look?
Nothing is forever, so I'm told,
But this is with me, till I'm old.

ABOUT THE AUTHOR

Rocky Barilla lives in the San Francisco Bay Area with his wife, Dolores, and dozens of feathered friends who visit the bird feeder daily, ranging from hummingbirds to red-tailed hawks. The couple spends part of the year in the paradise of Zihuatanejo, Mexico.

Rocky was formally educated at the University of Southern California and Stanford University. He also spent two academic quarters in Vienna, Austria. His passions are 19th century French literary fiction, Mexican history, global traveling, studying foreign languages, ceramic painting, and cooking. For fun and exercise, he and his wife do Zumba three times a week.

Rocky has been actively involved in human rights, immigration, and multicultural issues, especially involving Latinos and other people of color. He is heavily involved in the Oregon Sanctuary State movement that began in the 1980's.

His first book "A Taste of Honey" won second place at the International Latino Book Awards (2015) for Fantasy Fiction and won First Place at the Latino Books into Movies Awards (2015) for Fantasy Fiction.

"The Devil's Disciple" was Rocky's second book to win second place at the International Latino Book Awards (2016) for

Mystery, and it was also an award winner at the Latino Books into Movies Awards (2018) for Mystery/Suspense.

Rocky's third book, "Ay to Zi", is a romance about forbidden love that is set in Zihuatanejo, Mexico. It was the Second Place Winner of the International Latino Book Awards (2017) for Romance and an award winner at the Latino Books into Movies Awards (2018) for Romance.

"Harmony of Colors" (2017), his fourth book, won Second Place Winner of the International Latino Book Awards (2018) for Latino-Themed Fiction. It is a multicultural story about the search for self-identity and the realization that friendship and a sense of community can bring about a harmony of colors.

His mantra is "Life is Good."

Made in the USA
Columbia, SC
24 March 2019